The Vanishing Act

Sarah Ward is a critically acclaimed crime and gothic thriller writer. Her book, *A Patient Fury*, was an Observer book of the month and *The Quickening*, written as Rhiannon Ward, was a Radio Times book of the year. Sarah is on the Board of the Crime Writers Association, Derby Book Festival and Friends of Buxton International Festival. She is an RLF Fellow at Sheffield University.

G000320541

Also by Sarah Ward

A Mallory Dawson Crime Thriller

The Birthday Girl
The Sixth Lie
The Vanishing Act

THE
VANISHING
ACT

SARAH WARD

First published in the United Kingdom in 2024 by

Canelo
Unit 9, 5th Floor
Cargo Works, 1–2 Hatfields
London SE1 9PG
United Kingdom

A CIP catalogue record for this book is available from the British Library.

Print ISBN 978 1 80436 320 1
Ebook ISBN 978 1 80436 319 5

Cover design by Tom Sanderson

Cover images © Shutterstock

Look for more great books at www.canelo.co

Printed and bound in Great Britain by Clays Ltd, Elcograf S.p.A.

1

To Vicky Dawson

1

Friday

Elsa drove the car down the rutted road, the suspension on her ancient Fiesta groaning as it was thrown from grassy mound to pothole. She'd been told that old Tom Thomas, the legal owner of the strip of land, was too mean to spend money on getting the road in good nick, which can't have made the new owners of Tall Pines happy. Jon and Chrissie Morgan bought the place three years earlier, fully aware its access road was owned by another, but confident they could work their magic on him. It hadn't worked. In desperation, they'd offered to pay for the improvements themselves, as they wanted the holidaying families renting Tall Pines to be able to glide down a tarmacked road in their SUVs filled with booze and Waitrose goodies. Still, Tom had held out. He'd confided to Elsa one winter's morning that he liked the look of the pitted road with the shaggy green strip of grass down the middle. It had been like that, leading to his own farmhouse at the edge of the forest, for four generations. Why change now?

Elsa's car was so old it didn't have air conditioning, just ineffective blowers that pumped out hot air in the August heat. It would be fine once she was inside the house, as Welsh cottages were built to keep out the worst heat of the day, despite the best efforts of global warming. She wound up her window to keep the music blaring from Nation Radio station from disturbing Tom. Nevertheless, she turned her head towards Dan Y Derw, Tom's house, to see if he was sitting in his yard. That, at least, was something Jon and Chrissie liked. Tom, with his flat cap and pipe, gave the place a rustic feel – authentic Wales – and he was happy enough to pass the time of day with holidaymakers.

Elsa drew up outside Tall Pines, glancing up at its grey stone exterior. It was by far the least favourite place to visit on her roster. The remoteness of the location, along with its weird history, gave her the shivers every week when she arrived for her clean. She'd not felt able to say anything, though, to Chrissie when she'd first shown her around. Unusually, Elsa hadn't got the booking through her cleaning agency but via a contact of her mam's. Meeting the owner was more daunting than just being given a key, even though Chrissie had been nice enough. She'd suggested Elsa leave her car at the top of the track to spare its suspension but there was no way she was going to do that. The forest, its edge encircling the two houses, gave her the creeps too and she wanted a quick getaway from there if necessary. Whenever she got out of her car, it felt like someone was watching her. The forest did that to you – its uniform trees with the hint of something much darker underneath.

Elsa came to the house every Friday for the handover and, if guests were staying for more than a week, she would still visit to give the place a clean. It was a clause in the contract that renters signed – Chrissie wanted her investment maintained – but it also meant that Elsa had regular work. Chrissie had already told her the new holidaymakers would be staying for three weeks: a long holiday in a place with little to do. Admittedly, if you liked beaches and outdoor activities there was plenty to do around the coast, but Elsa couldn't understand why you wouldn't stay nearer the sea if you were going to spend your time on the sand.

Unusually, she'd already met the family staying in the house. The previous Friday they'd arrived early – they weren't supposed to get here until after four but had driven up the track around midday, as Elsa had been stripping the bedding of the previous holidaymakers. Realising the door was locked and the key not under the stone, as per their arrival instructions, they'd stayed by the car, a dark blue jeep. That had been odd. Although the heatwave hadn't yet started, it was hot enough and most would have rattled the door to ask to unload their gear.

Elsa, however, had been glad of the peace to finish her tasks. She'd been given strict instructions not to let clients in until she'd finished her clean and taken photos to show how she'd left the property. Nevertheless, she couldn't resist the occasional glimpse out of the window to see what the family were up to.

They made for an attractive fivesome. The father, she guessed, was in his forties, his grey hair clipped close to his head so he resembled one of those statues she'd seen on a recent coach trip to Rome with her mam. His wife had been more difficult to make out, as she stayed in the car, reading a magazine, and wide sunglasses obscured her face. She looked glamorous, like a Hollywood star from the Fifties, sporting frosted red lipstick which looked incongruous in this rural setting. It had been the children, though, that had held her attention. Two teenagers, a boy and girl, with the finest spun blonde hair similar to Elsa's own. They looked alike, although the boy was heftier than the girl. They'd got out of the car but had lacked the curiosity she'd have expected from holidaying teenagers. They'd shuffled around the car, talking in low voices. When they'd got bored, rather than walk around the garden or stray into the forest, they'd taken a blanket from the car and laid it out near the front door, lying on their back and continuing to talk in a murmur.

There was another child, younger than the teenagers, a girl aged about ten, Elsa guessed, with vibrant ginger hair cut into a short bob. She displayed more curiosity about her surroundings: once or twice she had taken steps towards the woodland, only to be called back by her father, while her mother remained immersed in her magazine. The girl's gaze kept straying to the edge of Brechfa Forest and resting on the crest of the pine trees that had given this house its new name. It had originally been called Pant Meinog, according to old Tom, but the new owners had foregone a historic Welsh name in favour of one easier for prospective renters to pronounce. At least, that was their story but Elsa suspected differently.

An attractive family, thought Elsa, who wouldn't be leaving a mess like the one she was cleaning up after now. The only anomaly was that the man was smoking. She watched in approval as he carefully stubbed the cigarette out on the rough path and deposited the stub into a tin. Elsa didn't think for a moment there would be the need to apply the deep cleaning fee most properties applied if she found evidence of smoking in the house. When she'd finished, and taken photographs of the gleaming bathroom and tightly made beds, she opened the front door and deposited the key under the hunk of stone. She could feel the eyes of the family on her.

4

'It's all yours,' she called over to them and only the youngest stepped towards her. 'I'll be back a week today to give the place a clean.'

'Pippa,' her father warned and the child halted as if playing musical statues.

Elsa beamed a smile in their vague direction, conscious of her sweaty clothes, and slid into her car, putting the family out of her mind until she'd arrived back today.

It had been a week of increasing temperatures; the thermometer in her car recorded twenty-four degrees Celsius this morning. As Elsa drew up outside Tall Pines, she saw that the jeep wasn't there. She climbed out of the car, rolled over the rock next to the door with her foot and saw the key was missing. She pulled her rucksack off her back, scrabbling around in its depths. She was so used to retrieving the key from under the stone after handovers that she didn't always carry the spare set on her. With relief, she found the key ring at the bottom of her bag, grateful she didn't have to call Chrissie to pick up a spare.

She opened the door, noticing it was unlocked anyway, and put her rucksack on one of the hooks in the hallway. The air smelt of orange squash and boiled ham, as if a children's birthday party was in the offing. As she pushed open the door to the kitchen, there were the preparations for a picnic on the counter. Cold ham and salami, a carton of tomatoes and a pint jug of prepared orange cordial ready to be poured into a bottle. Someone was in the process of buttering the bread; on one side lay two rounds, the other six still to be prepared. On the Aga, the kettle blew a steady hiss, the water boiling. Elsa lifted off the kettle and closed the hotplate to save the heat, which blew into her sweaty face. Odd. A chair had tipped to one side, and she automatically lifted it and placed it back behind the table.

'Hello...' she called.

The house was silent – perhaps one of the parents had gone out with the kids and the other was in the bathroom. She opened the utility room and saw the washing machine was on a cycle, with twenty minutes left to run. Retrieving the bucket of cleaning stuff, she decided to start on the bedrooms to give whoever was making the lunch their privacy. As she climbed the wide staircase, the silence of the house was oppressive. An awareness of total absence.

'Is anyone there?' she shouted.

On the landing, she looked out of the window onto the bottom of the drive but saw no one, not even Tom. She opened the door to the master bedroom with the king-sized bed and crossed to the window, looking out onto the patchy lawn. It was thin soil up here on the mountain and even grass struggled to thrive. Again, the lawn was devoid of activity and Elsa's eyes were once more drawn to the forest. Was it her imagination that the image of a woman stumbling through its undergrowth flashed into her mind? Perhaps it was a vision of the past, as the woman wore a white dress, her feet bare as she plunged on. Her aura pulsated terror, turning the sweat on Elsa's arms ice-cold. She shivered, pulling herself together. Time to get on with her chores, although she intended to keep an ear out for whoever had been buttering that bread.

It was sweaty work. She would strip all the beds first, pile up the laundry in front of the machine and then gather the clean bedding. As she went from room to room, she saw each bed was neatly made up. All three children had their own space. The teenage girl had a make-up bag and a novel with a cover of fluorescent lime green on her bedside table. The room had the smell of burnt toast and Elsa searched for the source of the odour. A set of hair straighteners had been left on, the tongs beginning to scorch the wooden tabletop. She switched it off at the plug but didn't make a move towards the bed, her mind turning over the signs of a hasty departure. She pushed open the adjacent door and saw that the older boy's room looked hardly touched but had that slightly sweaty smell Elsa associated with her brother's space. There was little here to cause alarm, only the sense that someone had just popped out.

The final space was the box room occupied by the child, Pippa. She had lined up a row of Lego ballerinas on the window, one of them holding a candy stick. The sugar fairy. Elsa held it up and smiled, her eyes dropping to the bed. Pippa had been drawing the woods and, once again, the woman flashed into Elsa's mind, her breath heavy as she pushed her way through the undergrowth. Elsa forced herself back into the present and looked at the girl's pictures. One drawing was half-completed, a green felt-tip pen resting on the paper, its lid missing. The other pens were neatly placed in a plastic folder, the colours fanning out like a rainbow. This was a child who looked after her things, so why was a pen left to dry out on the paper?

Back in the kitchen, with the dirty linen waiting to be placed into the machine once the cycle was over, Elsa worried. She opened the front door and shouted into the clearing.

'Hellooo. Is anyone there?'

Her eyes dropped to the stone. The door had been unlocked when she arrived. Had they all gone out and forgotten about the kettle, sandwiches and hair straighteners? What would make them leave so suddenly? In her haste to solve the mystery, she realised she'd forgotten to take the photos for Chrissie to prove her cleaning had been completed. She found her phone at the bottom of her rucksack and went from room to room, photographing her work. When it came to the kitchen, there was little she could do. The table still had two cups of tea cooling, one nearly full. In the end, she photographed the clean sink and the top of the Aga, which she'd wiped over with a clean cloth. She would have to explain to Chrissie that the family were still using the kitchen when she arrived, although that was hardly the truth.

Slowly, Elsa closed the door, her mind uneasy over the order of things. It continued to worry her as she deadheaded the blood-red geraniums in the terracotta pot by the front door, turning over things until she came to a decision. She got out her phone and scrolled through her contacts until she found what she was looking for. Elsa pressed the number, which was answered on the second ring.

'Hello?'

'Mallory, it's me, Elsa. Remember, from Eldey? There's something really weird going on here and I need your help.'

2

That summer, Mallory was embarrassed to find herself technically homeless. The lease on her rented Pembroke-shire flat had expired in April and, as she'd expected, the owners had wanted to rent it on a weekly basis to holidaymakers. What Mallory hadn't expected was the impossibility of finding anywhere else to rent, not only in St Davids but also elsewhere in the county. Tired of her job at the cathedral, she'd handed in her notice and begun to consider returning to London to look for work suitable for an ex-copper invalided out of the force. Wales, although beautiful, was expensive in the summer and rammed with holidaymakers that she had little in common with. She also really had to make a decision as to what she was going to do with the rest of her life, a not-unusual situation for former police officers to find themselves in.

It was her son Toby, however, who had forced her to confront the fact she needed to stay where she was. After a difficult school year, he wanted a July holiday in Wales mainly spent on the beach. Mallory had changed tack and decided to take the summer off from gainful employment, hoping her police pension would cover her everyday needs for the short term. She'd managed to find a seasonal let at Golden Sands Caravan Park in a small village called Tresaith in Cardigan Bay: a one-bedroom static caravan with a sofa bed in the living room. Accommodation-wise,

Mallory was on a downward spiral and only the thought that this was a temporary solution gave her the resolve to cope with the rest of the summer.

Mallory was contemplating an afternoon on the beach when Elsa called. Toby had enjoyed two weeks of sunshine with her but had returned to London to spend August with his friends there. She had downloaded an audiobook and was about to put on her headphones to walk to the sands, when Elsa's number had flashed up on the phone. Just the sight of the girl's name had given Mallory a momentary jolt. It took her back to the previous September and her fight for survival on the picturesque island of Eldey. She took the call and listened to Elsa, remembering her whimsy and practicality, two character-istics that rarely went together but gave the girl her unique charm.

The drive down to Tall Pines was slow. Everywhere was packed with holiday traffic, mainly caravans, and it was a relief to turn off the coastal road and head inland. Mallory hadn't visited this part of Carmarthenshire before and was struck by its greenness, in contrast to the rockiness of the coast. The forest, however, had a regimented feel to it: uniform rows of conifers suggested a government policy of replenishing woodland without much thought to the natural environment. She followed her satnav's instructions, turning left up a single-track road that had no obvious passing places, so she bloody well hoped she wouldn't meet a vehicle coming the other way. In her experience, it was usually she who had to do the reversing when she met another car head-on. She took her time, however, keen not to crash her ageing Volkswagen as she mulled over Elsa's call. She hadn't been making much sense; something about a family who'd gone out and left the kettle on, and should she call the police? Mallory had tried not to laugh but, realising that Elsa was deadly earnest, she'd offered to come up to the holiday house and see what the issue was. She still felt a residual bond with the brave teenager who, when stuck on Eldey with a poisoner, had come to Mallory's aid. It was as much wanting to see Elsa again, rather than any sense of unease, that made Mallory agree to meet her in the depths of Brechfa Forest.

Elsa had given her the postcode to a place in the middle of nowhere, although Mallory passed a gaggle of mountain bikers, so it must be on the tourist trail. The satnav was more confident about its destination, so Mallory gave herself over to the bossy male voice until she reached a rocky clearing, the type she hated driving down. At the bottom of the dead-straight drive, Mallory could see Elsa waiting for her, peering anxiously into the distance. As she inched the car closer, wincing at what the road was doing to her suspension, she could see Elsa had grown since they'd last said their goodbyes, or maybe she'd lost that hunched-up look she'd adopted on the island of Eldey.

Mallory parked the car and a rush of emotion engulfed her when Elsa approached. She hugged the girl, who tensed, reminding Mallory of her own son, Toby.

'So,' said Mallory, to alleviate the shared embarrassment. 'What's this about leaving the kettle on?'

'Oh Mallory, it's more than that. The house is like the *Mary Celeste*. We did it at school – it's a ship that was found completely abandoned, as if the sailors had just left minutes earlier. It's the same with this house.'

'Because of the kettle?'

'Because of everything. Come and see for yourself. There's five of them staying here. Mam, Dad, three children.'

'How old?' asked Mallory sharply.

'Teenagers, and one a little younger. She's the only one whose name I know. Pippa. I saw the family arrive a week ago today.'

'Right.' Mallory followed Elsa up the stone steps. She saw a sign to the right of the door – 'Tall Pines' – and in smaller letters underneath: 'Holiday lets by Daffodil Properties'. Mallory nodded to the sign. 'They your employer?'

'Yes, for this house. I also get work through an agency but I have a couple of places who employ me direct. Daffodil Properties is just a business name; it's Jon and Chrissie Morgan who own the house.'

'Like them?'

Elsa shrugged. 'They seem OK. Pay me on time, at least.'

'That's something.' The door opened onto a narrow hall, with a row of pegs to one side. 'Is this the side door?'

'The front and it's the one everyone uses. The key's left under the stone for guests and there's a spare left on the kitchen counter for them to take as well.'

'Do you have your own set of keys?'

'Yes, but I rarely use them. There's a key safe at most houses, but this place is so rural they just use the stone.'

Mallory sniffed. She was surprised there hadn't been burglaries, given the lack of security. She turned left and the room opened out into a farmhouse-style kitchen with cream-painted cabinets. Elsa pointed at the red Aga.

'When I came in, the kettle was on the simmering plate, steaming away. I moved it to the side so it wouldn't boil dry.'

Mallory picked up the kettle. It was about a quarter full. Elsa was pointing at the plate to the right, where a kettle that had been boiled on the hotter plate on the left could be left to simmer. Mallory turned and caught sight of a pile of bread, some of it already buttered. She touched the crusts that were already beginning to curl in the heat.

'Looks like someone was interrupted,' she said.

'Mallory, that's exactly what I thought. One of the chairs was on its side, as if someone had got up in a hurry. I should have left it where it was, but I put it back behind the table.'

'The chair was overturned?' asked Mallory, looking at the two cups of tea, one half-drunk the other barely touched.

'On its side, like there had been an argument.'

'Perhaps there had been. Teenagers fight. Sometimes it gets violent, as I've seen it before. The parents might be in the hospital with them now.'

'But what about the simmering kettle? They would have only just left, and I never saw a car on my way down here. You've seen the road.'

Mallory looked around. Strange, definitely. A mystery possibly, but she could see no evidence of a crime.

'Why don't you show me the rest of the house?'

Mallory followed Elsa, sticking her head through the doorway of each of the spaces. It was the two rooms belonging to the teenagers that gave her pause for thought. Where was the mess like the one Toby left behind whenever he came to stay? The evidence of budding lives. Perhaps they were made to follow the example of their parents, for whom everything had a place. Elsa was pointing at a set of hair straighteners.

'They were on. I had to turn them off because they were burning the wood.'

'So they might have been on for a while. Say, half an hour and forgotten about?'

'I… I suppose so.' Elsa bit her lip.

'Don't worry, let's see the rest of the house.'

When they got to the smallest bedroom, Mallory paused in the doorway, taking in the drawings on the bed. It was the little girl she was the least happy about disappearing. Adults and teenagers, in her experience, could usually look after themselves. There was again no sign of violence in the room, although there was a sense that its occupant had just slipped out and could amble back in any time. Without thinking, she reached out and touched the nib of the felt-tip pen missing its lid. It had begun to dry out, leaving little ink on Mallory's fingers.

'Let me have a look downstairs again,' said Mallory.

In the living room, there was not much evidence that the family had spent any time there, although that didn't necessarily mean anything, given their level of tidiness. Not everyone lived their lives as messily as Mallory. She could feel Elsa's eyes boring into hers.

'I had this feeling when I was in the upstairs bedroom… of a woman running barefoot through the woods. I think it was a vision but of an event long ago. The woman looked old-fashioned.'

'Oh Elsa.' Mallory was exasperated. 'You were obsessed with that ghost on Eldey. Are you having visions now?'

'I've always had them. If you're not a believer—'

'I am not,' retorted Mallory.

'Then I'll say no more.' Elsa folded her arms. 'You don't think anything amiss?'

'I suspect the family have just gone out. They were planning a lunch and something came up. An appointment made for a boat trip, for example, and just remembered. It's easy to forget you've left the kettle on and, as you're grabbing the kids, you're leaving a trail of items left on or discarded.'

'What about the chair?'

'Well.' Mallory looked round. 'Things can get knocked over in a rush. Don't worry about it, Elsa.'

'But I do. Suppose something has happened?'

They both jumped at the sound of a mobile ringing from above. Elsa pushed past her and raced up the stairs, returning with the phone clasped in her hand.

'It was in the teenage girl's room. It had slid down the back of the chest of drawers.'

'Answer it,' said Mallory.

Elsa slid her finger along the screen. 'Hello.' They listened to the silence. 'Hello,' said Elsa again, before the connection was cut.

'Pass it to me,' Mallory said but the phone had already locked itself, leaving little information about the caller's identity. 'Damn. It's probably someone thinking they've got a wrong number and ringing off. Leave it here on the kitchen table in case it rings again.'

Mallory glanced around the living room once more. It had the air of a tastefully furnished holiday home, the furniture robust but aesthetically pleasing. She couldn't understand Elsa's jitters.

'What are we going to do?' asked Elsa, still keen for Mallory to take charge of a plan of action.

Mallory sighed and looked at her watch. Just gone two. The family could be out all day in weather as warm as this.

'I tell you what: how about I come back this evening to check up on everyone? Do you have another house to clean this afternoon?'

Elsa nodded. 'A cottage near Poppit Sands. It'll take me half an hour to get there.'

'Are you still living in Tenby?'

'That's right. At home, just me and Mam.'

'Then, you go home when you've finished the next cottage. I'll come back here this evening around six and check that they've returned. You said the house was unlocked?'

Elsa nodded. 'Although I can't see either set of keys.'

'Then leave it as you found it. If there's no one here, I'll have another look around. They're due to stay another two weeks, you said?'

'Yes. It's a long time for this house. Two weeks max usually, as the weather can be funny.'

'Some families have three-week holidays. What does their car look like?'

'It's a dark blue SUV. I don't know what make, but fancy. It's always people in fancy cars that hire this cottage.'

'Fine. Leave it with me and I'll call you, OK?' Mallory hesitated. 'Do you have a number for Daffodil Properties if I need to ring them?'

Looking relieved, Elsa gave her the number for Chrissie Morgan. As they left the house, Mallory's eyes strayed to a chimney peeping through the trees.

'Who lives over there?' she asked.

'An old man called Tom Thomas. I talk to him sometimes, as I think he's lonely. Should we go and tell him what I've found?'

Mallory shook her head. 'No need to worry him and, anyway, the car's gone, hasn't it? They'll be somewhere out on the road. Leave it with me to sort out.'

It felt odd leaving the house unlocked but the spot was isolated enough. Elsa climbed into her car, which was even older-looking than Mallory's old banger, and drove away, the vehicle listing violently near the top of the road. At least the missing family would have had a comfier journey, wherever they'd rushed off to in their jeep. Perhaps, at this very moment, they were sunning themselves in Cardigan Bay, unaware what worry their departure had caused. Except, Mallory wasn't worried, was she?

3

At a loss for what to do for the next four hours, Mallory rang the only friend she'd made since arriving in West Wales: DI Harri Evans. Admittedly, the term 'friend' was a little strong. Colleague, maybe, but even that relationship had been a temporary thing. She'd reluctantly been seconded onto a murder inquiry in the winter, which had led to her son Toby being dragged into the unmasking of a killer. She'd told Harri that she was finished with contract work with the force and they'd hardly spoken since.

'Mallory Dawson. This is a surprise.' It was good to hear Harri's tenor Welsh accent again and he also sounded pleased to receive the call.

'I'm not disturbing you, am I? Are you at the station?'

'Friday off, thank God, although it does mean I'm working the weekend. Is everything all right?'

'Right as rain, but I'm in Carmarthenshire and I had a call from Elsa. Remember her from Eldey?'

'Not likely to forget her, am I? She in trouble?'

'Not exactly. She's still cleaning, but mainly holiday lets now. She was a bit spooked about a house near Brechfa, where she was doing an interim clean for a family staying another couple of weeks.'

'Spooked in what way?' Harri's tone was sharp.

'It's a long story but absolutely nothing to worry about, I'm sure. It's just that I offered to go there again this evening and speak to the family, but I'm kicking my heels until then. I'm living it up on the coast near Tresaith, on Cardigan Bay.'

'Left Pembrokeshire, then? You never told me.' He sounded hurt.

'It's the summer, I've had Toby to stay and, embarrassingly, I'm currently living in a caravan.' She heard him chuckle; Harri was always able to surprise her. 'I wondered if you fancied a coffee or something, but if it's your day off—'

'Brechfa, did you say? Tell you what, I'll meet you in Carmarthen. I've got to pick up Ellie at four from the cinema, but I could do with dropping a file off at the office. Do you want to make your way down to the town? We could have a chat then.'

-

Harri had suggested the Marks & Spencer cafe, as it had air conditioning. Mallory took the opportunity to dive into the toilets before meeting him, conscious that she'd left the caravan without even brushing her hair. The weeks spent on the beach had tanned her face, and she briefly toyed with the idea of buying a lipstick to spruce herself up. In the end, she found a can of deodorant at the bottom of her bag and sprayed her armpits to cool herself down. Harri was already in the cafe when she arrived, gazing at a group of women chatting at an adjacent table.

'People-watching?' she asked, sliding into the seat opposite him. 'I'd have thought you'd get plenty of that in your job.'

Harri smiled at her, reaching across the table to give her a brief hug, which took her by surprise. He looked thinner than when she'd last seen him, but healthier: the rings underneath his eyes had all but disappeared. He nodded towards the next table. 'They're discussing the job losses at a local factory. It seems family members are affected, which I can sympathise with, as my son Ben worked there one summer. Soon this place will only have tourism to keep it afloat.'

'How are the kids?' Mallory picked up a menu and looked at the drinks list.

'They're fine and enjoying the summer. I'm currently taxi-dad for Ellie. How's your boy?'

Mallory shrugged. 'Same as usual.'

Harri was tactful enough not to push it. 'Sorry I've not been in touch with you, Mallory. It would have been brilliant to have you back on the team as a civilian investigator, but tightened budgets – plus, thankfully, a lack of serious crime – mean we haven't actually needed your expertise.'

'And I wasn't exactly very enthusiastic about any potential work the last time we met.'

Harri waved it away. 'How are you finding living in a caravan?' The question was put casually, but she saw that Harri was watching her reaction.

Mallory made a face. Put like that, it sounded like she'd sunk as low as she could go without actually sleeping on the streets. But Harri knew she had her police pension, which meant she could technically afford to rent a bricks-and-mortar place, just not in high season.

'It's fine for me on a temporary basis. Toby's become obsessed with the beach – he came to visit in July and loved it.'

'Bit of a squash for the two of you, surely?'

It was said without criticism but Mallory was compelled to defend herself. 'He took the bedroom and I slept in the living room, which was a bit of a challenge, but we managed. It's not long term.' Mallory looked towards the counter. 'Do I need to queue for a coffee?'

' 'Fraid so. Want me to go?'

'Don't worry about it. Want another?' She gestured at Harri's cup, which seemed to contain peppermint tea. 'You on a health kick?'

'Something like that. Yeah, another mint tea.'

When she'd got the drinks, she told Harri about the house and the sudden departure of the family. As expected, he was interested but unconcerned.

'I think Elsa is worrying about nothing. There's something about holidays that makes you act outside your usual behaviour patterns. People who religiously lock their doors every evening will freely admit to having gone to bed with all their downstairs windows open in the rental and are surprised when they wake up to find they've been burgled. Or tourists take a dip in the sea with their wallet still in their jeans on the beach and return to find it isn't there. The family will turn up later.'

'I'm inclined to agree with you, especially as I'm now sitting here in M&S. To be honest, there's something about the way Elsa weaves a story that gets to you. She was telling me about a vision she had of a woman running in the forest. That girl's got one hell of an imagination.'

'Sometimes we get bound up in a place,' said Harri. 'I wouldn't worry.'

'You know, it *was* a strange house, stuck like that in the middle of a forest clearing with just another adjacent property, although it was nice enough inside. Money's been spent on the place but it's not somewhere I'd go for my holiday. Even my caravan feels more welcoming.'

'Holiday homes do a roaring trade round here, and if you employ a half-decent photographer, no one will know about the atmosphere of the place anyway. Where is it exactly?'

'In the middle of somewhere called Brechfa Forest. I'd never even heard of the place, let alone been to the area.'

She saw Harri bristle. 'It's a modern-day forest, planted to replenish the depleted resources following the First World War. It's row after row of conifers, but they've made the most of it with cycle and hiking trails. What you're feeling is due to the fact that it's planted on a much older forest called Glyn Cothi. Heard of it?'

Mallory shook her head. 'Of course not.'

Harri sighed. 'Of course not,' he repeated. 'It was once a Royal Forest and its history is woven into the story of Wales. The place is very atmospheric. And the house is in the middle of it, you say?'

'Two houses, actually. You take the road to Brechfa and start to climb the hill. It's a twisty road until you reach a terrible driveway on the right to get to the place. What's the matter?'

'The holiday home. It's not called Pant Meinog, is it?'

'It's Tall Pines.'

'That's not Welsh. Second homeowners are always changing the bloody name of their houses. Do you have a photo of the place?'

Mallory frowned at the tension in Harri's voice. 'No, but I can find the place on my phone if you give me a mo. The owners call their company Daffodil Properties. It must be featured on their website.'

Mallory found the house easily enough and saw it was showing as fully booked until October. She turned her phone to show a photo to Harri. She saw him exhale slowly, some of his high colour draining out of him. 'It *is* Pant Meinog. Well, bloody hell.'

4

The chatter of the busy cafe receded for a moment to be replaced in Harri's mind by memories he'd hoped he'd left in the past. The sensation was unpleasant, as he considered himself a practical man. He'd visited plenty of crime scenes over the years and seen horrors whose memories were hard to wipe away when he got home from work. Nothing like that had happened at Pant Meinog, where physical injuries had amounted to little more than a few deep scratches. All in a day's work when you were out on patrol attending incidents involving the vulnerable and wounded. He was kidding himself, of course. There was far more to the case than that, although he'd initially thought he was attending a domestic dispute, as he'd been told on the radio. He'd driven over with PC Delyth Jones, a promising young copper, and ambitious, like himself. He felt Mallory's eyes on him, waiting for the story he would have to tell her. He regarded his cup, wishing he had a glass of whisky in his hand rather than another bloody mint tea.

'I was called to Pant Meinog, now apparently renamed Tall Pines, when I'd been a copper for a year or so. The first time was innocuous enough. It was a hot summer's day, a little like today. Two sisters, Carys and Gwenllian Prytherch, had said they'd been watching TV in the living room, and had gone into the kitchen to get a fizzy drink and some snacks. According to them, they heard nothing untoward while in the kitchen, but by the time they returned to the living room, the place looked like it had been burgled. Two lamps had been thrown off the tables, the curtain pulled off its pole and a plant ripped from its pot, with the soil spread across the room. The pair were naturally terrified and the older girl, Carys, called 999.'

'How long were they in the kitchen?'

'About five minutes. I know that it's not long but, you know, it was just about possible that an intruder had come in, created havoc and left in that time. So we searched the place to check it was empty and found nothing. There was a younger sibling, Dylan, aged around eleven, but he was outside the whole time. Gwenllian said that she'd been able to see him from the kitchen window, kicking a football in the small courtyard at the bottom of the driveway while they'd poured out their drinks.'

He watched Mallory frown as she considered the conundrum. 'You think it possible that someone came through the woods and entered, presumably through the front door? I've been in the house, and the back door opens on to a passage leading to the kitchen. If the layout's not changed, there's no way someone could have entered through there and not been seen.'

'I guess that was our hypothesis, although soon things started to get even stranger. The younger of the two girls, Gwenllian, pulled me to one side and insisted that it wasn't an intruder at all, and that Carys should never have called us. She said they were being tormented by a poltergeist and that the house was under attack.'

'Oh God.' To his relief, he saw Mallory start to laugh and roll her eyes. 'Like the Enfield haunting, only in

Carmarthenshire. That's not in your training manual, is it?'

'It's not. I didn't know what to make of it, to be honest, and I was a bit suspicious that she'd confided in me. Delyth was nobody's fool and perhaps Gwenllian thought I'd be the softer touch. Anyway, we calmed the girls down and helped them set the room straight. It didn't actually take that long – the soil from the plant was the main issue – and we put it down to a teenage prank. Delyth gave the girls a stern talking-to, if I remember correctly.'

'But, don't tell me, it happened again.'

Mallory was as jaded as he was, but it hadn't always been like that. He'd been convinced that it was simply a case of two bored teenagers with time on their hands during an interminable hot summer and that single incident would be the end of it. He had been wrong.

'Over the space of that summer, there were multiple call-outs to the house. At first, there were events like the one we'd attended, where the girls would leave a room and return to find it in chaos. They were questioned closely and the pattern was always the same. Carys was panicking and would be the one to call the emergency services, while Gwenllian was calmer, but insistent that it was the poltergeist.'

'*The* poltergeist rather than *a* poltergeist. Did it have a name?'

'Don't laugh, please, or I won't tell you any more of the story.' Harri could feel his mood darkening, although it was hardly Mallory's fault. He felt the need to communicate his uneasiness about the whole episode, afraid it would diminish him in her eyes.

'All right, all right. Carry on.'

Harri drained the rest of his tea. 'Towards the end of August, things started to deteriorate. Officers would arrive at the house to discover bruises on all three children and, a couple of times, plates and ornaments flew through the air while we were present.'

'What?' asked Mallory. 'You're kidding. What did everyone think was happening?'

'It's difficult to say – everyone had their own theories – but when "incident at Pant Meinog" came over the radio, none of us were exactly fighting to attend the scene.'

'And where the hell were the parents at that time?'

'Lewis and Sally Prytherch were a hippyish couple into promoting sustainable living. Sally sold wicker baskets and her pottery at various markets around the area, while Lewis hawked some produce from his garden, although he also held down a job at the local school. Carys, Gwenllian and Dylan were left in the house for long periods of time, and there was no initial suggestion of neglect. Christ, most of the farming families encouraged their children to fend for themselves while they were working.'

'No *initial* suggestion?' asked Mallory, ever alert.

'To be honest, the kids weren't thriving, and neglect, as you know, can take many forms. Perhaps it was less about abandonment and more to do with a loose temper causing the injuries to the kids, which made them invent this poltergeist. That was my theory, at least.'

'You said Dylan was eleven. How old were the other two?'

'From memory, Gwenllian was fourteen and Carys fifteen, nearly sixteen.'

'And what happened next? Presumably, the children went back to school?'

'You're skipping forward too quickly. As you can imagine, news of the alleged hauntings began to leak out. People talking at the station, taking the stories home to their families. Before we knew it, we had the local press visiting the children and writing up accounts of the happenings. Then the *Daily Express* picked up the story.'

'Jesus.' Mallory sat back in her chair. 'It'd be the kids playing jokes on everyone. What makes people so gullible?'

'I suppose it was the fact that the girls had perfected a technique where objects could be seen flying while adults, such as my colleagues, were present. Plus, a local Baptist minister got involved, a woman by the name of Bev Christie. She made it her mission to persuade everyone that the girls' story was genuine.'

Harri looked at his watch, conscious he'd need to be picking up his daughter Ellie soon. Time to cut to the chase.

'It gave my boss a headache. How can you fight serious crime when your officers are being called out to the middle of nowhere for an imaginary ghost?'

'I see your point. You went the once, you said.'

Harri's stomach turned as he realised he'd been delaying recounting the final episode. 'I visited Pant Meinog once more, in what turned out to be the final appearance of the alleged poltergeist. An emergency call was made by Dylan, who was screaming down the phone, saying his sister was being murdered. This was unusual in itself, as Dylan was very much out of the claims made by the two girls. When questioned about previous incidents, he stressed he had witnessed little, except for the odd plate flying through the air. It strengthened the official line that we were being taken for fools by the sisters. This time, however, it was different.'

'How did Dylan sound?' Harri saw that her coffee cup was half-full, her focus completely on his story.

'When we replayed the recording, we noticed he was almost incoherent with fear. Then it sounded as if the receiver was being wrenched out of his hand, while he was trying to tell us what was going on. So, naturally, the dispatcher sent a patrol car to take a look, even though Delyth and I groaned when we heard about where we were being sent.'

'You said the Prytherch family were living there. Did they own the house?'

Harri looked down at his cup. 'No, it was owned by Tom Thomas, who lived next door, but the Prytherch family were related to him in some way. I think the father of Lewis Prytherch and Tom Thomas were second cousins or something like that.'

He saw Mallory's face look ever so slightly bored. Well, OK, the names meant nothing to her, but he wanted to show that families who were distantly related occasionally still entwined with each other. Sometimes that was a good thing. Sometimes not. 'Look, do you want to hear the rest of the story? I mean, it's going to have nothing to do with your absent-minded family who've gone AWOL.'

Mallory coloured slightly. 'Sorry. Go on.'

'When I got there with my colleague, Gwenllian was crying hysterically outside. Her face was covered in scratches, the deep grooves of someone scoring her face. I have to tell you, it was a horrific sight. Her face was in shreds.'

He saw he had her attention then. 'What had happened?' asked Mallory.

'This is where it gets very odd. There were no adults in the building. The children's parents, Sally and Lewis, were out at a local market once more, and the children had been left to their own devices.'

'So, what happened to Gwenllian's face?'

The image of the deep channels carved into the girl's skin came unbidden into his mind. He shook his head.

'She told us she had been assaulted by the poltergeist. Her story was that she'd been attacked from behind by a force that had pulled her head back and scored deep grooves into her face. The girl was frightened out of her wits, I'll give you that. We questioned both Carys and Dylan, and their accounts were essentially the same. Gwenllian had rushed out of her bedroom, screaming and with her face covered in blood. She'd run down the stairs, leaving a trail of blood in her wake, and fallen to her knees in the clearing outside the side door. They were adamant no one else was in the house.'

'That's it? Their sister is injured and they still persist with the story of the poltergeist?'

Harri made a face. 'They did at first. We called an ambulance and the paramedics cleaned Gwenllian up. If anything, the scores looked worse once the blood had been wiped away. Delyth, my colleague, went in the ambulance while I took a closer look around the house. I was glad to get the place to myself, given it was now becoming infamous.'

'And how was it?'

'Like any other family home with busy parents. It was a bit shabby, needed work doing to it, especially in the kitchen and bathroom but it felt just ordinary.'

'Any sign of an intruder?'

'None that I could see. My initial thought was that she'd done it herself. You know, you've come up with a story about the poltergeist and you have to keep making things more and more dramatic. But if that was Gwenllian's intention, she had a shock coming…'

'Her sister finally admitted to making things up! I think I've heard this story, although it was so long ago that I can't remember the details.'

'Yes, exactly. Carys and Gwenllian had hatched a poltergeist plan after one of the girls had read a book on poltergeists and how teenage girls can be the conduit for such things. I'd personally ban such crap but I know Ellie likes to read them too. I think Gwenllian's injuries shocked Carys into admitting what had happened, how they'd perfected the art, for example, of chucking a plate across a room without anyone spotting. As a result, the Brechfa haunting became the Brechfa deception, thank God.'

'And Gwenllian's injuries?'

'This is the thing. Despite Carys's confession, Gwenllian kept to her story about what had happened that day. She admitted to the other deceptions – she didn't really have any choice, given Carys had confessed – but she was adamant she was attacked by an unseen force in her bedroom that final time.'

'Could she have made those marks herself?'

'That's what Delyth and I thought, but if the girl did deliberately injure her face, she never admitted to doing so.'

'Any other signs of self-harm? On her arms, for example.'

'None that I could see, although a subsequent medical examination did reveal a number of bruises on the girl's torso and limbs.'

Mallory sat back and regarded him, frowning as she thought over the story. He noticed she looked better than the previous time they'd met, but a suntan can mask a range of physical and emotional knocks. He wondered, not for the first time, why the hell he hadn't just picked up the phone and called her. 'Well, it's quite a story,' she said finally. 'You look quite ruffled in the retelling. Why's that?'

Harri shrugged, embarrassed. He'd tried to convey the absolute otherness of both the place and the series of incidents. 'It's just stayed with me. Not the first visit but that second call-out to the clearing. When you spoke about the house and the forest, I just felt this creep up the spine.'

'So, what happened afterwards? Were there any more repeat attacks?'

'None whatsoever. I mean, it was all a big sham, wasn't it, to get the girls through the summer holiday? Our thinking was that things had finally gone too far and the girls had given up the play-acting.'

'And what happened to the Prytherch family?'

Harri shrugged. 'At some point they moved on. A couple of years ago, I did look them up. I was driving past with the kids and something made me take the turning to Pant Meinog. The place was being torn to bits and the old water tank was in the garden. Tom Thomas, who was still living next door, was keeping an eye on the work, and he told me he'd sold the place to a Welsh holiday-letting company. And that was the end of that.'

Harri sat back in his chair, a false smile on his face. He wasn't feeling cheery. Far from it, but how to explain to Mallory the horror of those injuries? He didn't think for a minute those wounds would have healed without leaving scars.

Mallory looked at her watch. 'Funny that it's the same place as my missing tourists, but I've learnt this area is full of coincidental meetings and discoveries. I'd better make tracks, as I need to do some shopping before I head back to the forest.'

'Sure.' Harri was engulfed by a wave of lassitude. Recently diagnosed with diabetes, he was still telling people about it on a need-to-know basis. He hadn't yet confided in Mallory but he had a yearning to do so at that moment. Those events of twenty years earlier had opened up a crack of vulnerability. 'You know…' He made his tone as relaxed as possible. 'I'd like to know that your family have returned safely – call it human curiosity.'

Mallory nodded. 'Of course.'

5

To give him his due, Harri never ceased to surprise Mallory. As ex-police, she understood that some places remained with you beyond the circumstances of the crime. There was one street in the East End of London that she'd never liked visiting after an elderly female vagrant had been found there, beaten to death. The stench, the desolation, had got to Mallory and she'd half-anticipated a similar story from Harri. What she'd actually got, however, was something stranger. The name Pant Meinog had initially meant nothing to her but as Harri's story unfolded, flashes of the press attention on the alleged haunting came back to her. The teenage girls assailed by flying objects, which culminated in the gouges on Gwenllian's face. Interesting that the older girl had confessed to the poltergeist being nothing more than a figment of their fervid imagination, but even more curious was that Gwenllian had stuck to her story after those extensive injuries. Mallory, struggling with the mental health of her own son, thought that Gwenllian had probably harmed herself. Admittedly, the face was an unusual place to do it, but she was no expert. She'd wanted to press Harri a little more but sensed a raw spot, so had instead just listened.

Mallory made her way back to the car park and sat for a moment watching a family of five piling into an SUV. Were these the missing holidaymakers? No reason why they would be, but equally no reason why not. Mallory wondered why she was giving so much weight to Elsa's concerns, especially when the girl had such an active imagination. Perhaps it was because Elsa had once already detected a sense of wrongness about a place. Instinct wasn't always to be dismissed.

Mallory started the engine and, after spending a leisurely hour at the supermarket, drove the half hour back towards Pant Meinog. She was once more struck by the narrowness of the roads. If the missing family had been heading down the hill after their hurried departure, Elsa would certainly have encountered them in her car. Instead, it looked like they had gone over the mountain, where the road was surely more twisty than the one downhill. As Mallory indicated left to take her car down the bumpy, rough track, she saw that nothing had changed. No blue jeep, no other vehicle in the driveway. Mallory pulled up outside the house and checked to see if the door was still unlocked. It opened easily onto the narrow hallway. Mallory chewed her lip, thinking. There was nothing to suggest the place was a crime scene and, as she'd already been in every room with Elsa, she'd have left a trace of herself anyway. Elsa had also changed the beds and cleaned the rooms. Forensic damage had already been done and if she had to explain to a returning family why she was in the house, she could claim to be checking Elsa's work.

In the kitchen, the kettle was now holding only residual heat on the Aga and the cups of tea on the table were coated in a viscous scum produced by coagulating milk. The mobile phone retrieved by Elsa lay on the table, still locked but indicating no other missed calls. The other rooms appeared unchanged – Mallory touched nothing, poking her head around each room until she was satisfied that no one had returned to the house in her absence.

Back outside, she hesitated by the car. The only other house in the valley was just visible through the trees; judging by the rooftop, it looked a smaller, squatter building than Tall Pines. She decided there was no harm in knocking on the owner's door. Harri had said the occupant was called Tom Thomas, who had once owned both dwellings. Elsa too knew the man, which suggested he was often outside and might have seen the family's hasty departure.

The path to the other cottage took her nearer to the forest, where the trees' desiccated lower trunks belied the huge canopy of green towering above her. Harri had been sniffy about the replanting of the ancient forest with a non-native species but the uniformity of the trees reassured her that a family was unlikely to get lost in the woodland. The house she came upon was a single-storey building covered in white render that, unlike Pant Meinog, needed renovating. The roof was missing a few slates and the paint peeled off the windows in curls. The door opened as she approached and a man stuck his head outside.

'This is private. It says at the entrance.'

Mallory had missed the sign and the man's tone suggested that others in the past had too. 'It was you I was coming to see. I'm sorry to disturb you but I was wondering if you've seen the occupants of the holiday home next door?'

He opened the door more fully and stared at her. He was a thin man with a headful of hair, in his late sixties or perhaps a little older, and dressed in smart trousers and a houndstooth jacket. 'Saw a young girl hanging about here a few days ago. A chatterbox but I was on my way out. She laughed at my car but said the colour was the same as theirs.'

He was pointing to a battered Volkswagen Beetle, the iron-red rust spread out like blood against the turquoise paintwork. Mallory frowned. Elsa had said the family had a dark blue jeep, and turquoise definitely wasn't the preferred colour of SUVs.

'Have you seen her today?'

'I told you it was a few days ago.'

Mallory raised her hands. 'Sorry. A friend of mine is the cleaner there and it looks like the family left in a hurry. I'm just checking they are OK. If I give you my number, could you give me a call if you see them come home?'

She ripped off a piece of paper out of her diary, and scrawled down her name and number. He took it off her.

'Think something has happened to them?'

'I don't know. The way the house has been left feels a bit… odd. They clearly left in a hurry.'

He snorted. 'That place has always been odd. I should know, I used to own it. I sold it in the end, as I didn't have the money to renovate it like the new people have.'

'I might give them a call if I don't hear from you this evening. I'll probably come back in the morning as well.'

'I'll call if I see them. *Hwyl*, Mallory. Goodbye.'

He shut the door on her and she could hear the sound of Radio Cymru seeping through the cracks in the window. Mallory used another piece of paper from her diary to scrawl a note for the family, asking them to call her when they got home. She put it in a prominent place on the kitchen table, trying to ignore the nauseating cups of tea. She'd done what she promised Elsa and, realistically, given the heat of the day, the family might not be getting home until after dark. Getting back into the car, she wondered if she'd had a wasted trip and why, deep down, she thought she hadn't.

–

Toby rang as she opened the door to the caravan, wanting to know if he'd left his earbuds there. Mallory searched the small space as she spoke to him, trying to extract news from her monosyllabic son. She was about to give up, certain that he'd left the pair on the train home, when she discovered them pushed down the side of the bed. She promised to send them on to him but the offer was met with silence.

'What is it?'

'It doesn't matter – just stick them in the post, would you?'

'Of course. I'll send them tomorrow.'

In the kitchen, Mallory opened her tiny freezer and surveyed the uninspiring ready meals which she'd bought at the supermarket. She pulled out a tray of lemon chicken and turned on the oven. Hot and sticky after her exertions, she got in the miniscule shower, leaving her mobile phone on the sink in case it rang. Through dinner and while she was watching a Netflix film on her tablet, she waited, her eyes straying to the phone, which failed to ring. Finally, she got a text message from Elsa with just a '?'. She replied 'nothing yet' and, for something to do, opened a bottle of white wine and poured herself half a glassful.

She took it outside and sat under the awning of the caravan. She'd managed to secure herself a six-month let in the less touristy area of the park largely used by owners, who were content to leave their caravans empty for the periods they weren't in residence. It meant that Mallory didn't have to put up with an ever-rotating cycle of new holidaymakers, but she was occasionally forced into idle chit-chat with her neighbours, which she found excruciating. Tonight, she had some peace, which she was grateful for, as she needed to mentally turn over the events of the day. There were two reasons why she was failing to write off the drama as a forgetful-family incident. Firstly, Elsa – for all her stories – had proved a hard-headed ally when confronted with a murderer, and Mallory trusted her judgement. Secondly, there was something odd about the boiling kettle, the half-made sandwiches, the chair tipped onto the floor.

The half-glass of wine gave her courage and she called the number Elsa had given her for Chrissie, one of the owners of Daffodil Properties. The call rang onto an answerphone so it clearly wasn't an emergency number. She left a brief message for the owner and was contemplating another glass of wine when Harri's number came up on her phone.

'Heard anything?' he asked. His voice was strained, breathless, as if he was walking quickly.

'Nothing at all. I left my details on the kitchen table, making sure the message was reassuringly casual. If the family had got home, I'm sure one of the adults would have rung me out of curiosity if nothing else. Are you OK?'

'Had anything to drink?'

'Half a glass of wine. Why? Fancy going to the house yourself?'

'Something has come up. I want you to pick up your friend Elsa and come down to a lay-by on the A485. There's a detour in place at New Inn but I've left instructions for you to be let through. There's been an incident here and I want Elsa to take a look at the victim.'

'Shit. A victim? Not one of the children?'

'A male in his forties, I'd say. No ID on him, which is unusual but he's dressed in shorts and T-shirt, so he may have been on the way to or back from the beach.'

'Is there a vehicle?'

'A blue jeep that's registered to a hire car company.'

'That matches Elsa's description of the vehicle outside Tall Pines. Is there any evidence of the other members of the family?'

'Not that we can see, but we're scrabbling around in the dark, Mallory, both literally and figuratively. I'll explain when you get down here.'

'Is it a road traffic accident?'

She heard Harri exhale deeply. 'No, not an RTC. I can't say more over the phone. Get down here as soon as you can and bring Elsa with you.'

6

'This is fucking weird.' Detective Constable Siân Lewis gave Harri an incredulous look as they watched the forensic team scrutinising the lay-by, dark blue jeep and the victim sitting inside the car. The road was the main connection between the towns of Lampeter and Carmarthen – not an especially busy route, but one with a regular stream of traffic, especially in holiday season. Harri had already been there three hours and suspected it would be a while before the scene was cleared for him to have a good nose around, which was what he was dying to do. However, he'd managed to persuade his boss that, given the profile of the vehicle, there might be a connection to a family staying at Pant Meinog, or whatever the bloody holiday home was called now. He'd sent a patrol car up to the place to have a look round and had got the message back that the house was still empty. That meant five missing people, three of them minors, which upped the stakes considerably. Superintendent Steph Morris, his guv'nor, hadn't taken much persuading when he'd asked for their sole witness, Elsa, to come and take a look at the victim.

Harri could only begin to guess how many hours the body had been sitting there. The scene looked for all the world like someone was taking a break from the grind of the monotonous, country roads. He reckoned a couple of hundred cars might have passed the lay-by and not thought about the occupant sitting bolt upright in the front seat. At ten past eight that evening, however, a lorry driver had pulled in for the night and needed an extra metre or two to slot his truck into the space. He'd rapped on the car window, assuming the occupant had gone to sleep. A harder knock had rocked the car enough for the body to jolt forward and the truck driver to spot the sickening expression on the man's face.

'Weird, it certainly is.' Harri scratched his neck, the collar of his shirt too tight in the muggy night air. 'Could it be natural causes, do you think? He wouldn't be the first driver in cardiac arrest to stop at the nearest parking spot.'

'Hard to tell from this distance. The officers who first attended the incident couldn't immediately see any evidence of injury. The paramedics also didn't spend much time here – he was declared "beyond help" immediately.'

Harri watched the pathologist, Paula Griffiths, lean over the body, taking photos with her phone. He might be able to get some pointers from her, although he usually found the doctor a little too stand-offish for his liking. She straightened and murmured something to one of the forensic team. The pair turned and caught his gaze, Dr Griffiths peeling away to make a beeline for him.

'I've finished for this evening and there's not much more I can do *in situ*. I'll schedule the autopsy for tomorrow; I can shuffle things about so this gets priority, which I'm sure is what you want.'

'I'd appreciate that. Any preliminary conclusions you're able to share with us?' asked Harri, his expectations low. The medic, however, appeared to have already been briefed about the possible disappearance of other members of this family and was keen to help.

'Well, I need to have a good look at him under laboratory conditions, but I don't like the colour of his skin.'

'What do you mean?' asked Siân, fanning herself with her tablet as she struggled with the heat.

The pathologist continued to address Harri. 'It has a reddish tinge. If I wanted to be more specific, I'd say cherry red, which is a strong indicator of carbon monoxide poisoning. It's usually seen in accidental deaths in houses or on suicides inside cars.'

'You think that's what we're looking at?' asked Harri. 'Suicide?'

Paula took a step back. 'As I said, it's something I want to look at back in the autopsy suite. I'll know more in the morning.' She turned and made her way away from the spotlights, towards the edge of the tape.

'What's the matter with her?' asked Siân. 'Aren't I important enough for her to address me?'

'It's how she always is, so don't worry about it.' Harri looked at his watch. 'Mallory will be here soon and I'd like to bring her up to speed as much as possible. First and foremost, we need an ID on the victim because, without that, we're scrabbling around in the dark, worrying about a nameless family. What are the hire car company saying?'

'It's out of hours so I'm still getting the recorded message which directs me to roadside assistance. It's a Cardiff company, not one of the nationals, and clearly the only emergency they envisaged is a breakdown. No option to select if there's been a death in one of their vehicles.'

Harri turned to look down the road. 'It'll have to wait until morning, then, which is bloody inconvenient. Perhaps if we get a positive ID from Elsa, we can get in touch with the holiday let company.'

'I've already tried. It's Daffodil Properties and their number goes straight to answerphone too.'

Harri swore. 'We do, occasionally, get serious incidents here. How come it's so difficult to get through to a human voice?'

Siân shrugged. 'Brexit, post-pandemic, the rise of AI – all make for an impersonal twenty-first-century holiday experience. Sorry, boss, but no one gets to speak to a human easily these days.'

Harri refused to be mollified. 'You're positive there's no wallet on the body?'

Siân shrugged. 'I haven't looked myself but the two officers who arrived on the scene searched the victim. They say he wasn't carrying a mobile or wallet, which is unusual in itself. You think he might be connected to the family near the forest?'

'It's got to be a possibility, hasn't it? The lack of ID could suggest a hurried exit. Let's see what Elsa has to say as, according to Mallory, she got a good look at both the family and the vehicle. They should be here soon.'

They waited in silence, Harri missing nothing. He looked up at the sky, the stars bright against the cloudless dark. It had been a winter of wind and rain but now he missed the damp on his hair, which would have been a welcome relief from the heat. Finally, a noise behind him made him turn and he watched two figures approach by torchlight along the path running parallel to the road. He recognised Mallory's silhouette, which meant that the other, shorter, figure must be Elsa. He remembered a bedraggled girl desperately ringing the tower bell to save Mallory, who was locked in a battle of wills with a poisoner. He'd been struck by her resolve, despite looking like a child – and now, as Elsa came into the beam shone by the police lights, Harri saw she'd grown up and was no longer that awkward-looking teenager.

'*Noswaith dda*, Elsa. Good evening, Mallory. Thanks for coming down. Elsa, did Mallory explain what we want you to do?'

'You've found a body.' Elsa's eyes strayed over to the jeep. 'Mallory said it was a man, and you want me to see if it's him from Pant Meinog.'

Harri noticed she used the old house name and tucked the knowledge away. It was perhaps of little relevance. The poltergeist of Brechfa had, after all, had its own flare of fame.

'That's right,' he agreed. 'I'm just waiting for permission to take you over to see the deceased man now but there are some things we can do from this distance. Mallory said that you noticed the car the family arrived in was a blue jeep, is that right?'

'Yes, it's that one.'

Despite the bright spotlight trained on the vehicle, night had fallen, turning the dark blue hue of the hire car an inky black.

'Are you sure it's the same jeep? Do you remember the registration number?'

Elsa shook her head. 'It looked like that one, though.'

Harri's gaze met Mallory's. He didn't like witnesses all too willing to identify cars – or, come to that, people – that quickly.

Mallory shook her head slightly. Give her a chance, she seemed to be saying. Harri got Elsa to tell him the story of her visit to Pant Meinog, step by step, and Siân and Mallory listened. Its essence was as Mallory had told him, but the sense of place came alive in Elsa's retelling. She had the story gene in her and Harri the Welshman was proud

– until, that is, she came to the woman running through the woods. Elsa could sense his disbelief but she held firm to her tale.

'I saw it clearly: a woman in a white gown, running barefoot through the forest. It was one of my visions.'

Harri was prepared, in this instance, to humour the girl. 'Did it look like the teenage girl or the woman in the front seat of the jeep?'

'Not the girl and I don't think it was the woman either, although she had been harder to see.'

Harri was saved from replying by a nod from the forensic lead, who was happy for Elsa to take a look at the body. He gave the girl a disposable crime-scene suit, which Mallory helped her to get into.

'I'm sorry, Mallory, but it's me and Elsa only at this point in time.'

Mallory, however, knew the drill and stepped away readily as Harri guided the girl towards the vehicle.

'I want you to have a look at the man at the wheel. Mallory has explained that he's dead but I'm pretty sure it won't be too distressing. His face might be a funny colour but that's it. I just want you to look at him and tell me if you think it's the same man you saw at Pant Meinog.'

Elsa turned towards him, her fair hair covering her face. 'You know the original name of the house too? It's not called that anymore.'

Harri cursed the slip of the tongue. He'd given away more than he intended and he was determined to say no more. They'd reached the open door of the car and a white-clad figure stepped back so that Elsa could take a closer look. She frowned and leant forward.

'It's definitely him. He looks like Julius Caesar.'

Harri frowned, wondering if she was taking the piss. He could swear the forensic lead was smirking. 'Julius Caesar?' he asked.

'It's the hairstyle. Mam and I went on a coach trip to Rome in June and the statues of the senators had hair like this.'

Harri remembered now the full extent of Elsa's eccentricities. Had it been anyone else, he would have been furious at their flippancy, but he could see she was deadly serious.

'OK, you're sure it's the man you saw a week ago outside the holiday home.'

'Positive. His face is the colour of Ribena, though. What happened to him?'

She was right. The pathologist had mentioned a cherry-red colour but the victim's skin was as if blemished by a port-wine stain. Harri gently pulled Elsa away. 'We don't know.'

–

Siân took a statement from Elsa, which would form the basis of both the investigation into the man's death and the search for the other members of his family. They were sitting in the back of Mallory's car, the three of them sweltering in the humid night while Mallory stayed outside, checking her phone. This time around, Harri was more interested in the manner of the family's arrival and how Elsa had sensed something was off. Pressing the girl, however, resulted in her focusing not on the victim, but on the mother, who had refused to leave the vehicle, and the teenage boy and girl who had displayed a distinct lack of curiosity for their surroundings. If anything, the dead man and the child, whose name was Pippa, were the two who'd appeared the most normal to Elsa although she'd noted that the man was a smoker. The girl's name was a helpful pointer, but nothing more at this stage without a surname. They needed much more on the family, although Elsa had a good memory for physical appearances. Two older children with straw-blonde hair and a smaller ginger-haired girl was something to be going on with. Harri hoped that forensics would be able to get something from the mobile phone now retrieved from the kitchen table, but experience had taught him it was almost impossible to unlock an iPhone without the passcode.

His mind kept straying back to the children. He hoped to God they were still alive and, hopefully, holed up with their mother. Even better if none of them were implicated in this death, even if it was suicide, although he wasn't holding his breath on that one. He could write a book on families and their secrets. Next to him, Siân continued her interview deftly and, to his relief, Elsa didn't mention the running woman in her statement. This case was complicated enough without adding Elsa's visions.

'We need to contact your employers as soon as possible,' said Siân. 'The number you gave Mallory isn't being answered.'

'It's the only one I have. Jon and Chrissie Morgan live in Carmarthen, if you want to speak to them. The office is near your police station.'

'There won't be anyone at the office now, though, will there?' said Siân. 'We need to speak to someone tonight. The Companies House website gives an address in Carmarthen too, a residential one. Do you think they live there?'

'I don't know.' Elsa was close to tears. 'I only ever go to the office and that's not often.'

'That's fine,' said Harri. 'I'll get Mallory to drive you home after I've had a word with her.'

He opened the car door and stepped out into the still warm night. Mallory put away her phone as he approached.

'What do you think?' she asked.

'Her ID was positive enough, if a little quirky. We need to find the other family members as a matter of urgency, especially as it appears there was only one car. The best-case scenario is that he'd dropped them off at Carmarthen station after some family emergency and was returning to the house to sort things out.'

'And where does carbon monoxide poisoning fit with this theory?' asked Mallory.

'Who told you that?' Harri looked around. She must have quizzed a member of his team while he was questioning Elsa. Bloody hell. 'It doesn't matter at this point in time, as finding the family is of key importance. I need to get back to the office and start briefing everyone ready for tomorrow. I'll send Siân down to the owners of the holiday let and get details of the family.'

'You know...' Mallory raised a thumb and indicated a uniformed officer in the distance. 'Charlie over there also knows about the history of the house. Maybe we should start looking at that angle too.'

Harri stared across at the officer. 'We? Sorry Mallory, you're here as a witness and nothing more at this point in time – and, anyway, Charlie needs to keep his bloody mouth shut. The fake haunting was in 2003 and nothing untoward has happened since.' He took a deep breath, aware of his irrational anger. 'Thanks for coming out, Mallory. Will you drive Elsa home?'

'Of course.' Harri saw her hesitate. 'If you need me, though…'

He nodded, experiencing a rush of pleasure at the thought of working with her again, although it wasn't exactly his call to make. 'All right, I'll see what I can do.'

7

Saturday

Mallory spent a restless night trying to sleep, until she gave up as the sounds of her neighbours rising early to pack their car for the trip back to their home in Birmingham filtered through the thin walls of her caravan. She stuffed two slices of bread in the toaster and checked the news sites on her phone. There was little there except on Twitter, where she found a couple of tweets about the road closure. She wondered if there had been any developments overnight on the missing family, but it appeared the decision had been made not to go public at this stage about the disappearance. As she moved on to check her emails, her heart leapt when Harri's number came up on the call display, but the news wasn't good.

'I've spoken to the Super and there's no budget for consultants yet. Our priority is to find the family and that's a region-wide issue involving scrutinising ANPR, CCTV, and so on. It's hard for people to disappear without a trace these days and we're confident we'll find them soon. We're about to put out an appeal for dashcam footage this morning, keeping everything low-key, of course.'

Mallory rubbed her eyes. The day was warming up and she felt sluggish after her fractured night. Perhaps it was a blessing she wasn't going to be co-opted onto the case straight away. She could doze on the beach and hope that, by Monday, if the family were still missing, there would be a role for her in the team.

'That's completely fine,' she said, not really meaning it. After the conversation with Harri in the cafe, she'd realised how much she missed his company. There was so much she didn't know about him – how he coped with raising two children after the death of his wife, how he felt about his job, and why he sometimes looked well and other times terrible.

Some of her disappointment must have transferred down the line. 'Sorry, Mallory,' said Harri. 'I'll let you know if this escalates but you'll excuse me if I say I really hope it doesn't. I've briefed the team already and really need to find the identities of who we're looking for. That's our priority this morning.'

'No problem.' Mallory wanted to cut the call but Harri was inclined to linger.

'Funny it was Pant Meinog, you know. It gave me quite a jolt when I saw the house on your phone yesterday. There's almost certainly no connection to this case, of course, and the Super is super keen, if you'll excuse the pun, to keep the location of the dead man's holiday home quiet. There's nothing like a haunting, even a fake one, to get the press interested. I do wonder what happened to Gwenllian Prytherch, though. She'd be in her early thirties now.' He paused, letting the silence settle. 'Anyway, have a good day, Mallory.'

Mallory smiled as Harri cut the call. Gwenllian Prytherch was an unusual name and Harri had casually dropped it into the conversation for a reason. He was too wily to accidentally let slip the name of a previous victim in a potential line of inquiry. Mallory did a quick Google search on her phone for Gwenllian, which threw up hundreds of hits: very few in relation to the original haunting but plenty in the intervening years. That in itself was curious. Despite Harri stressing that the press had taken a keen interest in the case, this wasn't reflected in online coverage. What had happened, however, was that the so-called Brechfa haunting had been kept alive by a keen band of internet fans and podcasters with names such as Weirdasfuck and Hauntedly Yours.

Mallory was pretty sure she had Harri's tacit approval to do a little digging, as he wouldn't be going down this route in the first instance. It sounded as if he had his work cut out even establishing the identity of the family. She also understood his boss's reluctance to rake up the past when there was no evidence of any connection to yesterday's death. Steph was on the up career-wise and wouldn't want to be dragged into what had turned out to be a deception by the girls. Harri too would be unlikely to push this angle until he was forced to, reluctant to articulate how much the alleged haunting had affected him. He'd been clear the previous afternoon that his disquiet wasn't because he believed in ghosts, but due to the impact of such an act of violence on a teenage girl.

Mallory glanced out of the window and saw it was going to be another hot day. She was itching to get out and contribute to the hunt for the missing family. She was an experienced former detective who understood there was little she'd be able to do in relation to the murder investigation unless she was officially brought on to the team. Trawling through websites wasn't doing it for her, but she did have some tidying to do, so she could listen to one of the podcasts to get their take on the case from a historical perspective. Harri, after all, had only given his recollections that, given his police status, provided a one-sided overview.

She clicked on a link to a random podcast but as soon as she started listening, she realised her mistake. The voice grated on her and it was full of woo-woo over-the-top theatrics that she hated. She happily put the duster away and sat down to read some of the internet articles. Three sites stood out for the in-depth neutral coverage they gave to the hauntings. They had also come to a similar conclusion – Gwenllian and her older sister Carys had made up the poltergeist – but they were sure that something was wrong with the house, and the final attack on the younger sister remained unexplained. None of them gave any updates on the whereabouts of the family. She sent a message to all three website hosts via their social media accounts, explaining she had a few questions about the Brechfa poltergeist and asking if they were available for a chat.

One, Luke Parry, who ran his own website and podcast called Haunted Wales, must have been online, as he replied immediately. He'd looked at Mallory's Instagram page, which she kept meaning to make private but couldn't work out how. Her account contained only two images of the caravan site, but Luke recognised it immediately. He lived in the nearby town of New Quay and suggested meeting in person. Perhaps on the beach for a swim? Mallory rapidly reassessed her view of true-crime bloggers as people who hide away in darkened rooms. His profile made Luke sound more surfer dude than goth, but she would reserve judgement until they met.

A benefit of having had Toby to stay was that she'd bought them both wetsuits for what had been a chilly

July. This meant that at least she wasn't interviewing a random man in her old floral swimming costume. She put the wetsuit on under her clothes and filled a beach bag with sunscreen, towel, water and her notebook. She doubted Harri had had interviewing on a beach in mind when he'd mentioned Gwenllian's name, but at least she was doing something. She shut the door of her caravan and slid into her car, noticing a fine layer of yellow dust that had spread over the bonnet. The winds from the Sahara had brought the particles up through Europe, and they landed on the fringes of Wales.

She forced herself to listen to Luke's podcast about the Brechfa poltergeist on the drive to the coastal town. This might be the only chance she'd get for an interview with someone who had researched the case, and she needed to know which questions to ask. The podcast gave Mallory a decent enough summary but appeared to be overly critical of the police. He pointed out that a relaxed approach to previous incidents had contributed to the escalation that culminated in the attack on Gwenllian. Poor Harri, thought Mallory, who'd decided Luke's analysis was a little tough.

Luke's conclusion was that, in the absence of any useful suspects, there probably was a malign influence in the house. He was pretty good at summing up the atmosphere of the place – perhaps he'd visited Tall Pines, or Pant Meinog as Harri remembered it, in advance of the programme. Where the podcast fell down, as far as Mallory's investigation was concerned, was in expanding on the ramifications of that final attack. Gwenllian had apparently spent a few days in hospital but after that... silence. The house had remained in the Thomas family, which Mallory already knew, as she'd met Tom the previous day. What *had* happened to Gwenllian after the incident? Perhaps she'd moved elsewhere and the attacks had continued. It was impossible to find out. The podcast cut off abruptly to be replaced by a blast of music, the type Toby liked to listen to, and Mallory hit the off button.

Finding somewhere to sling the car was harder than she expected in New Quay. The one huge car park with its grassy bumps was filled to bursting point, with a queue spilling out onto the road. Mallory drove fruitlessly around for about twenty minutes, until she finally found a space on the street, with an hour's permit. She'd need to be quick to get all the information required in the short window of time.

The slope down to the beach was steep, the descent pulling at her leg which an old injury had weakened. Luke had told her the exact spot where she'd be able to find him and, sure enough, close to the lifeboat station, she saw a man in his late twenties reading a Lee Child paperback. Mallory plopped down beside him and pointed at the book.

'Glad you gave me your reading material to identify you. I couldn't find a picture of you at all on the internet.'

'That's deliberate.' Luke put down the book and held out his hand. 'Luke Parry. The thing is, I studied media at university and you can go down two routes – making it all about yourself or about the subject. I prefer the latter.'

Mallory propped herself against her beach bag and pulled down the visor on her cap so it shaded her eyes from the sun. 'I listened to the podcast in the car. It was helpful but only half an hour long – I'm sure there's a lot more information than what you were able to put in the programme.'

'Do you know... I'm not sure that is the case. There's plenty online about the whole Brechfa incident but it's all a bit vague. Gwenllian's scratches, for example. I wanted to flesh it out – sorry, bad joke – a little. How deep were the gouges? Was the girl's face permanently scarred? But no one would talk to me and I found no trace of the family. I went up to the house but it's a holiday let now and the old man next door wouldn't even open his door. I even tried to contact the police officer who first arrived on the scene. He's a DI now but you should have heard his language when I spoke to him on the phone.'

'DI Harri Evans?'

Luke glanced at her. 'That's right. You know him?'

'A little. I don't think I've ever heard him swear.'

'Anyway, he didn't want to talk to me. Probably lumps me alongside journalists and irritating members of the public. So, anyway, I used what I could find online. I'm sorry if you've had a wasted trip, but there's not much more I'll be able to tell you. What's your angle on this, anyway, and how come you know the detective inspector?'

Mallory hesitated and decided a half-truth was better than nothing. 'A friend of mine cleans the holiday cottage where the alleged haunting happened. She told me the story and I was interested.'

'Why? Why were you interested? And that doesn't answer the question about knowing Harri Evans.' Luke had turned over onto his side and was eyeing her lazily.

Mallory was amused at his attention. 'I'm a retired copper, so I love a good mystery, and I met Harri in an investigation as part of my job.' Again, a half-truth. She was suggesting a long-finished association with Dyfed-Powys police, whereas she'd worked with Harri earlier that year. Luke, however, was only concerned about any ramifications for his chosen profession.

'Right. Well, as long as you're not planning on a rival podcast, I don't mind talking to you. You'd be amazed how many people have tried to pick my brain in the name of research, and the next thing is I see a podcast that goes by the name of Spooky Wales or Welsh Haunts. Not a million miles from the name of my podcast.'

'I absolutely promise you that I've no intention of writing a podcast or a book about the house. I'm genuinely interested in what went on. It must have felt like a gift when you realised it had taken place nearby.'

'D'ya know what? I'd never even heard of the incident until I contacted Bev Christie when I was writing about another case. It's a little before my time so I rely on a network of friends to tip me off about cases in the past. Bev is one such contact – have you heard of her?'

'Umm… I'm not sure,' said Mallory. 'Who's she?'

'She calls herself a deliverance minister. Like an exorcist, but not as scary. People get in touch with her when they feel something is going on in their house that's a little strange. She's harmless enough, famous around these parts, and I interviewed her over the phone about something that was happening in a derelict former coaching inn near Haverfordwest. Anyway, she mentioned this story, as she'd had contact with the family at the time. She's worth a chat, too, if you're going down the "there's an actual haunting" route.'

Mallory smiled. 'You're a sceptic? I'd have thought you were a believer after listening to your podcast.'

'I do believe in hauntings, but I also want to attract an audience who are sceptical about these things. What I'd really like on my programme is a Scully to my Mulder, if that makes sense. A rationalist to counteract my enthusiasm.' He paused, his eyes on her legs. 'You're not interested, are you?'

'Me?' Mallory laughed. 'I don't think so.' What she really wanted to do was get involved in a possible murder investigation, and that wasn't going to happen if she became involved in a podcast about the supernatural.

Luke smiled at her. 'Shame. I can give you Bev's number if you want, as she's good for a story but, beware, like everyone else, she'll have her own angle on this.'

'And you really didn't find out what became of the family?'

Luke pursed his lips, his eyes on the horizon. 'All I know is that they all moved away. I really couldn't get further than that, which was a shame. The podcast would definitely have benefitted from one of the original residents of the house.'

'You didn't like the place, did you? I got that from your podcast.'

Luke turned to her, his expression difficult to read. 'Wales is full of such settings. Layer upon layer of history. It's not the only building where I've picked up negative energy.' He sighed. 'Fancy a swim? The sea is usually warm after the hot weather.'

'Sure.' Mallory stripped off her clothes, trying to ignore Luke's eyes on her as she undressed. She must be at least ten years older than him. Maybe fifteen. Oh well, it was only a swim.

8

Mallory arrived back at her car to a ticket on the windscreen. She looked up the long line of vehicles, each covered with a square of yellow.

'It's a fair cop,' said the occupant of the car next to hers, slitting open the square to see the fine. Mallory ripped off the offending item from beneath her wiper and stuffed it into her bag. The two hours spent with Luke had been much more enjoyable than she'd expected. For once, she wasn't swimming by herself or with her son, but with another adult. Maybe, she thought, I need to start dating. As if sensing the direction of her thoughts, her mobile rang in her bag and she saw that it was Harri.

'Where are you?' he asked. 'I've been trying to get hold of you.'

'At the beach.' Mallory felt her mood darkening at his tone, given she'd been trying to help him. 'Is anything wrong?'

'Everything's wrong. We got in touch with the hire car company this morning and we have a name. The car was hired by Robin Stevens, which also matches the name on the rental agreement for the cottage.'

'That's good news, isn't it? What did you discover about the family?'

'Nothing. The ID is fake.'

'What?'

'Mr Stevens's wallet was stolen on 29 July, when he was out on the town in the centre of Cardiff. He'd got around to cancelling his credit cards but not reporting his driving licence missing. The fake Robin Stevens hired the car with this document and paid cash.'

'Cash?' Mallory's voice rose and a passing family turned to stare at her. She opened the car door and slid inside. 'Can you still hire a car with cash?'

' 'Fraid so. That's what these smaller companies pride themselves on. Helping out if you've got a credit rating issue. I did a search online and there's multiple sites offering the same service. You turn up and take what car is available on the day, but that's about the only difference to a regular car hire company. It's the licence they're more interested in to check you have a UK address and are authorised to drive.'

'So what about the holiday rental?'

'Paid for in cash again. Now, you're usually not advised to do that because, if the house listing is a scam, for example, then the potential holidaymakers leave themselves exposed to fraud. Giving up their money for a house that doesn't exist. But if you're willing to take the risk then there's nothing to stop you paying for your rental plus deposit with cash. Apparently, it's not that uncommon.'

'Jesus.' Mallory turned on the engine. 'How did the cash reach the owners, though?'

'Well, this is something. It was brought in by a man answering the deceased's description two days before the family took over the house. The reason it didn't arouse any suspicion was that they'd had a cancellation, and everything was last-minute anyway. I think the owners were pleased to get another booking, given the short notice.'

'So what are you calling me for?' Mallory tried and failed to keep the appeal from her voice.

'This case has just widened considerably. Not only do we not know the real identity of the fake Mr Stevens, but we're also looking for the woman who is possibly his wife or partner and the three children. We're calling in extra personnel and one of them is you. Can you be here for tomorrow's briefing? It'll take personnel this afternoon to get your paperwork in place to join the team. Sorry it's not on the beach.'

A flush of happiness washed over Mallory. 'No need for the sarcasm – I was following the trail of Gwenllian Prytherch. I thought that was the reason you mentioned her name on the phone.'

There was a silence at the other end. 'Right. Let's leave the past be, for the moment. This afternoon, I'm sending a forensic artist to Elsa's house in Tenby to put together some images of the family she saw. She'll get to Elsa's around four and I think it'd be a good idea if you went down there. You know how nervy she is.'

'There's nothing nervy about Elsa – she has the heart of a lion – but I'll happily visit. You don't have anything else to go on?'

'Not yet, unfortunately. The phone, as expected, is a no go, although we're keeping it on in case it rings again. There's a lot riding on Elsa's descriptions and I'd like you there. Then, first thing tomorrow, come into the station. I'll sort out your pass and anything else you need. We'll be expecting you.'

After Harri cut the call, Mallory looked down at her damp clothes. She'd put her shorts and T-shirt back on over her wetsuit after getting out of the sea, thinking she'd be heading home to get changed. The fact that

Harri not only wanted her on the case, but was also co-opting her this afternoon gave her a warm feeling but there was a sense of something left undone. Harri's urgency suggested that once she was on the case, there'd be very little time for pursuing the Gwenllian Prytherch connection, and Mallory wanted to at least see through what she'd discovered today. She pulled out of her back pocket the phone number that Luke had given her and typed in the digits.

–

Rightly or wrongly, Mallory had formed a poor opinion of the clergy. She'd spent time as a shop assistant at St Davids Cathedral earlier in the year but had made sure she had little day-to-day contact with religion. She'd liked the volunteers and tourists who came into the shop but had been a little wary whenever she saw a clerical collar. Bev Christie, therefore, was a surprise. She knew the Church of England had an official 'deliverance' priest, but Bev was a Baptist minister dressed in jeans and a floral blouse which gaped at the buttons. She lived in a tall townhouse in Carmarthen, its brickwork painted in muted grey. She took in Mallory's expression and laughed.

'Don't tell me! I'm not what you expected.'

'I… No, you're not,' admitted Mallory. She stepped over the threshold into the high-ceilinged hall. 'Thanks for agreeing to see me. You must constantly be pestered by the curious.'

'Not the curious, no. The desperate usually. Come into the living room – there's a pot of tea waiting for us that I've just brewed and I've also had the fan going all day.'

Bev took her into a room where an elderly chocolate Lab was snoring heavily on the threadbare sofa. Bev and

Mallory took armchairs either side of it, as if venerating the ancient animal.

'I was surprised to get your call, to be honest. I have plenty to keep me occupied in relation to present-day hauntings, without digging around in the past. Who did you get my name from?'

'A podcaster called Luke Parry.'

'Ah. I remember. He telephoned me about a case he was investigating and asked me if I could recommend any other cases that might be suitable for the podcast. He specifically wanted something local and I mentioned, of course, the Brechfa haunting. He was a little young to remember the events.'

Mallory shifted in her seat as the dog lifted an eyelid to regard her. Over the phone, she'd given Bev the same story she'd told Luke: that she was interested in the case after a chat with Elsa. 'That's one of the strange things about this. I mean, there have been quite a lot of famous hauntings. The teenager at Enfield, for example, and one at Brecon. This one in Brechfa Forest got a brief flare of publicity but everyone largely fell out of the public eye. Why do you think that's the case?'

'How many cases of possible supernatural activity do you think I get asked to investigate?'

Mallory shrugged. 'I don't know. One every couple of months.'

'Every couple of weeks, more like. Sometimes weekly. Do you hear about these incidents? Of course not. People don't want to advertise that their houses might be haunted or they've been a victim of a poltergeist. How's that going to look when they come to sell the place? You've got to declare these things, so people want to rationalise the situation by proving it's the wind or ancient central heating.

When all these attempts have failed, they contact me but they're not looking for publicity or a slot on someone's podcast. They just want to get rid of the phenomena.'

'Every couple of weeks?' Mallory couldn't hide her disbelief. 'Is it something about this area?'

'I really don't think so. I suspect it's being replicated all over the country.'

'And what proportion of these incidents are genuine?'

'Genuine?' Bev put a spoon into the teapot and gave it a stir. 'Well, that's not a term I find particularly helpful. If you're scared to be in your house or in a particular room, then that's an honest emotion, isn't it? What I suspect you're asking me is what proportion of people who contact me are fakes. The answer is very few, but it does happen occasionally.'

'How do you find them out?' asked Mallory.

'It's a mixture of things. Their attitude, the presence of pins, string that sort of thing. Not everyone who calls me is behind the scam. They might have a teenager who thinks it's a good idea to play a joke on their family. They're usually easy to spot.'

'Like the two sisters at Brechfa.'

'Exactly. Although, I understand the younger girl stuck to her story about the scratches on her face.'

'So, how did you get involved?'

Bev picked up the teapot and busied herself with pouring out the cups. 'I'd taught alongside Lewis Prytherch, the father of the children, although I'd already left to pursue my ministry by then. He remembered me and telephoned me after a journalist had turned up on his doorstep.'

'Do you think he suspected that the girls were playing a joke?'

Bev handed Mallory a cup. 'Lewis was difficult to read. The whole family were, to be honest. I decided to put that to one side and concentrate on the fact that Lewis had called me in. I went over to speak to the girls at Pant Meinog and I'm not sure I came away with a definite feeling of what was going on.'

'You thought there was a possibility the haunting might be true?'

'Something was going on, but I don't think I ever really got to the bottom of it. The thing was, nothing actually happened while I was there. That can have two explanations. Firstly, that spirit is quiet because it doesn't wish to come into the open while I'm there or, secondly, the girls have been making it up and don't wish to demonstrate their shenanigans in front of me. As I said, I'm sharp at spotting the fakes.'

'So, what did happen?'

'I said my usual prayer and suggested I come back and do a much more formal ceremony, which they readily accepted. Gwenllian in particular was quite nervy, I thought. She kept asking me about deliverance from evil.'

'And how did that ceremony go?'

'It never happened. There was the incident with Gwenllian's face, after which the girls admitted to making up the poltergeist activity. That's where my involvement ended.'

'So you're only interested in cases that aren't fake? You actually believe in the hauntings?'

'Why not? I'm an ordained minister. I believe in life after death. It's not that big a stretch to say that sometimes those who have passed over have trouble leaving the earth plane behind.'

Earth plane? thought Mallory. Jesus. 'OK, look, I think I need to explain a little more about why I'm here. I want to dig a bit more into that final incident. I can't tell you why, but I'm here in a semi-official capacity.'

Bev looked across at her. She had dark eyes that gave nothing away. 'I can keep a secret but I also respect them. Go on, how can I help?'

'I'm interested in the possibility that Gwenllian made those scratches herself. Why do you think that might have been?'

'How old was she? Fifteen?'

'Fourteen.'

'Well, it's a difficult age, isn't it? People self-harm for complex reasons. I'm really not the person to ask about that.'

Unbidden, Mallory's thoughts turned to Toby and his issues with eating. Was that a form of self-harm? She'd never really thought about it in that way before, focusing instead on his iron control on what he put inside his stomach. But, whether intentional or not, his body had the appearance of being punished.

'Have you seen something similar in your line of work? Where people are harmed by spirits, real or imagined.'

Bev shook her head. 'Never scratches on the face only. In fact, most injuries are due to something being thrown at the resident of the house. A flying plate can do a lot of damage, I can assure you. I've also heard of people waking up with injuries on them, but the cause of the violence is unknown. Gwenllian said she was attacked, though, didn't she?'

'By an unknown force, apparently.'

Bev shrugged. 'It's possible.'

'What about siblings in cahoots? Gwenllian's story on that final day was backed up by her siblings.'

'Definitely possible. In relation to the Enfield hauntings, people believe the two sisters made it up between them.'

'So there could, for example, have been an intruder whose existence, for reasons that aren't clear, both brother and sister decided to hide.'

'If you were looking for a rational explanation, that would be my guess.'

'And you can't give me any more insight as to what happened at Pant Meinog?'

Bev stood, brushing down invisible crumbs from her trousers. 'Can't help you at all.' Mallory wondered what raw nerve she'd touched on, as the previously hospitable woman was suddenly keen to get rid of her.

'I'm sorry for bothering you,' said Mallory at the door. 'You didn't keep in touch with the family at all, did you?'

Smiling, Bev shook her head. 'I never took to Lewis and Sally Prytherch, and I later heard they'd moved away. It's all a long time ago, in the past. The only thing...'

Mallory turned. 'What is it?'

'Be careful how you go, Mallory. Be open to the fact that some things are very hard to comprehend.'

9

After the team briefing, Harri was desperate for his morning cappuccino, which was now delayed as he'd been called to see his boss, Superintendent Steph Morris. She was worried about the death on the layby, and was nervously chewing her lip as they discussed the pros and cons of a news conference so early in the case. Harri, unusually for him, was all in favour of the move.

'We have a victim that, despite all the resources at our disposal, we cannot currently identify. Until we get the genetic testing results back, we won't know if he's on the DNA database, and the car and holiday rentals are a dead end. We're fairly confident he fits the description of the man at the holiday cottage, which suggests there are others missing, including minors.'

Steph groaned, massaging her temple. 'Don't remind me. I've been awake half the night thinking about them.'

'There is, of course, a risk that by making our appeal public, we might be putting them further in danger, but that's a chance I'm prepared to take. We need to track them down and the best way of doing so is to find out who they are.'

'I agree.' Steph looked far from happy. 'I'll start putting things in motion for a briefing at three p.m. today, although I think everything will take longer because it's a Saturday. We don't wait for the forensic artist to visit your witness. Let's get the details of the missing persons out there straight away, then we'll take questions at the news conference and we can release any images we have later today or tomorrow. What time's the autopsy?'

'It's taking place at the moment. Siân's down there, observing, and will call me as soon as it's over.'

'You're sure you can't get anything more out of the hire car company?'

'I'm afraid not. No CCTV, only a vague description of the man who hired the vehicle, which is no help, except that it matches the victim. The guy who works at the desk said he never saw any evidence of a family. We assume the fake Robin Stevens took the car and picked up the woman and children from elsewhere. The house rental company has given little more. There was that initial contact when he paid, but nothing out of the ordinary and, after that, he was told to pick up the key from under the stone to gain access to the building.'

'You know,' Steph folded her arms, 'there should be a law against idiots running holiday lets. Think it's legit?'

Harri shrugged. 'If they were hoping to take the cash to bypass the tax office, they'll certainly be declaring it now, but for our purpose I think they're on the level. They've no idea who he was.'

'What about ANPR? Can we track the family's movements over the week?'

'We're starting it now, but it'll take time.'

'Shit.' Steph began chewing her lip again. 'Let's try to get something else before three. I don't want us to look completely at sea in front of the reporters.'

Steph stalked off, the heels of her boots tapping on the laminated wooden floor. Harri dug his hands in his pockets and pulled out a five-pound note, wondering if he could ask a member of his team to get him his coffee. He'd have to ask a bloke, otherwise he'd be accused of sexism but, in his experience, his male colleagues didn't like running errands for him. There was a knock and DC Freddie Carr hovered in the doorway. Freddie was English and had come to Wales, most thought, for a more relaxed lifestyle than the one he'd got in Greater Manchester Police. Well, his wife and kids might be having an easier life, but Freddie had already been involved in a murder investigation and had nearly been stabbed after a run-in with a local thug. He looked none the worse for his misadventures.

'Any news?'

'Just something that's set my senses twitching. The emergency comms centre has just received a call from a shopkeeper in Brechfa who thought a distressed child was stealing food from near the door. He shouted after her but she obviously thought she was in trouble and legged it. He called it in because he was concerned about the child. Didn't look like the usual delinquent. Said she had short red hair, which matches Elsa's description of the missing girl. What do you think?'

Harri's spirits rose a fraction and he reached for the five-pound note on his desk. 'Let's go.'

Freddie looked surprised. 'You want to come with me? I can whizz down there and report back if you're busy here.'

Harri shook his head. 'I've a banging head, due to lack of caffeine, and I'm just sitting here waiting for Siân to ring. I need to get the hell out of here.'

—

The Convenient Life was the type of store that was popping up around the country, replacing the traditional corner shop selling wilted cauliflowers and biscuits of the same variety favoured by Harri's grandma. Instead, young entrepreneurs — usually, Harri pictured them as bearded types — were opening hipster-type stores with an array of fresh fruit and vegan pasties. Harri, as he entered the shop, was assailed by the aroma of spices. It was a woman behind the counter, her hair in two plaits, who clocked them.

'Llion,' she shouted. 'It's the Old Bill.'

Freddie shot Harri an amused glance. From behind a curtain, a man emerged, sporting, Harri noted, the requisite beard.

'*Bore da*,' he said. 'Do you want to come in the back?'

The storage room was a mess of unopened boxes and strewn paperwork. Llion gave Harri the only chair, while he and Freddie perched against a long counter.

'Is everything all right?' asked Llion. 'When I rang you, I thought I was doing my civic duty. I didn't expect a visit from detectives.'

Harri watched the man as Freddie took the lead on the questioning. 'We are concerned about the welfare of a missing child who matches the description you gave to our colleague. You said she had red hair?'

'Yes, very red. Carroty, in fact. She walked into the shop and seemed agitated. I looked behind her for an adult, but there was no one there.'

'What about a teenager?' asked Harri.

'No one at all. She seemed to be on her own. I saw her stuffing apples and some bran bars into her pockets. I made the mistake of calling out and she ran off, but she looked terrified.'

'And that's why you called us?'

'I'm worried about the child. Like other shops, we occasionally have a shoplifting problem here, but it's the more expensive stuff – vitamins, bottles of wine. Middle-class theft, if you like. I'd never have made an issue of some apples. The child was clearly starving.'

'Do you have any surveillance cameras?' asked Freddie.

'Our ethos is to take people on trust,' said Llion. 'You won't find cameras anywhere in the village.'

Outside the store, Harri and Freddie glanced up the quiet road. 'We need to get some people down here as soon as possible,' said Harri. 'This place is walkable from where the jeep was discovered and it's possible they've found an empty holiday cottage. The child stole food but not water, and it's bloody hot this week. I want you to start knocking on doors and ask if anyone's seen the family or if they know of any empty houses in the area. Once we have the photofits, you do it all again.'

Harri heard the low rumble of his stomach and reached into his pocket. 'Go and get me one of the pasties and one for yourself. I've missed my morning coffee and I'll be damned if I forgo my lunch too.'

As Freddie went back into the store, Harri glanced upwards towards the hills in the distance. The sighting of the child was a good lead but he suspected the answers lay in the clearing up the mountain. All paths, he thought, led to Pant Meinog.

10

Elsa still lived with her mother in a small terraced house on the outskirts of Tenby. As Mallory drove through the winding streets, she noticed that many of the houses looked empty – probably holiday lets – and, sure enough, she saw a sign hammered into a patch of grass that said, *dim mwy o dai haf*: no more second homes. Despite the lack of full-time residents, parking was a nightmare and the forensic artist had already started work in the homely sitting room by the time Mallory eventually arrived. Elsa's mother was out, which was a shame, as Mallory had heard a lot about 'Mam' who, she thought, was a mine of local gossip. However, Elsa looked cheerful as she ushered Mallory into the room, her fair hair pulled back into a ponytail.

'This is fun. You know what? I think they look like a nice family in the sketches. I don't know what struck me as wrong when I looked at them through the window.'

It wasn't the right time for Mallory to tell Elsa to stick to her instincts. She'd been right to spot something was odd with the situation in the house and right to call Mallory.

'This is Jeanette, the forensic artist. We're nearly finished.'

A woman wearing a beautiful sundress sat on the couch, fiddling with a tablet. She looked up and gave

Mallory a smile, having clearly been briefed about her position in the investigation, and turned her attention back to the screen. Mallory wondered what Saturday activity had been interrupted by the call from Harri. The woman looked as if she were dressed for a garden party, in contrast to Mallory's clothes, still rumpled from the beach.

Mallory saw that Elsa was in her element as she chatted to the artist and revealed a good memory for faces. She was observant, for a start, which was no surprise to Mallory, but more than that, she had the censoriousness of the young. She looked, noted and judged. Mallory hoped Harri would appreciate the value of Elsa's recollections, because it sounded like they had precious little else to go on.

The artist was putting some finishing touches to one of the portraits. When she was satisfied, she turned her tablet to Mallory. 'Want to take a look? I asked Elsa to begin with the father. Obviously, we have a body, which she identified, but that was only her second sighting of him. I asked her to recreate him so we could judge how accurate her recollections were. What do you think?'

Mallory gasped when she saw the picture. She'd not been allowed anywhere near the dead body, so she couldn't comment on accuracy, but the face that stared out at her was full of intelligence and something else. Determination, perhaps.

'Wow. That's brilliant. Is that how he appeared to you, Elsa? He looks almost as if he's on a mission.'

Elsa beamed. 'Jeanette has definitely captured his likeness. It was as if he was in charge of everyone. Now look at his wife.'

Jeanette moved to the next image on her tablet. It showed an auburn-haired woman wearing oversized sunglasses and with a streak of red on her lips. Mallory frowned.

'You could tell she was wearing lipstick from the upstairs window?'

Elsa pouted. 'Yes, I could. I remember thinking it was a weird colour for someone with red hair to wear, and out of place in the forest. She was glamorous, like a Hollywood film star.'

'Fair enough. Was it sunny when she was wearing the glasses?'

'Of course. It's been hot all week, hasn't it?'

'It has. Let's look at the children.'

The first image was of a boy of about sixteen, the same age as Toby. He had none of Toby's leanness, though, with a chubbiness about the face and fine blonde hair.

'I can see you've given him fuller features. Was the rest of his body chubby?'

'A bit. He didn't strike me as someone who did much exercise but, saying that, neither did his sister, although she was thinner.'

Jeanette obligingly swiped the tablet screen to show a girl with her hair pulled back into a neat ponytail high on her head. Mallory remembered the hair straighteners – this was a girl who took care of her appearance even on a rural holiday. Although her face was a different shape to the boy's, their nose and lips were a similar shape.

'These two definitely look like brother and sister,' commented Mallory. 'Did you think that when you saw them?' She was concerned that a lot of emphasis was currently being put on the five being a 'family'. They might have looked like a unified unit, but appearances could be deceptive. Elsa, however, was sure of herself.

'They had an air of being twins, and they definitely did look alike. But I also think I got that impression because they sort of stuck together once they got out of the car. I mean, the youngest wanted to wander off, I could tell. She was being pulled towards the forest, which I can't blame her for at all. Brechfa Forest has—'

'Never mind about that,' said Mallory. 'Let's look at the third child, then. Pippa. You said she had red hair.'

'Very red.'

Then she ought to be distinctive, thought Mallory. Perhaps Pippa would be the key to finding the others.

Jeanette presented to her the final image. It showed a girl of around ten, with bright ginger hair cut into a bob. She had a pale freckled face and was smiling.

'Why is she smiling? Is that what she was doing when you saw her, Elsa?'

'Yes, she couldn't stop smiling. Maybe they'd had a long car journey, or it was the excitement of the first day of holiday, but she was definitely happy to have arrived. Unlike the others, she wanted to go and explore, but her father wouldn't let her.'

Mallory picked up the tablet and gazed into the girl's face. Jeanette misread Mallory's scrutiny as criticism of her work. 'I've also done one without the smile, as she's unlikely to be in the same mood as when Elsa saw her. However, smiles can be distinctive and it felt important to capture it.'

'Of course, I completely understand. Are you sending these to Harri? I mean, DI Evans.'

Jeanette nodded. 'There's just been a press conference, which I missed. I was at a hotel lunch with family when my services were requested, so it took me a while to get here. I'll be sending these through to him now – I'm sure they'll be distributed to journalists in due course.'

'With the exception of the dead man's, surely,' said Mallory.

'That's up to the boss, isn't it? I understand they don't have an ID on him, so it may well be they send that out too. It's not my call to make.'

They drifted towards the front door as Jeanette stuffed the tablet into her bag. 'Nice to meet you finally, Mallory. I've heard all about you.'

Mallory flushed. 'Really?'

'Sure. I think the team will be all the better for having you in it. I've heard you attract trouble like flies on jam.'

Mallory laughed. 'Thanks for the vote of confidence.'

As Jeanette's car pulled away, a woman appeared in view, walking up the narrow street, carrying a heavy shopping bag.

'Mam, I said I'd come with you later.' Elsa rushed forward and grabbed the bag off her mother. 'This is Mallory, remember? From Eldey?'

Mam shot Mallory a look that was half-admonishing, half-curious. 'Finished with your drawings, then?'

'I'm pretty impressed by Elsa's recall, Mrs er…' said Mallory, trying to remember Elsa's last name and now unsure if she'd ever known it.

'Call me Carol. Coming in for some tea?'

What Mallory wanted to do was go home and watch the press briefing on S4C, but here was an opportunity she might not get again.

In the small kitchen, the woman filled the kettle. 'I'm glad Elsa had someone sensible to call when she found the house left in that state.'

Mallory took a seat at the table next to Elsa. 'You already knew the story about Pant Meinog, didn't you? You never said anything when we were looking around.'

Elsa glanced at her mother. 'I didn't know for sure and I wanted to check with Mam before I told you. Mam realised it was the same place after I showed her the picture on the website. You spotted it straight away, didn't you?'

Carol looked pleased. 'It's the same house as in my book, *Haunted Wales*. I recognised it immediately.'

For a moment, Mallory thought that Carol had written the book herself, she sounded so proud of it. She briefly left the room and returned holding a huge book, the type you'd leave on your coffee table, although maybe no one did that anymore. She opened the page to a large black-and-white photo and gave it to Mallory. The image showed a house that was definitely the place now called Tall Pines. It looked less cared for, more gothic, but the outline of the building was there. Even the large rock where Elsa said she left the key was to the right of the door. Mallory turned the page.

'No pictures of the family.'

'Oh no, it's about haunted places, not people, and anyway those little madams made the whole thing up. There were photos of the two girls in the newspapers at the time.'

Mallory retrieved her phone and searched again, this time focusing on images. 'This them?' she asked, showing a photo to Carol.

'Looks like them,' she agreed.

Mallory scrutinised the photo. It showed two teenagers very similar in age and it must have been taken before the attack on Gwenllian, as their skin was unblemished. It was difficult to tell which girl was which. The one on the right was taller, but looked younger. Perhaps that was Gwenllian. Mallory saved the image on her phone and picked up her cup, wondering if it was possible to visit a Welsh home without being given a cup of tea.

'It's a strange place, isn't it? Very remote. No wonder the girls were inspired to make up stories.'

Carol sniffed. 'Lots of legends around there. Glyn Cothi Forest has its own myths. It was a beautiful place once, filled with apple, alder, oak and willow trees. Now it's just pine, but the animals are still attracted to it. Ever heard of the Beast of Brechfa?'

Oh no, thought Mallory, not another story. 'I'm afraid not.' She hoped her tone was suitably discouraging, but Carol intended to tell her tale.

'There's a black cat that's been seen in the hills since the Seventies. The farmers know about it, as it's been killing their sheep. Recently, some researchers came down and made casts of the footprints. They think it's some panther or puma.'

'Right.' Mallory was unimpressed. It was neither frightening nor supernatural, so she wondered why Carol was so affected. 'Have you ever seen it?'

Carol looked put out. 'Of course not. It's called the Beast of Brechfa because that's where it's seen. It doesn't come down to Tenby.'

'Why is it so famous? I mean, it sounds like something that's escaped from a zoo or private collection.'

'Because no one has ever managed to photograph the animal, so we can't be sure it exists. I heard of a farmer who claimed to have seen three of them stalking his sheep when he got up early one morning. By the time he went for his phone, they were gone.'

'Is it associated with bad luck or anything? I mean, black domestic cats are considered unlucky.'

'I don't think so, but I personally wouldn't want to come face to face with it. Can you imagine what injuries it could cause?'

Mallory frowned, remembering Harri's description of the marks on Gwenllian's face, the deep grooves that couldn't have just come from a human's fingernails. Had Gwenllian tried to appropriate the legend of the beast for her own means? Anything was possible, thought Mallory, when it came to teenagers.

11

Sunday

Mallory usually dreaded Sunday mornings, as it was a day of overexcited kids and stressed parents at the campsite. Used to the wind blowing from the west, the cloudless skies meant that sound carried across the campsite and a lie-in was impossible. At the station in Carmarthen, she was grateful for the distraction of the team briefing, although she wondered how many officers, with their leave cancelled, were feeling the same. It took her a while to get into the building. The personnel department naturally didn't work at the weekend and, in the end, she was given a temporary visitor's pass. She saw Harri was in a determined mood as she took her seat in the briefing room. He introduced her to the team – Siân she knew, but the others were a blur of faces barely remembered from the previous case. Harri pointed to the printed images of the five faces prepared by Jeanette, which had been pinned up onto the glass screen.

'Let's recap. On Friday, 4 August, Elsa Jones, the cleaner of the holiday let Tall Pines noticed that the family residing there had left in a hurry. She telephoned Mallory here, who thought there was likely an innocent explanation. Mallory and I had coffee together while she waited for the family to come home, but on returning to the holiday let, there were no signs of them. Still aware there could be an innocent explanation, Mallory went home. Is that a fair summary?' Harri looked at her.

'I think so. It did look like the family had left in a rush, but my guess was that some emergency had occurred, possibly to do with the children.'

'OK. That was my view, too, until a male in his early forties turned up dead in the lay-by on the Lampeter–Carmarthen road. Both the deceased and the vehicle he was in were positively identified by Elsa on Friday night as being a close likeness to what she had seen through the window the previous week. No evidence of the other occupants of the jeep was found. Yesterday we put out an appeal, although these images weren't yet available to us. How are we doing, Sioned?'

A woman with cropped grey hair leant forward.

'As of this morning, twenty-three calls. It's actually fewer than we were expecting, but I wouldn't read too much into that. It's holiday season, so people aren't in their usual places and aren't necessarily looking at the news. All it suggests is that it hasn't been noticed by the family's nearest and dearest that they've disappeared. It also suggests that they've not been seen in the immediate area around the crime scene. That's got to raise the possibility that they're no longer alive.'

Mallory winced but Harri kept calm. 'We have what we think is a valid sighting of Pippa in Brechfa. It suggests that she, at least, isn't dead. We didn't mention the inform-ation in the briefing, as we want to try to narrow possible sightings to that area in the first instance. Do we have any, Sioned?'

'We have two other sightings of the girl in Brechfa, which we're following up as a priority. Both witnesses saw the red-headed girl on the street.'

'Right, keep me informed as to how that goes. OK, the question is, if the sightings are genuine, why hasn't Pippa or any of the other family members come forward? It suggests that they may already be aware of the fact the victim is dead. We've put out an appeal for dashcam footage on the A485, as we want to see at what time the car arrived at that spot. A patrol car passed the lay-by at 10:50 a.m. and it definitely wasn't there then.'

'Elsa arrived at the house around eleven a.m., so the car could have got there shortly after,' said Mallory. 'Say 11:15?'

'Which is why we need other dashcam footage. The lay-by is secluded enough, but we should be able to spot the vehicle if it's there. Siân's already given us an update on the results of the post-mortem. An initial hypothesis of death by carbon monoxide poisoning, due to a cherry-red colouring of blood, organs and skin.'

'Also, pulmonary oedema and general congestion of the organs,' said Siân. 'Interestingly, his left anterior descending artery was eighty percent blocked. He was suffering from heart disease but might not have been officially diagnosed. Elsa said he was a smoker, which is one of the main causes of the condition. The doc thinks it might have accelerated death.'

'Any signs that the poisoning might have been deliberate?' asked Mallory. 'A hosepipe, for example.'

'None, but the car's being examined by automotive forensics. If they do find evidence of tampering with a view to someone ending their life then we've got a number of scenarios, not least the possibility that our

84

victim killed the missing persons and then took his own life.'

'Christ, what about someone else tampering with the car? Is that possible?' asked Mallory.

'According to forensics, yes, but we'll have to wait for their conclusions.' Siân looked across at Harri. 'They're not working today.'

Harri shrugged. 'It's a Sunday in August so we'll have to run with what we have. Let's move on to identities. An initial DNA was taken from the victim and run through the DNA database, which didn't throw up anything. We're now waiting for forensics to match it with forensics from the house. What do we think about them actually being a family?'

'From those e-fits, I think those two eldest children look similar.' Freddie leant forward. 'And possibly a little like our victim.'

'I agree,' said Mallory. 'I noticed it as soon as I saw the pictures yesterday afternoon, and Elsa confirmed it.'

'Then we'll proceed on that basis while keeping an open mind about blended families,' said Harri. 'The hire car and holiday cottage, as we know, were rented in a false name. Assuming they're not local, why choose Tall Pines?'

'Links to the area, came here as children, looking for somewhere remote with few surveillance cameras, luck of the draw as the property was available at the time...' Freddie counted off the suggestions on his fingers.

'According to the rental company, he specifically asked for the house, although it was showing as free on the Facebook page, due to a cancellation. That's sounding suspicious to me,' said Siân.

'I agree,' said Harri. 'Get in touch with the people who originally booked and find out their reason for cancelling. I want to see how random the selection of the house was.'

'What about the stolen wallet?' asked Siân. 'The theft occurred in Cardiff, so perhaps that's where the family are originally from.'

'Agreed,' said Harri. 'Freddie, I want you to liaise with the South Wales force. See if they've had any reports of a family's holiday or trip that felt a bit odd. The problem is that the schools are shut, so the children won't have been missed, but there might have been something from a neighbour. Perhaps a hurried departure. Ask them to relook at the CCTV around where the wallet was stolen.'

Freddie nodded. 'The owner of the wallet looks a little like our victim, so we can assume he was targeted.'

'Right.' Harri turned to the faces staring up at him. 'We regroup at four p.m. this afternoon and see where we've got to. We have a number of lines of inquiry and the door-to-door of our uniformed colleagues. It is of utmost urgency we try to find out what happened to the children – and don't forget the female adult may also be vulnerable.'

'Hold on.' Mallory raised her hand. 'What about the history of the house when it was called Pant Meinog? Would you like me to take that forward?'

Harri made a face and Mallory noticed that the team already seemed to be aware of the history of the house.

'First, let's try to see if the house was deliberately targeted for the holiday. We may discover the victim had approached other rentals, as not everyone would take cash. However, I agree we need to keep an open mind about the house's history. I really don't like coincidences in this job.'

Mallory felt the intensity of Harri's gaze, as if he was trying to tell her something. He looked at his watch. 'Siân, Mallory, I'd like a word with you in my office.'

–

Mallory, Harri and Siân squeezed into the small space, which was at least cool thanks to the air conditioning. Out of the large picture window, Mallory could see the sun high in the sky. She was sick of the heat, but summer would soon be coming to an end and she'd need to find another place to live. The thought exhausted her – how long could she carry on living like this? Harri, she saw, also looked tired, his apparent good health on Friday having dissipated in the early stages of the investigation. He wanted to drill down on what Mallory and Siân thought the family might have been up to in the first week of the holiday. Siân had all the facts to hand.

'We've put together as much as we can in relation to the family's movements up to Friday lunchtime. Given they were supposedly here on holiday, they spent little time on the road. ANPR picked them up on the Tuesday around Carmarthen, where they presumably went for provisions. They're seen entering and exiting the Tesco car park, and we have CCTV of them inside the store.'

'All five of them. That's odd in itself, isn't it?' said Mallory. 'It's nigh on impossible for me to get Toby, my son, to come shopping with me, and yet all five of them made the trip to Tesco.'

'Perhaps they were intending to make a day out of it,' said Harri.

'They bought ice cream and frozen pizzas. It suggests they were intending to return home after their morning shopping trip. None of that food would survive a trip to the beach.'

'Which indicates they didn't want to leave the kids alone in the house, which in itself is odd,' said Mallory. 'Why might that be?'

'Perhaps the answer lies in the reason for the fake ID,' said Siân. 'They're worried about a threat from someone.'

'Which would also account for why there's not much that came up on cameras. Are we suggesting that, apart from the Tesco trip, they stayed at the cottage? What were they doing the whole time?'

'Not sure,' said Siân. 'It's possible they did go out. There are precious few cameras on the roads, but we can look at petrol stations, the larger cafes, and so on to see if anything comes up.'

Harri, Mallory saw, was downbeat. 'I wouldn't bank on it. If the deceased went to the trouble of hiding their identity when hiring both the car and the cottage, they'll have thought about cameras on the road.'

Siân said, 'We went back to interview the neighbour Tom Thomas but, apart from that short exchange he had with the little girl, Pippa, he says he never saw the family. It was a hot week so why would they stay inside the house? It suggests again an attempt to conceal themselves.'

'Think Mr Thomas is telling the truth?' asked Harri.

Siân shrugged. Harri looked at Mallory. 'Go and use your magic on him. Talk to him again.'

Mallory noticed Siân looked affronted, as well she might. Mallory didn't think she had any more charm than Siân – in fact she was sure she hadn't – but she was happy to give it a go.

'Any leads whatsoever on the family?' Mallory asked.

'Our Cardiff colleagues haven't come up with anything yet, but even that might be a false lead,' said Siân. 'All we know is that the stolen wallet came from the capital. The family could have been passing through.'

'I'm not so sure about that,' said Harri. 'The wallet was stolen but then the ID used to rent Pant... I mean, Tall Pines. There's been planning around all this and I think our victim would have liked to do it close to home.'

'The girl, Pippa, told Tom that her car was turquoise, which is our only clue about the family's real vehicle,' said Siân. 'It's called teal in the motor trade and it doesn't help much. Virtually every make of car has a teal option, but it's something we could use to corroborate any information we receive.'

'Damn.' Harri picked up his tea, scowling into the cup. 'You know, the reason I got the two of you in here is that we do need to seriously consider the house's history. I don't want the team sidetracked but I'd like to thrash out some scenarios with you two.'

Mallory felt her spirits rise. This was more like it.

'Of the five family members,' said Harri, 'only the mother could possibly have lived in the house back in 2003. Our victim is too old to be the young boy, Dylan. Early forties the pathologist thought and, based on what I saw, I agree. Gwenllian Prytherch, however, would be about thirty-five now, which might match the age of the woman Elsa saw. I've asked for a National Insurance number for Gwenllian and any other information that could help track her down. If she's paid tax in the last year, we'll be able to find her employer.'

'You think the mother might be Gwenllian, rather than Carys?' asked Siân.

'Gwenllian is a good place to start, because of Elsa's comments about the dark glasses. I thought of her scars immediately, although I can't see why she'd want to return to the house after everything that happened there. We need to dig deeper into this.'

'I'll do it, boss,' said Siân, shooting a look at Mallory.

'I'm not allocating this to anyone until I find out where Gwenllian is and she's been contacted by the relevant constabulary.'

'What about her siblings? The youngest would be in his early thirties now, wouldn't he?'

'Dylan would be almost thirty-one and Carys thirty-six.' Harri tapped the file. 'I've got the information here. I've also asked for their addresses.'

'You know...' said Siân slowly. 'Even if one of our missing victims isn't one of the Prytherchs, there still might be a connection to the case. The owners of the house, Jon and Chrissie Morgan, told me that they do occasionally get a ghost hunter or just an interested group of friends renting out the place, despite the fact they don't advertise the house's history. They even once considered making a feature of it, you know – come and stay with the poltergeist – but they decided against it. It's a little niche and it might put regular tourists off.'

'So they didn't rename it to hide the house's history?' asked Mallory.

Harri made a face. 'The traditional names of Welsh houses are being changed to make them more palatable to a tourist market. It's just part of a trend.'

'I can't believe,' said Mallory, 'that tourists might want to visit a house where a fraud took place.'

Harri shrugged. 'Everyone has their passion. Fortunately, communicating with the dead isn't mine. Look,

I'd really like to pin down the whereabouts of the three Prytherch kids, who will all be adults now, and also find out why the family who originally booked to holiday in the house cancelled. When I have that information, I can decide whether I can leave the events of 2003 there.'

'What about Tom Thomas?' asked Siân. 'You said he was related to the family. He might have an address for them.'

'I wouldn't be so sure about that. I'm pretty certain he was unimpressed by the girls' story even before they admitted to making it all up.' Harri paused, his eyes on Mallory. 'However, blood is thicker than water, isn't it? You know what? If we push it, we could get there and back in an hour. You up for some company?'

12

Harri was quiet in the car up to Brechfa. The first forty-eight hours were usually crucial in a case, and they were coming up to the end of that period. Mallory doubted, however, that they were in it for the long haul, as far as the missing family were concerned. She could easily envisage a situation where an adult woman proved elusive to find, but children were harder to conceal – the youngest most of all. If the sightings were true, however, and Pippa had been separated from her family, she'd possibly spent two nights out in the open and the thought of this squeezed Mallory's heart. Thank God for the hot nights.

'I didn't overstep the mark talking about Pant Meinog in the team meeting, did I?' she asked Harri. 'I just got the impression right at the beginning that you wanted me to look into the whole deception that took place.'

Harri glanced at her. 'It's fine, but I don't want the wider team distracted too much. If they come up with something to link the two cases, it will make any evidence more compelling if I haven't been steering them in that direction. It's important we do this right.'

'Sounds fair enough,' said Mallory. 'Are you sure you can't do anything with the phone we found in the teenage girl's bedroom?'

'Unfortunately, the SIM is locked, so we can only extract basic information. However, I've put in a request to use Cellebrite, the data extraction company we've recently signed a contract with. It'll take a few days but that way we should get contacts, photos and anything else stored on the phone. My best guess is that it was one of the other family members in the car ringing the number. You know, when you get a family member to ring your mobile to find out where you've put it.'

The track to the house had been sealed off with yellow police tape but there was no sign of any police presence. Mallory drove slowly down the bumpy terrain, her eyes on an elderly man standing near the front door of the house, leaning onto his stick as he stooped down to search the ground with the other hand. He must be partially deaf, as he only caught the sounds of their approach as they drew up beside him.

'The key's gone, if that's what you were looking for,' said Harri as he wound down his window. 'And we've changed the locks.'

The old man straightened, looking unrepentant. 'I think the family on the news might be the ones staying here. The young lady here knocked on my door on Friday, didn't you?'

'I did. If you have any information, have you rung the hotline?' asked Mallory.

Tom snorted. 'Hotline! What for? It must be them – there have been police cars here all day.'

Harri got out of the car, soon followed by Mallory, who was shaking her leg that had gone dead, her old injury aching in the heat.

'I can let you in,' said Harri. 'We're going to take another look around the place. Do you want to come with us? My guess is that you know this place better than anyone else.'

Tom looked taken aback. 'I haven't been inside the house since it was sold. You don't mind?'

'I'd appreciate your eyes on how the place has changed. One line of inquiry is that the house was deliberately targeted by the family. You might have some ideas of who might want to do that.'

Mallory watched as Tom froze, casting an anxious glance at Harri, who was opening the door with new keys. They stepped inside, piling into the hallway and heading towards the kitchen. Mallory's senses were on high alert, as the feeling of something seriously askew was more pronounced after the passage of time. Forensics had left everything as they'd found it – the bread with the crusts now curled, the cups of tea with the milk congealed on the top. Even the kettle remained warm on the side of the Aga. Harri and Mallory watched Tom take it all in.

'Left in a hurry, did they?' he said finally.

'It certainly looks like it, doesn't it?' said Harri. 'Can I ask you not to touch anything, but I'd like to go through what forensics have drawn from this room. They believe at least three people were here in the kitchen – one of them the adult, unless they'd roped in a teenager to butter the bread. It's not impossible, but based on the other rooms, we think the two adults are most likely to have been in here.'

'One buttering the bread, the other drinking tea,' said Mallory.

'Or sitting on that chair, which had fallen sideways,' said Harri. 'Elsa righted it, but it was this one here. There's another cup of tea opposite, but my kids like a nice cuppa, so it may have been the other adult in the fallen chair.'

'If we're going to ascribe gender roles, possibly the victim, but that can only be a guess.' Mallory resisted the urge to throw the sandwiches in the bin. 'So, let's say the adult female was buttering the bread – any clues in relation to an order of events?' asked Mallory. 'I mean, the chair on the ground is facing the kitchen window. Perhaps they spotted someone coming down the drive.'

'It's definitely a possibility.' Harri frowned. 'The person buttering the bread is standing next to the cooker with the boiling kettle, and one of the children has their back to the window. It's possible that whoever was sitting in the upended chair saw something and called to the other occupants of the room. The problem with this theory is that the hire car will have been parked out front. If you were leaving in such a hurry, you'd hardly rush towards whatever was scaring you.'

Tom was listening to the exchange with relish. 'Maybe it was the Beast of Brechfa,' he said, his eyes alight.

Mallory watched Harri roll his eyes. 'Go on,' he said.

'It's the wild cat that's been seen a few times on the mountain. I'd be rushing out of the house if I saw it.'

'I think locking your door would be a better strategy.' Harri looked furious. 'We're not looking for the Beast of Brechfa.'

'One thing you're wrong about,' said Tom, 'is that the car had to be parked at the front. There's an old track at the back that leads to the road at the bottom of the hill. I keep it cut back, as it still belongs to me.'

'Where's the track?' asked Harri.

Tom took them into the living room and pointed across the lawn. 'You go down the trail and through the gate, which I never shut. A jeep would make light work of it.'

Mallory glanced at Harri but he'd already got there. 'Is the track common knowledge or would you need to know the house?'

Tom shrugged. 'It's no secret, but most visitors don't use it.'

Harri nodded, his eyes still on the entrance to the track. 'Shall we go upstairs? Unless you want to see the little parlour off this room, Tom.'

'I'll just stick my head around the door,' said Tom gruffly.

They waited for him as he glanced into the space that was used as a study, bare except for a sofa bed.

'Changed a lot?' asked Mallory and she was shocked to see tears in the old man's eyes.

'I spent my childhood in this room,' he said. 'You'd never recognise it. I've seen all I need to see.'

Harri led the way up the narrow staircase into a small room with a single bed, desk and a chest of drawers. On the bed was a drawing half-finished – a good representation of the woods outside, but a child's nevertheless – and underneath, three other drawings of the same subject. The pen on the bed was still missing its top and Mallory wondered how long it'd be before a clean-up finally took place.

'You think she was disturbed while drawing?' she asked.

'It's a possibility, isn't it? The problem is that the nib was dry when the forensic team arrived at the house. They dry out quickly, I suppose, so there's no way of telling how long the pen had been missing the lid.'

Mallory glanced out of the window, which had the same view as the kitchen. Whatever the person sitting in the chair had seen, Pippa would surely have spotted too. Finding Pippa might unravel much of the mystery, as the girl was clearly observant, drawing the woods as she saw them from this window. Harri had already led Tom to the other bedrooms, but he gave them only a cursory glance. After viewing the old parlour, he seemed anxious to get out of the place, his memories distressing.

Back outside, Tom relaxed a little, screwing up his eyes as he regarded Harri. 'I know you, don't I?'

'I came here a couple of times, back in the day when the house was still Pant Meinog.'

'Oh.' Tom took a step back.

'Gwenllian and the rest of the family OK now?' asked Harri with a casualness that didn't deceive Mallory.

'Not heard from those bastards for years,' said Tom, turning his back on them and starting to move away.

'You don't, for example, think she was staying at this house?'

Tom turned. 'Gwenllian? There's no way that lass would come back here. You saw what happened to her face.'

'Sometimes people are inclined to revisit their past. Maybe Gwenllian was doing that.'

Tom shook his head. Mallory called after him, 'The girl, Pippa, spoke to you. Did she look like Gwenllian – or Carys – as a child?'

'I don't remember,' said Tom, walking slowly back to his cottage.

13

As soon as Harri got home, he opened a can of non-alcoholic beer from the fridge, desperate to get some cool liquid into his overheated body. It had been a frustratingly slow day – no surprises, given it was a Sunday – and the holiday spirit evident on the roads on his drive home had put him in a foul mood. His sister Fran wandered into the kitchen, glass of wine in hand, and glanced at the can.

'I'm glad someone is drinking that stuff,' she said. 'It's been lying around in the fridge for weeks.'

Harri looked at his watch, noting it had just gone six. He pointed at her glass. 'Bit early for you, isn't it, even on a Sunday?'

Fran grimaced. 'It's been one of those days. A client is driving me mad, emailing me on my day off. I actually tried to work out today how long it is until I can retire.'

'Jesus.' Harri pulled out a chair and sat down heavily. 'Don't wish your life away. Look what happened to Paula.'

The face of his wife, dead from cancer for more than a decade, flashed into his mind. At least these days he was remembering her as she was when they met and not at the end. He didn't like people trying to rush through the years – Paula had desperately wanted to live to see their kids, Ben and Ellie, grow up and that privilege had been given to him only. After his health scare earlier in the year, he had found himself thinking about death more and more, worrying about his children's future without him.

Fran caught his eye and mouthed 'sorry'. She took the chair opposite him. 'Do tell me about your day. Please say you've found those poor children.'

Harri shook his head. 'No, and I'm beginning to feel much less confident about the chances of them making it out alive.' He paused. 'Remember the Brechfa Forest haunting?'

Fran snorted. 'Of course, and I think you had a little part to play in the drama too.' She stopped, aghast. 'Don't tell me that's connected to this.'

'It's not, as far as I've been able to prove, but the family were staying in the same house.'

Fran's eyes widened. 'You're kidding me.'

'Bit of a coincidence, don't you think?'

'Coincidence my arse! I bet they were tourists who booked that place just to see what happened.'

'According to the owners, there have been a few people doing so and they even thought of making a feature of it.'

'Everyone likes a good spooking.'

Harri glanced across at practical Fran. 'You don't actually believe the stories.'

'Of course not,' she scoffed. 'I'm just saying that kids, especially teenagers, love that sort of thing. In fact, I can imagine you throwing a hairbrush across the room when we were that age, claiming it was the spirit of Great-grandma.'

Harri laughed and felt himself relax, the tension of the previous few days seeping away. 'What I'm worried about is that it's more than curious people. I'm trying to track down what actually became of the family living there.'

'Wow.' Fran sat back, her arms folded across the chest. 'You all right? You seem a bit, I dunno, out of sorts.'

'You know, as much as I hate to admit it, the whole set-up gave me the creeps and going back to the house has brought it all back. Even after the two girls admitted to making the whole thing up, I've never really felt comfortable about the whole scenario.'

Fran took another sip of her wine, taking her time to answer. 'You know, I do believe there are some forces in this world that are from outside it. I know it's a clumsy way of putting it but that's what I feel.'

'And at Pant Meinog?'

'Well, you never did get to the bottom of those scratches on the girl. What was her name?'

'Gwenllian,' said Harri grimly. 'Wasting a lot of police time although, of course, there are some who believe the scratches were made by an unseen force.'

'I personally think that's one mystery you're not going to be able to solve.'

Harri sighed. 'I might have to if I'm going to work out what's happened to that family.'

Ellie came into the kitchen then, her cheeks flushed. By unspoken agreement, Harri and Fran changed the subject.

'You been overdoing the blusher?' asked Harri before realising with horror that his daughter was close to tears. 'What's the matter, *cariad*?'

'Nothing,' muttered Ellie, turning away from them. 'I'm going to my room.'

Harri twisted in his chair, trying to gauge his daughter's mood. 'Has something happened?'

'Just leave it, would you.' Ellie pulled open the door and said in a rush, her back still to them, 'If you want to know, I've been dumped.'

Harri, embarrassed, caught Fran's eye. She stood, threw the rest of her wine down the sink and crossed to Ellie, giving her a hug. 'Oh Ellie, love. I'm sorry, do you want to talk about it?'

They both glanced at Harri, who took his cue. 'I'll have a shower. The Chinese takeaway is on me tonight.'

Harri, whose answer to most of life's problems was to have something nice to eat – a habit which had probably contributed to his diabetes – felt at a loss as to how to comfort his daughter and was glad to leave the room. Paula again swam into his mind. Fran was excellent as a confidante to his children but she'd never tried to assume the role of their mother. What would Paula have done? He wasn't sure, but he'd probably have been sent from the room in a similar manner. At fifteen, Ellie was old enough to have a boyfriend, of course, but it was a reminder that she was growing up fast. Once she and Ben left home, what then? Maybe time for him and Fran to have a chat about what the future might look like. A ten-year plan or something like that, although he wasn't much into long-term decisions. However, he might end up in this big house on his own, a depressing thought.

His mobile rang and Siân's number came up on the display. She began talking before he'd even spoken.

'Carys Prytherch has been easy to track down. She's living in Carmarthen and I've just sent a car to check up on her, but the flat is currently empty. The neighbour says she's single and gone away for a few days on a painting holiday. I showed her the artist's pictures of the family and she says she's seen no one like that around here.'

'That's good news. What about the others?'

'Nothing on Dylan, which is strange, but we're carrying on looking. We do, however, have a lead on Gwenllian Prytherch. She was married in 2012 to a David Anderson and, in 2013, a Philippa Anderson was born, mother's maiden name Prytherch. Now, a Gwenllian Anderson has been hard to track down, as she has no online presence. At first, I thought she'd changed her first name but we've had luck with her National Insurance number. She was recently employed in a shoe shop in guess where—'

'Cardiff,' said Harri.

'Exactly. I also have an address and the house is getting a knock on the door as we speak. I'll let you know what they find, OK? If we think it's them, do you want me to go to the house?'

'Yes, and take Mallory with you.'

He'd expected some note of disapproval, but she was inclined to be magnanimous in her triumph. 'Of course. You all right about us going tonight if it looks like the house belongs to the family?'

'The sooner the better. Keep me informed.'

14

Mallory, desperate to have a late-afternoon snooze to catch up on her restless nights, discovered that it was not only her evening plans that were being thrown into disarray, but also her summer. She was putting a salad together, made up of some wilted lettuce and wrinkled tomatoes, half-heartedly throwing in some tinned olives, when she got a call from her ex-husband Joe. Her spirits dropped as she picked up his morose tone. It usually meant their son was in trouble.

'Toby wants to come back to stay with you for the whole of August. I don't understand why – he's already spent two weeks in July with you.'

Mallory bit back the retort that she'd hardly seen her son over the school year, but she was also gripped by a sinking feeling that, now she was deeply involved in an investigation, she'd struggle to make time to see him.

'Well, that's great,' she said to Joe. 'When's he planning to come?'

'Tomorrow morning,' said Joe, listening to her groan with satisfaction. 'He's desperate to get back there and I don't blame him. London is like a furnace in this heat. At least you can cool off in the sea there.' He paused, keen to get a snide comment in. 'It'll be cramped for the summer with the two of you in that caravan.'

Mallory, as usual, rose to the bait. 'I got the caravan because he wanted to spend his holiday with me on the beach.' She was rapidly making calculations. She desperately needed her sleep, which had been impossible while Toby had the main bedroom. Perhaps she could suggest that he slept in the living room for this stay, which would also give him the freedom to come and go. Despite his eating issues, he made friends easily, and she was sure he would hook up with some new pals to surf with.

'Well, fine. Text me his travel details when you have them and I'll drive down to Carmarthen to meet him.'

'OK. Hmm, look, I might go away myself if Toby's going to be with you.'

'Well, that's OK,' said Mallory, wondering why he was telling her.

'It's just that if there's an issue, we might be more difficult to contact.'

Mallory stopped herself from sighing. 'I'll be fine.' She paused. 'We?'

'Well, the thing is, I've just started seeing someone. I've not introduced her to Toby yet, but we've been talking about taking a break somewhere. I thought it might have to wait until half-term but now he's with you...'

Brilliant, she thought. You just live your best life while I steam inside my tin hut. She cut the call and had just started to tidy the living space when her phone rang again – this time, it was Siân.

'We've got a break, Mallory, and about time too. Gwenllian Prytherch – now known as Anderson – lives in Cedar Close, Cardiff, with her husband David and their three kids. Two of them his, the other from their marriage. A neighbour has just identified them from the photos. Harri wants you to come with me to the house.'

'Why not?' said Mallory, surveying her wilted salad. 'Is there a McDonald's en route?'

Siân picked her up from the caravan park, although Mallory would have preferred to have made her own way there, so she could have gathered her thoughts before Toby's visit. They drove south-east across Wales, the night growing darker until they hit the bright lights of the capital city, where Siân reluctantly stopped at the burger chain so Mallory could grab a Big Mac.

Number three, Cedar Close was on an estate with attractive suburban-looking, red-brick houses. The close reminded Mallory of something out of a soap opera. *Hollyoaks* maybe. Number three was a neat, slightly boring-looking family house although, realistically, she was in no position to be sniffy about anyone else's accommodation.

There were lights on in the building and a uniformed officer stationed at the door. Malloy and Siân showed their ID, the officer frowning at Mallory's visitor pass, and were let through into the house. A man came forward, tall and with a thin moustache.

'DC Lewis?' he asked.

'That's me.' Siân stepped forward. 'This is Mallory Dawson, a civilian investigator who has been co-opted onto this case.'

The man gave Mallory a brief nod. 'Pleased to meet you both. DS Singh. We've looked through the house but there's no sign of the family. The neighbour to the left says Pippa, the little girl, told her they were going on holiday for three weeks, so they weren't unduly concerned.'

'The photofit of the family was made public this morning,' said Mallory. 'Did she not spot the photos on the news?'

DS Singh shrugged. 'Apparently not, but it's a Sunday and it's not like the old days when everyone sat down for the teatime programme. She recognised the family readily enough when I showed her the photos, though.'

'So, what can you tell us about them?' asked Siân.

'The parents are David and Gwenllian Anderson. David had two children from a previous marriage, Matty and Ava, who are twins. The mother's around but for some reason the kids want to live with their dad.'

Mallory felt herself flushing but Siân didn't look in her direction and instead said, 'Go on.'

'There's also a little girl called Pippa, aged ten. Goes to the local primary school. Very chatty, according to Mrs Watson, the neighbour. She gets more out of Pippa than the other four put together.'

'Is there a reason why the family are so reserved?' asked Mallory.

'She didn't know of one. Kept themselves to themselves, she said. You know, if I had a fiver for every time someone said that to me, I could retire before my thirty years is up. Who actually keeps themselves to themselves? We all have to interact with someone.'

'In this family's case, it might be true,' said Siân. 'They seem to have kept themselves very much to themselves while on holiday.'

'What car do they drive?' asked Mallory.

'A teal Passat, which we're trying to track down. My guess is that it's likely to be near to where they hired the jeep.'

Mallory glanced around the house, which was as dull on the inside as its exterior. It could almost be a show home, with little to suggest the presence of children. 'We need to get some actual photos of the family as soon as possible. Are there any around the house?'

'None at all.'

'What?' asked Mallory and Siân in unison.

'It's not that unusual. Everyone keeps their photos on a mobile phone these days, don't they?'

'Seriously?' said Siân. 'Surely there must be one of Pippa, as a baby even.'

DS Singh shrugged. 'I can't find any photos in the house at all.'

'Mind if we look?' asked Siân.

'Be my guest. For the kids, though, I think a better bet would be their mates and we'll be talking to their respective schools tomorrow. Even during the holidays, we'll be able to track down friends.'

'Plus, social media profiles,' said Siân.

'Well, I've already had a quick search on my phone and I couldn't see anything on Facebook or Twitter.'

'Those sites are for our age group,' said Mallory. 'My son wouldn't be seen dead on Facebook. It'd have to be Instagram or TikTok, or one I've never heard of, and they'll also likely use a pseudonym.'

DS Singh rubbed his face. 'All right. We're on it. In the meantime, feel free to have a look around. I'm not treating this as a crime scene, given that David's death clearly didn't happen here. But we are looking for anything that might help you with your investigation. Is there something in particular we should be looking for?'

'Have you found out much about David? What he does for a living, for example?'

'According to the neighbour, he works at the university but that's all we know.'

Mallory looked at Siân. 'We're particularly interested in the backstory of Gwenllian and an incident in her past. Siân, here, will update you. I'm going to speak to the neighbour.'

'Sure.'

Mallory went out into the cooling night and knocked on the door to the left. It was answered immediately by a woman in her eighties who had been hovering by the hall window, her shadow pressed against the glass.

'Mrs Watson? I'm with Dyfed–Powys police. Could I come in?'

The woman opened the door and let Mallory into the hallway, but no further. It suited Mallory, who had been dreading the offer of a cup of tea and a biscuit. Tired and irritable, she didn't want small talk, only facts.

'I know you've already spoken to my colleagues next door, but I wanted to check some things with you about the family.'

'All right.'

Mrs Watson sat in the upright hallway chair, grunting as she took the weight off her feet.

'First of all, I believe you've been shown the five pictures drawn by the artist and you've identified them as the family.'

'That's correct. The artist did a good job.'

So did Elsa, thought Mallory. 'Is there anything else you wanted to add to those images? We've not been able to find any pictures in the house although, of course, we're hoping the children's friends will be able to help us. However, it's important to see what Gwenllian looks like without those big sunglasses.'

'You're wasting your time with that. She always wore them, come sunshine or snow.'

'She wore them in the winter?' asked Mallory, pretty sure she knew where this was going. 'Do you know why?'

Mrs Watson gave her a wink. 'Well, one day I was putting out my washing. It was due to rain, but a little light shower doesn't hurt, as long as the sun comes out later. Anyway, I don't think Gwenllian expected me to be in the garden and I saw her outside, smoking a cigarette.'

'She smoked?'

'Once in a while. I don't think it was a regular thing with her. But anyway, it was cloudy and she didn't have her glasses on. You should have seen her face.'

'What was it like?'

The woman grimaced. 'She had three, maybe four deep scratches across her cheeks.'

So, as Harri had expected, the scars hadn't healed over the intervening years.

'She never spoke about them?'

'She hardly ever talked to me at all. None of them did, except little Pippa and that was when she was sure the rest of them were out of earshot. It's that family that's gone missing in Carmarthenshire, isn't it? I saw it on tonight's news, after speaking to the policeman. I saw them all drive off the other week and never thought anything of it.'

'OK. Thanks,' said Mallory. 'I'll let you go.'

Mrs Watson, however, was inclined to linger. 'You know what he did, don't you?'

'Who? David Anderson?'

'Exactly. He was an academic, but not like Emrys down the road, who teaches physics.'

'What was his subject, then?'

Mrs Watson was enjoying her mystification, Mallory saw. 'Paranormal psychology. I found out after he was in the paper. There was a car crash on one of the local roads and there were stories that one of the victims was haunting the place. I saw him standing there when I was waiting at the bus stop. I thought it was strange, so he told me he was there in a professional capacity.' Mrs Watson snorted. 'Professional indeed.'

Mallory stared at the woman. 'Why didn't you tell DS Singh about this?'

'He never asked and, besides, how was I to know whether or not it was important?'

How indeed was she to know, thought Mallory. She didn't want to give any ammunition to this already nosy woman. She might know David Anderson's business but Gwenllian, given her private nature, was likely to be an unknown quantity. The key was to discover how Gwen-llian and David had met, and Mallory had a pretty good idea it was to do with his job. But there was more, she saw. Mrs Watson was dying to tell her something else without appearing indiscreet.

'Well…' Mrs Watson's voice lowered to a hush. 'I heard that he'd been involved in a scandal.'

15

Monday

Steph was understandably aghast as Harri gave her a morning update. The non-alcoholic beer from the previous evening had given him a dry mouth, which was the last thing he needed before a team briefing. Steph hardly helped his mood, as she tapped her foot on the floor, her nerves making her jittery.

'We've not only got a dead body, but he's some kind of weird scientist married to a woman who was once attacked by a ghost. Oh, the press are going to love this.'

Harri, used to putting up with his boss's moods, felt his own sour. He didn't much care for the fact that David Anderson was involved in studying the paranormal – from the little research he'd done that morning, it was a legitimate academic discipline. Parapsychologists invest-igated paranormal or psychic activity using a range of scientific models and were also well-versed in the history of paranormal activities. From Harri's point of view, this was preferable to the waffle that Mallory had been forced to listen to in the podcasts, and David was a qualified psychologist who'd specialised in the subject.

The scandal that Mallory had managed to wheedle out of his neighbour was interesting but not shocking. David had been accused by his colleagues of jettisoning his academic neutrality over whether paranormal activity actually existed, coming down heavily on the belief that some hauntings were genuine. This had been going on for years, until students who were firmly on the side of scepticism found themselves being sidelined in lectures and tutorials. David was warned and disciplined, and then suspended from his academic post.

'Do you think,' asked Steph, 'that David's loss of neutrality coincided with him meeting Gwenllian?'

'It's difficult to say at this stage, as we don't know when he met her. Assuming it's around 2011, based on their marriage date, I guess it's possible, although I suspect something has happened more recently to bring things to a head. We need to do more digging – we only know about this issue because of a curious next-door neighbour.'

'This is a bloody nightmare,' said Steph. 'Have the press got hold of any of this?'

'Unfortunately yes,' said Harri. 'We've had to move the news briefing to a bigger venue because of press-pass requests.'

'Fuck.' Steph eventually sat down, continuing the tapping of her foot. 'OK. Recap what we think, and do it slowly, because I'm a bit stupid.'

She was anything but and Harri wondered what she'd have done if he'd nodded in agreement.

'Of course. Our theory is that David and Gwenllian Anderson made plans to return to the house of Gwenllian's childhood. The reasons for that are unclear, although we could speculate that David was adopting a confessor/psychologist role and encouraging her to confront a childhood trauma. Another possibility is that David saw Gwenllian as a way to finally prove the presence of paranormal phenomena. Gwenllian, we assume, was happy to go along with this. Another scenario is that Gwenllian was the instigator and the family came along for the ride. Perhaps she wanted to revisit her teenage home for whatever reason.'

'Christ,' said Steph. 'What is this modern obsession about confronting the past? I'm inclined to leave my former misdemeanours right there in history.'

Harri was inclined to agree with her, as the past was a painful place for him and he had two children to bring up. But part of him understood the draw of Pant Meinog and, at least in that respect, he had some sympathy for Gwenllian.

'In any case,' Harri continued, 'they came back. What I can't understand is why they did it incognito. David could easily have booked the holiday rental in his own name and driven down with the family without attracting any attention.'

Steph drummed her fingers on the table. 'Maybe it's due to that elderly neighbour. He knew Gwenllian, didn't he?'

'Yes, but he has no connection to the letting company or the car hire. Adopting a fake name wouldn't have stopped Tom seeing Gwenllian once she was there. One look at her face and he'd have been sure who she was.'

'So why the bloody hell did he steal a wallet, and rent a car and the house for cash?' Steph was, in fact, calming down, he saw. She looked genuinely puzzled by the mystery.

'Find that out and we'll be nearer to catching his killer and finding the family.'

'Do you think they're in hiding because they fear for their lives or because they're hiding from justice? Surely, if

David's death is murder, the likeliest killer is whoever was in the car with him.'

'Possibly, but I'm still concerned about the rushed departure. There may be an external threat that we haven't yet been able to identify.'

'Good, keep at it. How's Mallory getting on?'

'Fine and I'm giving her the lead on digging into the Prytherch family. The answers, I suspect, lie in the past and I just want to have a quick review of the case before I brief her.'

Steph blew out a long breath as if the conversation had exhausted her. 'Right, I'll see you at the press conference at six. Call me if you discover anything in the meantime.'

–

The records from 2003 were readily available on the Police National Computer and Harri spent the morning refreshing his memory of the Brechfa poltergeist. He'd only been present for two of the seven call-outs; the rest of his knowledge was station gossip and newspaper reports. Freddie Carr had already begun to sift through the endless notes, but Harri made his own list of who he wanted Mallory to interview. She'd asked for the morning off to pick her son Toby up. Harri would have preferred her at the station but knew all too well the calls that children made on a parent's time. He hoped Toby's issues wouldn't impact too much on Mallory's focus on the case. Hopefully, the lad would spend his time on the beach and find some friends, leaving his mother to her own devices.

A knock on the door and Siân came in.

'No luck with the door-to-doors in Brechfa yet. There aren't actually that many empty homes – it's probably too far from the coast. The ones we know about, we've checked and there's no evidence of anyone staying there.'

'What about the other potential sightings of Pippa?' asked Harri. 'Did they see what direction the girl was going?'

'Away from the shop, towards Abergorlech, but that's not much help.'

'No, no, it's not.'

Harri sat back in his chair. 'Was there anything in the Andersons' house that struck you, yesterday? Any clues to their likely behaviour?'

Siân made a face. 'I'm not sure what your place is like, but mine is a tip and I don't even have kids. The house in Cardiff was beyond neat – it looked as if there was nothing in it to tidy in the first place. A place beyond presence.'

'I can understand a traumatised Gwenllian, and even David, liking order, but the kids? Have you been able to track down the twins' mother?'

'She lives in Italy and there's been no contact there at all for years. She left and says motherhood didn't suit her.'

Shocked, Harri swallowed the flash of fury that Siân's comment had produced. 'What mother would cut contact with her kids?'

Unusually, Siân, who was the most censorious of his team, came to the woman's defence.

'I spoke to her and she told me straight. If you haven't bonded with your children, don't love them even, why stay?'

After Siân had left, Harri forced his attention back to the screen to read through the files. First up were Gwenllian's siblings, Carys and Dylan. Carys was still away but they'd discovered from her plane ticket that she was due back that day. Dylan, her younger brother, was proving harder to trace but it was surely only a matter of time until he was tracked down.

The Prytherch parents, he knew, had died in a car accident in 2014 on a mountain road in the Brecon Beacons. A corner taken too fast had resulted in a crash into a roadside barrier and a plunge down the mountain. A diligent admin assistant had made the connection to the 2003 hauntings and added a note to the file. Joining the dots between one tragedy and another. Harri had been inclined to move on, but he stopped. Car accident? Was it coincidence that a vehicle had been involved in those deaths too? Harri didn't much like coincidences but he couldn't for the life of him see a connection between a road traffic accident in a national park and a murder in a lay-by.

Harri jotted down the names of others connected to the family. He was pretty sure Tom Thomas knew more than he was giving away, but the other people he really needed to look at again were Gethin – Tom's son – and his wife Cathy. They had been living with Tom at the time of the haunting incidents, and Harri had been left with the impression that they were friendly with their young neighbours. On the second visit, after Gwenllian had been assaulted, Gethin and Cathy came into the courtyard and helped to comfort the children. The events had taken place before Harri's kids had come along and he'd not been brilliant with juvenile victims. He'd been glad of Cathy's presence in particular, but it was Gethin who'd made the strongest impression on him: a younger version of his father, with swept-back sandy hair. Harri added a final name to the list – a name he'd have to explain to Mallory in person. Nevertheless, she would need to be contacted. He looked at the list with distaste, aware that he was the subject of his own haunting and, like Steph, he very much wished the past would stay where it belonged.

16

Mallory and Toby both yawned all the way back to the campsite. Mallory, who'd finally got home at dawn, thought she had a good excuse for her tiredness, but she wasn't sure why Toby looked so lethargic. He stepped down from the train, carrying a huge sports bag which made his thin frame stoop. Mallory experienced a pang of guilt at not having anywhere for him to leave his stuff; he'd have to push it under the sofa during the day, which wasn't ideal. She resolved once again to find some permanent work soon to tide her over until Toby reached the age of eighteen. He deserved his own space when he came to stay with her during the holidays, not a converted bed in a mobile home.

'So, you couldn't keep away from the caravan,' she said as he yawned again without putting his hand over his mouth.

'Not the caravan, to be honest, Mum. Although, I have to say, it's pretty cool living so near the beach.'

Not that I get to see much of it, thought Mallory sourly. 'I'm worried we're going to be a bit squished for the next month. There's not much room and I was wondering if it might not give you a bit more freedom, as you come and go, if you slept in the living room.' She saw him frown. 'I mean, you can have the bedroom if you want, but I know you were out late most nights in July. You might prefer the living room.'

'That'll be fine and don't worry about me. I've got a job, so I'll be out of your way much of the time.'

'A job?' Mallory swerved the car as she turned to look at him. 'Your father never said anything about that.'

'He doesn't know, because I didn't tell him. He's been a bit distracted recently.'

And I know the reason why, thought Mallory. 'Where's the job?' she asked.

'It's at the dolphin-watching centre at New Quay. Don't worry, I won't be going out to sea, although I wish I could. I'll be behind the desk, selling tickets to the tourists.'

'Behind a desk? Not touting them on the street?'

'I told you, I'll be inside. They're training me up to use the till and I'll be working eight-hour shifts, with an hour unpaid lunch. I can walk to it from the holiday park.'

It sounded all right to Mallory, and perhaps a bit of freedom would help Toby's mental health. 'Who got you the job?' she asked.

'My friend Megan.'

Mallory wasn't deceived by his casual manner. So, there was a girl involved. Well, that too was fair enough – and also probably accounted for Toby's reticence to talk about his job offer. She remembered Megan: tall and dark-skinned. A Greek mother, she thought, or maybe Spanish. She suspected she'd be seeing more of Megan. 'When do you start?'

'Tomorrow at ten.' He was fiddling with a bracelet, bright beads of coral against his pale skin.

Mallory laughed. 'No wonder you wanted to get down here quickly. I was worried you wouldn't be seeing much of me, as I've been contracted by the police again to help with an investigation.'

'The missing family?'

'That's right. Have you been reading about it?'

'Only on my tablet on the train. I mean, the teenagers are probably the same age as me, right? Where do you think they are?'

Mallory realised, with a jolt, that Toby was right. Matty and Ava Anderson were around Toby's age, but were they as streetwise as her London-based son? She thought it unlikely. 'I wish to God I knew.'

–

Back at the caravan, Toby stashed his bag under the bench in the main living space. He'd probably worked out for himself that sleeping in the living room would give him more opportunities to come and go, and he was eager to get out of the caravan.

'I'm meeting Megan and some pals at the beach. Can I go?'

'I'd like you to eat something first.'

Toby scowled, picking at the hem of his T-shirt. He'd confessed to an eating disorder during his winter visit to her and had been seeing a therapist, who'd diagnosed moderate bulimia nervosa. Mallory had spent anxious evenings reading up on it, and the consensus was that the condition was treatable through counselling. He'd made good progress but still over-exercised and had the telltale leanness of deprivation and iron self-control. Mallory had been told by Joe not to make negative comments about body shapes and weight in relation to anyone, nor to focus too much on food. The former she was relaxed with, not caring much about how anyone looked, but food was a thornier subject. She couldn't just never mention it.

'Sit down and eat something. I've prepared a salad.'

She'd managed to get to the local shop as it opened that morning and bought every salad veg they offered. She pulled a bowl from the fridge and added some sourdough bread to his plate, noting he was happy to consume the veggies but not the carbs. She'd make croutons for the next salad, although she couldn't force him to eat something he didn't want to. He was perfectly capable of picking at his food.

Her eyes dropped to his bracelet again. 'I like that. Is it new?'

'Megan bought it for me,' he said, talking with a full mouth. 'Before you say anything, it's ethical coral. She's careful about that kind of thing.'

When he'd finished, he grabbed his phone and headed off. He wouldn't come to much harm at the beach and Mallory was glad he wasn't going to be spending the trip in front of the tiny TV in the caravan. The new model she'd bought for his winter visit was now languishing in storage. Feeling weirdly bereft by Toby's absence, Mallory rang Harri for an update.

'There have been no more sightings of Pippa, which is disappointing, and none whatsoever of the rest of the family. I'm going to widen the search area again, and ask ramblers and bikers to look out for patches of ground that might have been disturbed.'

'Christ,' said Mallory. 'You don't think they're dead, do you?'

'I hope to God they aren't, but where are they hiding if they're alive? Look, I've got meetings all afternoon. Steph is doing her nut. Siân is preoccupied with tracking the movements of the family after they left Cardiff. Can you visit Gwenllian's sister, who should be back from her holiday today? I've made a list of others we'll also need to interview, which I'll discuss with you when we meet. Start with Carys, though. I want to know when they were last in touch, if either Gwenllian or David made contact with her recently, or for that matter the children. And we need to know where Dylan is. Don't let her lead you too far into the past – I'm trying to find the rest of the family.'

–

Mallory was a little miffed by Harri's tone but decided to be magnanimous, putting it down to stress or pressure from his boss. She was glad to get out of the caravan but struggled to dress in something that looked professional but would also be comfortable in the heat. Last night had been an urgent call-out so she'd got away with her drawstring skirt and tank top but that wouldn't work for interviewing potential witnesses. The chances of her getting to Carmarthen for a shopping trip were fairly small so she'd have to sweat it out in one of the two linen dresses she owned.

Carys Prytherch lived in a new-build flat overlooking the river in Carmarthen, about half a mile away from Bev Christie. Carys taught photography at the local college and had, according to Harri, just returned from a summer vacation. The apartment, however, was empty when Mallory rang the intercom, and she was happy to stand on the bank of the river, watching the muddy waters eddy and swirl as she waited for Carys to return. She'd need to inform her that David and Gwenllian had returned to Pant Meinog while she was away and, unless the sisters had lost contact with each other, this was unlikely to be a coincidence. With Harri's instructions ringing in her ears, Mallory waited, her mind turning over various scenarios until she heard the sounds of a car drawing up, and a woman with strawberry-blonde hair pulled back into a ponytail climbed out of the vehicle and retrieved two shopping bags from the back seat. Her expression was closed with worry, her eyes fixed on the front door to the apartment building.

'Carys?' Mallory asked, pulling out her ID.

'I've no comment to make,' the woman snapped. 'Leave me alone.'

'I'm with the police. I need to ask you a few questions.'

Carys stopped. 'I've only just got back from my holidays and discovered what's happened. They're not with me so you're wasting your time.'

Mallory, after years of police work, wasn't shocked at the woman's failure to mention her dead brother-in-law, tucking away Carys's reaction to mull over later. 'Can I speak to you for a few minutes, though? We really need to track down the family and I want to talk to you about Gwenllian in particular.'

'Of course you do. It's always about Gwenllian.'

She took Mallory up to the first floor, refusing her offer of help with the shopping. There was little evidence in the flat that Carys had recently returned from abroad, only the sound of a washing machine and a separate dryer churning in tandem. Mallory glanced around the space, noticing it was as neat as Gwenllian's house, although large framed black-and-white photos on the wall gave it a more personal feel.

'You live alone?' asked Mallory.

'I do now.' Carys took her into the kitchen and filled the kettle. 'My partner left a few weeks ago. Found someone else, apparently, which was a bit of a shock but not devastating. We'd booked to go on holiday together and when he bailed, I decided to go anyway. I'm still trying to decide if it was a good idea.'

'I'm sorry about that. I know how it feels to be betrayed. Infidelity stings, however rubbish your relationship.'

Carys glanced at her. 'I guess so. Got any kids?'

'Just the one. My son Toby is fifteen.'

'That's nice. You had the air of being footloose and fancy-free yourself, that's all.'

'I guess I am in a way – Toby lives with his father most of the year.'

Carys's face crumpled but she kept her voice even. 'That was the problem with us. He wanted them – kids, I mean – and I didn't, so there was basically no future for us. What's the point of staying together if you can't resolve that one?'

'You don't like kids?' asked Mallory, thinking of Carys's job at the local college.

'I don't like or dislike them. It's just, as the eldest of three, I was left alone with my siblings a lot while my parents did their hippy thing. I feel I've done my child rearing without any tangible benefits and I'm not looking to repeat the experience.'

Mallory looked at the steaming kettle. 'Could I just have a glass of water? It's a bit hot for tea. I didn't realise your childhood was like that, although I had heard you were left on your own a lot.'

'Well, it was,' said Carys, turning on the tap. 'I had a chaotic upbringing and I've now created my own sanctuary – as, in fact, did Gwenllian.'

'So, you were in touch, then. Did you know Gwenllian was coming back to Pant Meinog?'

Carys winced at the name. 'I didn't, and it was a bloody stupid thing to do. It must have been her husband's idea. Shall we sit down?'

'You think it was David's idea?' asked Mallory, pulling a stool from underneath the kitchen counter.

'Well, that was his forte, wasn't it? Digging deep into people's psyches to see if there really is such a thing as the supernatural. There's no way Gwenllian would have gone back to the house without him pressuring her to do so.'

'It sounds like you didn't like him.'

Carys raised her eyebrows. 'David is, I mean was, a little intense. I felt he invaded my space a little too much, but it wasn't particularly threatening. Just, you know, intrusive.'

'He questioned you about what went on in 2003, then?'

Carys shifted on her stool, uncomfortable with the question. 'He tried to, but I didn't want to talk about it. I still don't. It was a stupid prank that went too far.'

'Including the scratches on Gwenllian's face?'

Carys froze. 'Yes, even that.'

'You thought it was a prank? Who by? Gwenllian?'

'I think so, yes. I'd begun to get a bit tired of the whole thing – I was growing up and wanted to do other stuff, but Gwenllian kept shouting that there was evil in the house. I know this sounds a terrible thing to say, but part of me was relieved when her face was scratched – not because of the injury, of course, but because it put a stop to everything.'

'And after that you moved away. Whose idea was that?'

'Mum's or Dad's. I don't know. Or maybe it was Uncle Tom, because he was furious with us when it all came out. He knocked on the door the evening of Gwenllian's accident and I heard shouting.'

'He might have given your parents notice?'

Carys frowned. 'It's possible, as he owned the cottage. I never found out why we moved but I was glad we did.'

Mallory remembered Harri's warning not to get stuck in the past. 'So how often were you in touch with Gwenllian?'

Carys shrugged. 'As much as you can be, when your life has gone in different directions. For Gwenllian, it was all about family and she was devoted to hers, although I don't think she found her step-kids easy.'

'She told you that?' asked Mallory.

'She hinted at discord, although teenagers are never easy, are they?'

'They are not,' said Mallory with feeling. 'What did Gwenllian do for a living?'

'Not much recently, I don't think, but she did work in a high-end shoe shop for a while in St Mary Street. She married David in her twenties and I think he was happy to support her.'

'Seems an old-fashioned arrangement. When did you last see the family?'

'I was invited down to Cardiff for Pippa's sixth birthday. I only went because it had been about two years since I'd visited, and we were in danger of losing touch. Despite our childhood, there's still some residual affection. As you can imagine, a kid's birthday party wasn't exactly doing it for me.'

'And how were they?' Mallory finished her glass of water and set it on the table.

'Fine, everyone seemed fine. It was a little manic, as these things are, and Matty and Ava scowled in the corner for most of the celebration. After that, Gwenllian and I kept in touch via WhatsApp and text. Wishing each other happy birthday, that sort of thing. I hadn't seen her recently.'

'She didn't confide in you about how her relationship with David was?'

'I've told you we weren't close at all, but everything looked fine on the surface.'

'We understand,' said Mallory, watching for Carys's reaction, 'that David had recently been suspended from his post.'

Carys gaped at her. 'I never knew that. What happened?'

'There were complaints that he'd become too partisan in his theories. Specifically, he didn't appreciate a sceptical approach from his students.'

'But that's nonsense,' said Carys, angrily. 'What the hell was he playing at? You don't… You don't think that's why he's dead, do you?'

'We've got to keep an open mind. Do you think he might have taken Gwenllian back to Pant Meinog because he believed her story that not everything was made up?'

'Fool.' Carys stood, her eyes blazing. 'I knew he was no good for Gwenllian. I bet it was his idea to go back to Pant Meinog. It's all beginning to make sense now.'

'I'm glad you can see some sense in it, because we can't. What do you think happened?'

'I think he probably asked Gwenllian to go back to the forest to "dig around in her past". In other words, to get to the bottom of what happened on the day she was injured. Believe me, I never could work out what happened. David's belief, however, would be that it was some supernatural presence, and I'm telling you there was no such thing.'

Mallory regarded Carys. 'You obviously didn't like Mr Anderson.'

Carys flushed, an angry red staining her neck. 'That's not true.'

'The thing is,' said Mallory, 'I'm just finding your reaction a little strange. For example, I appreciate that you were on holiday and that you might not have known it was your family who was missing, but you clearly knew it was David who had been discovered in the car. Why haven't you tried to contact us?'

'I assumed you'd call me. In fact, I was a bit miffed when I discovered you hadn't. I assumed you'd found Gwenllian and the kids, and hadn't updated the press yet.'

There was something definitely off with Carys's story, but in Mallory's experience, siblings weren't always close. She decided to push a little harder. 'Would you be happy for me to look around your flat? I just need to be sure that they're not here.'

Carys laughed. 'It'll take you less than sixty seconds. This place is tiny.'

Mallory slid off the stool and walked through to the small bedroom with its neatly made bed, put her head into the shower room and finally looked around the living room. There was no evidence of the family nor, come to that, of Carys's former partner.

'What about your brother Dylan?' asked Mallory. 'Do you have an address for him?'

'We're not in touch, I'm afraid. Our lives went in different directions and I have no idea where he is now. I haven't seen him since my parents' funeral.'

'Did Gwenllian keep in touch?'

'Possibly. You'll have to ask her when you find her. If she spoke to Dylan on a regular basis, then she never mentioned it to me.'

Mallory gazed at a small table in the corner of the room where a manuscript lay in a neat pile.

'Writing your memoir?' she asked flippantly.

For the first time, Mallory saw Carys relax. 'I'm writing a book – well, when I say book… It's a series of photographs celebrating the landscape but the accompanying text is taking up all my mental energy. Do you want to see?'

Carys crouched down and pulled a large portfolio from under the couch. Christ, her sister and niece were missing, and she wanted to show Mallory photographs of hills and trees. Perhaps she was right not to have children, thought Mallory, aware that she was being a little judgemental. Carys wouldn't have been the first witness she'd interviewed to focus on displacement activities. Mallory dutifully looked through the photos, which were as intense and cold as the person who had taken them.

'They look great. Do you have photos of Pant Meinog, taken when you were living there?'

Carys looked disappointed at Mallory's swift appraisal of her book. 'I have some on a CD-ROM from back in the day when I had a little digital camera. I'll go and get them.'

While she was waiting, Mallory sat back on the sofa. Neither Gwenllian nor the children were here, and there was no indication that they'd been in the flat recently. There was nothing suspicious in that, she supposed. Mallory had a brother she rarely saw and texted probably once a year. No great drama but if Mallory had been holidaying near her sibling, she thought she might have at least contacted him, even if she knew he'd be away. It was possible that the family had specifically wanted Carys to be kept in the dark about their visit. Was she a threat?

Carys came back with a disk in her hand marked PM. 'There's probably more but there'll be plenty of images on this one. I should put it onto a hard drive or something, but I just can't bring myself to go through the past.'

Mallory took the disk and tucked it into her shoulder bag. 'There's one more thing I need to ask. What precipitated the hoax?'

Carys grimaced. 'We were bored, hormonal, looking for attention. It was fun at first, chucking things about the house. When the police turned up, they kind of added a frisson of the excitement we were missing.'

'And the final time and the attack on Gwenllian's face. How was it done?'

Carys shook her head and looked at the floor. 'I don't know, so you'll have to ask Gwenllian when you find her. She's the only one who knows.'

17

Carys looked out of the window at the driving rain, wishing she was anywhere other than this miserable valley. She had been born here and was pretty sure she would die in this godforsaken place if she didn't do something about it soon. Her parents, Lewis and Sally, were not much use. Her father, when he wasn't stressed about the school he worked in – where all the boys wanted to do was work on their father's farm – spent all his time in the garden hoeing the thin soil for the runner beans and tomatoes he sold at the market. Her mother, in Carys's opinion, was the more successful of the two. At least the art and basketwork she created sold well, although it meant she was usually buried away in the room behind the kitchen, covered in oil paint or dust from the twine she used.

Upstairs, she could hear Dylan thumping around. He'd been given a football as a present and was always playing with it, whether it was rainy or fine. She was surprised he was kicking it around in his bedroom, as the shelves were packed full of his favourite superhero models, and woe betide anyone who damaged one of those toys. The noise of the ball continued to grate on her, the thick walls of the house muffling the sound to a dull thud. She had no idea where Gwenllian was. They'd almost exhausted their repertoire of jokes to play on the family and now Gwenllian had a new idea. She wanted Carys to take a photo of her jumping from her bed, angling herself as she leapt to make it look like she'd been propelled by an unseen force through the air. Carys wasn't entirely sure her camera skills were up to this. They might need a few goes and Gwenllian had a habit of throwing herself completely into a part. She might end up injured, which is where Carys drew the line.

As she was examining the digital camera she'd managed to persuade her mother to buy for her birthday, Dylan came out of the kitchen, eating a packet of crisps. Carys frowned at him.

'I thought you were kicking the football around upstairs.'

'Not me,' he replied, his mouth full of Monster Munch. 'She'd better not be in my bedroom.'

'Shit.' Carys pushed past him and ran up the creaking stairs with the loose banister to Gwenllian's bedroom but it was locked. Except, it couldn't be, as there wasn't a lock. Instead, it seemed something was jammed up against the door. Carys banged hard on it.

'Gwennie. Let me in.'

'Help me, Carys,' screamed her sister. 'Help me!'

Carys put her shoulder to the door. Lewis and Sally were out at another bloody market, this time in the Botanical Gardens, so it would be hours until they got back.

'Dylan. Get the hell up here.'

Dylan came charging up the stairs, his eyes wide. 'What's the matter?'

'Just help me push against the door. Run at it if you can.'

Dylan, ever the live wire, pushed his head down and charged, bouncing off the door.

'Ouch. That hurt.' Dylan rubbed his shoulders. 'What's she got behind there?'

'Her wardrobe, I think, or maybe a chest of drawers.' Carys was out of breath from the exertion. Gwenllian continued to scream from inside the room as Carys fruitlessly rattled the door handle.

'Hold on, Gwennie. I'm going to get Gethin from next door.' The screaming came to an abrupt halt and there was the sound of furniture being dragged across the floor.

Carys flung open the door and found Gwenllian sitting on the floor, her face red as if it had been repeatedly slapped. Carys looked around the room but saw no one.

'What happened?'

'It's a thing,' said Gwenllian wildly. 'It's a thing.'

18

As Mallory opened the doors of her car to let some of the heat out before climbing in, she saw she'd missed a message from Harri. *Ring me – urgent.* She fumbled for the number, made clumsy by the anxiety over the children, and listened in despair as he updated her on the discovery by three mountain bikers. Gwenllian had been found and Mallory's presence was needed at the crime scene.

As she drove up the winding road from Brechfa, Mallory decided she would be happy if she never entered the forest again. There was a reason why she had chosen to live by the sea – first in Eldey, then St Davids and now at Cardigan Bay. She liked the sound of the crash of waves far in the distance and the scent of salt in her nostrils. The forest had a dark, sly feel to it, its aroma in the August heat fragrant but cloying. After parking her car on the narrow road, keeping her fingers crossed that her wing mirror would still be intact when she got back, she had a job getting past the officer guarding the crime scene. Civilian investigators were a new one on him and he hadn't liked the look of her pass. She was eventually scooped up by Siân, who was also just arriving, after she had left her car further down the hill.

'This puts a new complexion on matters,' she said. 'We have three children now definitely out there somewhere on their own. If they're still alive, that is.'

Somewhere, in the forest, the body of Gwenllian Anderson — formerly Prytherch — lay, a sickening sight after four days exposed to the elements.

'Any more news on the sightings?' Mallory asked Siân.

'Nope, but I personally don't think they're together. OK, a lone child around Pippa's age is easier to spot than teenagers, but these two siblings are distinctive-looking and appear to go round as a pair. My guess is they're somewhere other than with their younger sister, although I can't even begin to guess the reasons for this. Shall we take a look at Mrs Anderson?'

They walked along a gravelled track marked with deep grooves made by logging and tree-management vehicles. Another uniformed officer, standing to one side, pointed the way off the path. They headed towards the lights that had been erected and the crowd parted, as if expecting them. Harri turned and inclined his head.

'You only need a brief look. It won't tell you much.'

'Is it definitely her?'

'Can't tell from looking, but the pathologist says we'll definitely be able to match dental records quickly if it's Gwenllian, rather than wait for DNA results. The bones haven't been scavenged yet.'

Mallory took one glance at the body and turned away. On the drive over, she'd reasoned that, given that David Anderson had been killed on Friday, the discovery of Gwenllian's body on the following Monday would suggest a more recent killing. The victim, however — her body in active decay — looked as if she'd died days earlier, even allowing for exposure to the elements.

Harri had also reached the same conclusion. 'She may well have been killed around the same time as her husband, although the pathologist is saying it's going to

135

be almost impossible to determine time of death. Even the cause of death is looking unlikely, given the condition of the body.'

'Christ,' said Mallory. 'Trying to focus on anything concrete is proving almost impossible. How long has it been now? Four days? It shouldn't normally take this long to get something to go on.'

'It's frustrating but we plough on. What's the matter?' asked Harri.

Mallory's eyes were on the white nightdress, bloodied and dirty. The blood might give forensics more clues than the body, but Mallory remembered Elsa's vision of a woman in white running across the forest.

'It's nothing. Could she have run here from the house? I was just looking at the condition of the nightdress.'

'Easily, if you know the old track that Tom mentioned, which Gwenllian will have done. The blood's a worry, though, and I suspect Gwenllian's death was more violent than David's. Are you OK?'

'I'm fine, why do you ask?'

'You must be exhausted after last night's trip. Don't let this case consume you, Mallory.'

In his eyes, she saw concern and something else, difficult to read. He didn't, Mallory noticed, suggest she take any time off.

'I'm fine. I saw Carys Prytherch earlier today. She claims not to have set eyes on the family for a few years and can't give me an address for her brother.'

Harri shrugged. 'Not that unusual, although it's funny we too are having difficulty tracking down Dylan Prytherch. He had a series of low-wage jobs until 2016 and since then he's gone off the radar. I've sent a car to his last address but it's just a flat in Swansea. There have been plenty of tenants since he stayed there, and the landlord knows nothing. He left no trace – the only reason we know Dylan lived there is his employment record from bar work.'

'Any recent photo ID?'

'No driving licence, no passport.'

'You think he might be dead?' asked Mallory.

Harri's eyes strayed to the body on the ground. 'It's a possibility, isn't it?'

Mallory took a deep breath. 'I'd like to be involved in the hunt for Pippa. Interviewing witnesses of a past crime is all well and good, but I want to be on the ground, looking for the children. Siân thinks they might have got separated and I'm inclined to agree.'

Harri turned to her. 'You are involved, aren't you? That's what we're all working towards – finding the kids and identifying the killer. In that order.'

'You're sending me to visit people from Gwenllian's past. It's the present I'm interested in. If Pippa's stealing food, then she's not with someone she knows, family or otherwise. I want to help look for her.'

Harri shook his head. 'I've got a good team looking for Pippa. We can't do any more. You don't know this area, so you're not going to be bringing any local knowledge – you'll just get in the way.'

'Well, that's great.' Mallory folded her arms, remembering why she'd found the civilian investigator role so frustrating in the past. 'Always on the periphery, never right at the centre.'

But you don't want to go back to the police, do you? said the little voice in her head. Harri wasn't in the mood for arguments either.

'Come on, Mallory. You're good at winkling things out from the past. I've seen you in action before.' Harri reached into his back pocket and handed her a sheet of paper. 'I've looked through the 2003 case again and here are the people I think might be involved in the current case.'

Mallory unfolded the paper and looked at the six names:

Carys Prytherch

Dylan Prytherch

Tom Thomas

Gethin and Cathy Thomas

Bev Christie

Mallory gasped as she looked at the final name on the list.

'I went to see Bev Christie on Saturday. Why is she on your list?'

'Because, as far as I recall, she was at the house a lot during the alleged poltergeist incidents.'

'All right, but I saw no evidence of the children when I visited her.'

'Did you search the house?'

Mallory flushed. 'Of course not. We weren't even sure at that time whether the children were connected to the Prytherch family, and I wasn't officially on the case.'

'Take it easy, Mallory. She's on my list and you can go back to see her. Bev is well known in this area and has a kind soul. She's a person I'd gravitate to if I was in trouble, so she's on the list.'

'OK,' said Mallory, mollified. 'Who are Gethin and Cathy Thomas?'

'Tom's son and daughter-in-law, who were living with Tom at the time. We should have asked Tom about them when we met him, as I got the impression that the couple were close to the children.'

'Interesting, then, that Tom sold Pant Meinog rather than pass it on to his son. Suggests the next generation of Thomases didn't want to live there.'

'Yes, and I'm not really surprised, although housing for locals is in short supply. I'd be interested to hear what they have to say.'

Mallory's phone shrilled in the quiet forest and she groped for it, in case it was Toby. A withheld number came up and it turned out to be a duty officer in the detective room trying to connect an urgent call. Carys had been trying to track her down.

'I've been thinking about your visit since you left. You know… You have searched Pant Meinog properly, haven't you?'

Mallory frowned, trying to erase the image of Gwenllian's body from her mind. Carys would be getting yet another visit from police sooner rather than later, before news could break on social media. 'There's been a thorough forensic search. I've been there a few times too. Why do you ask?'

'Because Gwenllian and I had a hiding place: a loose floorboard in the airing cupboard. I doubt the cupboard is still there – I mean, who has them these days?'

'It is,' said Mallory. 'The hot water tank is in there, but the house has been renovated. I can't imagine the board being loose any longer.'

'No, that's true.' Carys's voice registered disappointment. 'It's just me being stupid. But I've been going over in my mind… Gwenllian returning to the house and what I'd look for if I was inside the building.'

'What did you keep there?'

'You know, the usual things: stones, feathers, bits of paper. It's only just come back to me. Look, forget it, I feel a fool.'

'No… no. Look, I can take a quick look. Why not? Did anyone else know about it?'

'I don't think so. In fact, I'm pretty sure it was just Gwenllian and me.'

'Then I'll look.'

19

Harri waited in the car for forensics to finish their work. Siân joined him, shivering even though it wasn't cold, and handed him a cup of tea she'd managed to procure from somewhere, possibly the pub in the village. Harri's spirits revived a little as the warm liquid trickled down his throat. Gwenllian's death had hit him harder than David's. That was hardly a surprise, given he'd actually met the victim, but there was something else besides this. He'd been absolutely sure up to that point that Gwenllian had been behind the family's disappearance. She'd already shown herself to be skilled in the art of deception in 2003, when she'd had the gullible fooled. He'd been convinced she was playing her tricks all over again, but he'd been wrong. Or, if she had set out to deceive, it had gone disastrously wrong.

'Think they died together?' asked Siân, articulating what was already in his mind.

'It's possible. Or not long before or after. Perhaps Gwenllian died first and David, filled with remorse, killed himself by ending his life in the car.'

'I've just rung down to the office for an update, and forensics aren't happy with what they found in the exhaust. They've discounted a leak because, although carbon monoxide is odourless, the other gases pumping out – if there was a hole in the exhaust – would stink the car out,' said Siân. 'However, there's an issue that occurs in the US when snow clogs up a tailpipe. People trapped in their snowbound cars don't realise they're dying.'

'They think that's what happened? The exhaust was bunged up with something?' Harri felt unwell and tried to remember if he'd taken his diabetic medication that morning. It was fifty–fifty, as he wasn't exactly on top of his medication.

'Exactly. They've found a kind of cloth or blanket pushed into the tailpipe. They're testing it now, but it would have caused a lethal obstruction.'

'Which doesn't rule out suicide.' Harri breathed out. 'But where do the kids come into it?'

'I don't know. Perhaps David was intending to take them with him and they're hiding because they're scared. They don't necessarily know that Gwenllian is dead.'

'It's all so bloody slow.' Harri's eyes swept the woodland.

'We're doing our best. Most of Carmarthen are out looking for them. It's not that easy to live off-grid. They'll be harder to find if they're staying with someone, but that doesn't look to be the case with Pippa. We'll find them.'

–

Back at the station, Harri read through a summary of DNA found at the holiday home. As expected, despite Elsa's expert cleaning, the house was a forensic nightmare, given it was occupied by holidaying families throughout the year. Ditto fingerprints, but Harri signed off the request to begin the laborious job of matching results to guests. More hopeful was the interview from the holidaying couple who'd cancelled their three-week stay in the house. They'd been contacted by David Anderson, who'd explained that he was desperate to get away, following his wife's illness. He offered the family double the value of the cottage rental if they could find somewhere else to go. Unsurprisingly, the family had taken the money and thought no more of it until the police turned up at their door. That explained how David had been able to book the place at such short notice. Cash. There was no update about the state of the Andersons' finances, but the university said he was suspended on full pay so, although perhaps not flush, there was an income coming in.

Harri picked up the timeline assembled by the team, detailing the movements of the Anderson family in the week prior to their deaths. A camera in a petrol station on the approach to the M4 had picked up the jeep refuelling on the day before the family went missing. Harri turned and looked at the map he had on his wall. He preferred this over the digital maps his colleagues used on their tablets. The south Carmarthenshire coast was one of the most beautiful areas of not only Wales, but also the British Isles – but there was no evidence that the family had visited these beaches, unless they'd used a small place where they could sunbathe in peace. From experience, though, Harri knew that on a beach you looked at the families either side of you, even if you didn't speak to them. Following the appeal, no one had come forward to say they'd seen the Andersons. So where had they gone?

20

Only a single plume of smoke from Tom Thomas's house indicated inhabitation of the land around Pant Meinog. Although she didn't know a word of the language, Mallory preferred the Welsh name for the house. Its translation, which she'd looked up in her dictionary, was 'stony valley', which suited the location and gave her a greater understanding of the deep affection felt by locals for original names of houses. Although it was a hot summer's day, Mallory was unsurprised by Tom's fire, knowing now that people liked to keep warm in the evenings inside their thick-walled homes where the heat of the day often never penetrated. This place was also, Mallory thought, a cold spot: the fine light in the clearing failed to infiltrate the forest surrounding it. Even though it was light, Mallory took a torch from the back of her car and walked to the edge of the forest, shining the beam towards the trees facing the kitchen window of the holiday home. The light bounced off the uniform trunks and Mallory made a slow arc, until she was confident no one was there. She'd had to stop at the station to get the key and it lay heavily in her palm, as if warning her not to enter the house.

As she opened the door, a rush of stale air came down the hallway. The place would need Elsa's ministrations before it could be let again. Mallory switched on the lights and made her way up to the airing cupboard. It was at the end of the upstairs passageway, a warm enclosed room with a pull light from the days when people dried their clothes near the hot water tank. Now there was just a row of empty shelves with a few blankets folded on them. The place had been given a lick of paint and a new tank had been fitted, but it looked largely unchanged.

Mallory tested the bare floorboards with her feet. As she'd expected, they held firm. A renovation company might not be minded to make many changes to the inside of an airing cupboard, but they weren't going to leave anything loose or damaged. When she was satisfied that all the boards were secure, Mallory looked around the tiny cupboard. Carys had remembered their hiding place and, she suspected, so might have Gwenllian. Childhood dreams and secrets are hard to shrug off. Mallory took a look round but saw no nooks that might act as a repository for secrets. She suspected she was walking in the footsteps of Gwenllian, testing each floorboard with her foot until she'd realised, in this cupboard at least, there was nothing to be found.

As she was switching off the light in the room, she heard a muffled sound coming from along the corridor. It sounded like an animal scratching against the door. Something larger than a cat and, despite her scepticism, the image of a large panther came to Mallory. The Beast of Brechfa. Ridiculous, she thought, her senses in high alert. There was a killer on the loose, not some kind of mythical being.

Aware of the danger she faced, she darted into the bathroom, her eyes scanning for something she could pick up to defend herself. A bathroom, especially in a rented property, is pretty useless in the hunt for weapons and Mallory was forced to stand still as she listened for the approaching steps, which never came. Stillness was to her advantage and she heard the sound again. A muffled movement that was coming, she decided, from the room Pippa had slept in.

Only when she heard a stifled sob did Mallory's instincts kick in and she rushed down the landing towards the sound. She pushed open the door and took in the slim frightened figure, crouching in a corner, staring at her with wild eyes.

'Oh, Pippa.'

The slim figure sprung forward, brandishing a piece of jagged glass in her hand. 'I won't let you kill me.'

The girl was trembling, her legs threatening to buckle beneath her. Mallory reached into the pocket of her jacket.

'Pippa, we've been looking everywhere for you. How did you get in here?'

'Through the back window.'

So much for the place being secured, thought Mallory. 'I'm going to show you my police ID so you can see that you've nothing to be frightened of, OK?'

Pippa gave a slight nod of her head as Mallory pulled out her pass. As the girl scrutinised the lanyard, Mallory saw her grubby face was lined with tracks of tears and snot, and she wanted to reach out and pull Pippa towards her. She was pretty sure that, if she wanted, she could overpower her and take the shard out of her hand. She also knew that getting Pippa to trust adults would be key in getting her to speak freely and what she did now, in the next few minutes, might alter completely the direction of the case. She waited, hardly daring to breathe until she saw Pippa's arms drop; the little girl then rushed to her, putting her arms around her waist. Mallory responded, hugging the child tightly.

'Are you OK?' she asked Pippa. 'Are you injured at all?'

'I'm really hungry,' Pippa replied. 'There was food here but it's all gone.'

The forensic team had finally removed the stale bread, and must have also emptied the fridge and cupboards of their contents, a decision that had been disastrous for Pippa. Because the family had been running from Tall Pines, it had never occurred to the team that Pippa or her siblings might come back here. Mallory hunted around in her bag but came up with nothing.

'I'm going to call for help but I'll also ask the man in the house next door for food.'

Pippa took a step back. 'I don't want to see anyone.'

Mallory swallowed. She really wanted to hold on to Pippa. If she went to Tom Thomas's house there was a possibility she might slip away, which would be disastrous. Given she wasn't actually a medical emergency, Mallory decided to forgo a visit to Tom until help arrived.

'I'm going to ring a colleague. He's a nice man and will send help. Do you trust me, Pippa?'

The girl shrugged, embarrassed, as Mallory made the call, still holding on to her hand.

'Harri, it's me. I've found Pippa. We're at Pant Meinog.'

Mallory heard a sharp intake of breath. 'Is she OK?'

'She's all right but hungry. Can you send a car as soon as possible and have them stop for some food en route?'

'We'll be there in less than twenty minutes. Can I have a word with Pippa?'

Mallory looked down at the girl. 'I have my boss on the phone who wants to talk to you. His name is Harri. There's no need to be afraid of him.'

Mallory saw Pippa tremble but she took the phone and listened as Harri spoke reassuring words to her. Mallory heard her say, 'I don't know,' twice and she suspected he was asking about her siblings. Mallory studied Pippa's face and saw what looked like anger when she answered Harri's questions, and wondered what the two teenagers had done to her. Jesus, Mallory felt sick. Surely it wasn't the teenagers who were the killers of their father and stepmother?

Pippa handed back the phone to Mallory, but Harri had already cut the call. He knew she wouldn't question Pippa until more people arrived, and he trusted her to look after the girl's welfare in the meantime.

'Shall we get ourselves a glass of water? After a fright we often forget to drink and get dehydrated.'

Pippa nodded and followed Mallory down the stairs.

'Do you know that Auntie Carys threw a vase from the top of these stairs and pretended it was a poltergeist?' she asked Mallory.

'I didn't.' Mallory kept her voice even. 'It sounds like they had a lot of fun playing jokes when they were children.'

'They weren't children,' said Pippa firmly. She took a glass of water from Mallory and drank deeply. 'They were older than me, and I'd never play such a trick.'

'Did your mum ever talk about it?' asked Mallory, wondering if she was venturing into territory she shouldn't really go to.

Pippa shrugged. 'Sometimes.'

'Shall we sit at the table?' In the distance, Mallory could hear a siren, which was understandable but could frighten the girl. Pippa clearly heard it.

'I won't go to prison, will I?'

'I promise you won't go to prison. The siren is because we've all been so worried about you. The car will get here quicker with the siren on.'

Pippa nodded. 'I wish I'd been allowed to bring my iPad. I like looking things up but it's hard when you can't get on the internet. It was just something Mum said.'

'I have my phone here now. Is there anything you want me to look up while we wait?'

Pippa nodded, her eyes huge pools in her face. 'What does cuckoo in the nest mean?'

21

There were strict protocols for interviewing children. In fact, there were rules for interviewing all witnesses, but when children were involved more agencies had a say in how things progressed. Children, of course, were an essential source of information in many crime investigations and prevailing opinion was the contrary to popular opinion: children made robust witnesses. Before Siân and Freddie were able to speak to Pippa, an interview adviser was consulted, along with a social worker from child protection services. Once an interview strategy had been prepared, Siân, who had been trained in interviewing child witnesses, was allowed to meet Pippa.

The wait for clearance was agonising for Harri, as he was sure the evidence provided by the little girl would be the breakthrough this case needed. He was relieved when they got the go-ahead, even though it was six p.m. – late in the day to interview a child. However, the fact that there were two other children missing meant no waiting until the morning. The assessment of the social worker was that Pippa had no additional vulnerabilities apart from her age, and her communication skills were above average.

There was no opportunity to obtain parental consent and it was decided the social worker would sit in on the interview. Harri watched on the screen as Siân and Freddie entered the room. Pippa was sitting on a chair with her social worker next to her, a young woman in her twenties with an efficient air. Pippa's hair was her most striking feature – Elsa had been right. Someone had used the word carroty but that failed to convey its golden burnish. Over time, it would fade, but the memory of that lustre would remain. Harri thought it was one of the most beautiful hair colours he'd ever seen.

Pippa was pale-skinned, with a flush across her cheeks that crept down to her neck. She'd clearly been crying – her skin had that tired, stretched look – but was now composed, glancing occasionally at her social worker, who seemed to bring her comfort. After introducing herself and Freddie, Siân took her time to frame her first question.

'I know it's been a hard time for you, Pippa, but I'd like you to start by telling me a bit about your family and this holiday you took together.'

'It wasn't a holiday.' The girl had a middle-class accent, her tone clear as a bell.

'What do you mean? If it wasn't a holiday, what was it?'

'A confrontation with the past.'

Harri felt his flesh creep at the girl's words.

'What do you mean by that?' asked Siân.

Pippa shrugged. 'I don't know, because Mum wouldn't tell me.'

'And your father, David. What did he say when she used those words?'

Pippa looked directly at her. 'She said it to me, not him. It was our secret.'

Harri grimaced. He didn't like it when adults used children as confidantes. It resulted in a loss of innocence, forcing them to keep secrets.

'Do you know what she was referring to?' asked Siân.

Pippa shrugged and made a mark on her face.

'Sorry, I didn't quite catch that. Why did you touch your face, Pippa?'

'It... It was to do with the scars. Mum... She had scars.'

'And she'd come to Brechfa to confront what had happened?' asked Siân.

'Yes, but Dad thought we were coming for another reason.'

'And what was that?'

Harri heard the door open behind him and turned slightly to see Steph enter the room. She raised her eyebrows at him and looked at the screen. Pippa was giving Siân's question some thought.

'I think he wanted to... to prove... that the poltergeist really happened. He was always going on about it, even though Mum told him to stop. I... I think he thought by going back to the house he could prove there was an evil spirit there.'

Siân paused and Harri felt for her. This scenario, he was sure, would never have cropped up on her training course. Pippa, interestingly, leapt in to fill the silence.

'I don't think he knew how bad things were.'

'What do you mean by bad, Pippa? Bad in what way?'

'I think Mum was scared about something. She was the one who told him to hire the car in secret.'

'How do you know that?' asked Siân. 'Was that something you overheard?'

Pippa nodded. 'They were talking about going away and Dad couldn't understand why we had to pretend we weren't who we actually were.'

'You sure it was your mum's idea?' asked Freddie.

Pippa nodded. 'Very sure.'

Siân exhaled. 'OK. Pippa, I have lots more questions for you but we'll take things very slowly. What I need to ask you is if you know where your brother and sister are? You told the officer who found you that you last saw them on Friday around lunchtime. Is that right?'

At first Harri thought the little girl was having a panic attack – she took three deep breaths – but he realised she was trying to compose herself. 'They just *left* me.' The outrage carried across the interview room, making even Steph flinch.

'Where did they leave you?' asked Siân but Pippa shook her head. It was a rare misstep for her. She'd taken things too fast. Freddie, spotting this, leant forward.

'Let's go back to your trip down to the house,' he said. 'Were you with your dad when he hired the jeep?'

Pippa shook her head. 'We waited by a factory. It was really boring but then Dad turned up and we put all our things in the other car.'

'What reason did he give you for swapping cars?' asked Freddie.

'He said it would be more fun to go on holiday in a jeep. And it was – we were all high up. Mum was happier too.'

'That's good,' said Freddie. 'So, you all drove down to the house in the forest. Tall Pines.'

'Yes.' She made to say something but stopped herself. Harri thought she might have been inclined to correct his use of the name Tall Pines, rather than Pant Meinog, but had thought better of it.

'And what did you do for your first week?'

'We mainly stayed at the house.'

'What, all week?'

'Yes, even though it was very hot. Dad told us that the first week would be work and then we'd be able to go to the beach. It was very important he get his investigations done first. He has these things – monitors, microphones, recording machines – that he placed around the house.'

'We didn't find those there, Pippa, when we searched the property,' said Freddie. 'Do you know what happened to them?'

Pippa was fiddling with a plastic cup of water in front of her. 'Dad went away on the Thursday and took all the equipment with him. He… He looked like he'd been crying.'

'Why do you think that was?'

'I'm not sure. He was out all day and when he got back, he was upset. He said the holiday was about to start but he was angry with Mum and didn't want to be with us.'

'Why?' asked Siân, smiling. 'Why do you think he was angry with your mum?'

'Because she had a visitor and Dad wasn't allowed to see them, and there was a huge row.'

22

Toby was nowhere to be seen when Mallory got home. He'd been back to the caravan to change – a wetsuit dripped over the drying rail outside – but hadn't bothered to leave her a note. She was fine with him getting a summer job, pleased even, but she wondered how he intended to fit his social life around paid work. Perhaps, thought Mallory, she herself wasn't presenting the best role model in terms of gainful employment. Harri hadn't even asked her to come to the station to accompany Pippa, who'd shown no reaction to being taken from the house. If anything, she'd been a little excited about the ride in the police car.

Annoyed that she'd been sidelined from the interview with Pippa and had little to occupy her until the morning, Mallory pulled out her ancient laptop and slid in the CD Rom given to her by Carys. Harri *had* given her a list of people connected to the 2003 case to work through and she supposed she could spend the evening looking at them. She'd met Bev Christie, but this was before the discovery of Gwenllian's body, so it would be interesting to hear her views on that development. First, however, she'd see if the disk given to her by Carys threw up any useful insights into the family's dynamics in 2003.

It had been a while since she'd used the programme on her computer but the thumbnail menu was easy to open, enabling Mallory to flick through the images. Carys, even as a teenager, had been obsessed with the scenery around her. Her connection with the landscape could find its roots in the forest which, to Mallory's eyes, looked the same all year round. No watching the changing of the seasons amongst the evergreen conifers. Carys, however, had shown a flair for photography at an early age, capturing the essence of the tall, dark pines. Mallory moved on, looking for images of people.

The first was a close-up of Gwenllian, the picture taken a little too close for comfort, and the girl looked uneasy. The two sisters, although alike, would never be taken for identical twins. Gwenllian's face was softer, her alabaster skin unblemished. Elsa had said that she was wearing red lipstick last week, which suggested she'd been proud of her appearance. There was a lot you could do with make-up for scars these days, so perhaps Gwenllian had been able to pass in the street without comment.

Another photo showed a hippyish couple in their forties, the man with greying hair in a ponytail, and the woman sporting dreadlocks. Their appearance suggested an alternative lifestyle which wasn't that unusual in this neck of the woods. This must be Gwenllian's parents, Lewis and Sally, looking carefree. Mallory squinted at the time stamp on the images: 28 July 2002, about a year before the deception. It was difficult to see either Gwenllian or Carys in this couple: their eldest, as an adult, came across brittle and no-nonsense compared to Sally's laughing casualness. Mallory knew appearances could be deceptive, however, and she wondered if the parents could be responsible for the bruises attributed to the poltergeist. Admittedly, the parents had been out of the house on the final day Gwenllian was attacked but that didn't mean they didn't have a hand in creating a mood of fear and deceit in the family home.

Mallory ploughed on through the photos, looking for an image that would capture the family. Another group photo showed a couple in their early twenties standing alongside Tom Thomas, unexpectedly handsome with his thick hair swept back, a Ted Hughes-like figure. Mallory squinted at the couple, noticing that the man looked like his father. This must be Gethin and Cathy Thomas, who had spent the beginning of their married life with Tom. They made for an attractive couple: Cathy was wearing tiny denim shorts and smiling broadly into the camera, with none of Gwenllian's unease. After a few minutes fiddling with various icons, Mallory found a way to send the image to her email and continued her sweep of the photos.

A lone image of a younger child in the thumbnails caught her eye and she opened it up. It showed a fair-haired boy, his features innocent, as his pale grey eyes and freckled face stared into the camera. She sat back in her seat.

'Bloody hell.'

—

Mallory found the number she'd called days earlier, but it rang out, unanswered. Grabbing her denim jacket, she scribbled a note for Toby, telling him there was food in the fridge and would he *please* eat something. Feeling guilty, she mentally tallied what snacks she'd left for him so she could check when she got back if he'd actually consumed any of them. It would be easy enough, of course, for him to say he'd got a bag of chips from a takeaway and she'd be none the wiser.

She drove down the coastal path to New Quay, where Toby was due to start his job the following day. The evening was balmy but it was fresher by the coast and Mallory quickly put on her jacket as she made her way to the beach. If Toby was here rather than in one of the other coves, he'd be mortified to see her. It wasn't him she was looking for, however. The beach was still busy: workers who'd spent the day in the office were desperate to top up their tans and cool off in the water. Mallory scanned the horizon, not expecting to find the person she was looking for, until she saw the familiar form reading the same novel as when she'd first spotted him.

She walked over, feeling sand spill over the edges of her trainers. Luke looked up as she approached, his smile freezing as he saw her expression.

'Hello, Dylan.'

Mallory sat down next to the young man and they contemplated the sea in silence.

'Was anything you told me on Saturday the truth?' she asked him.

Luke shrugged, putting his book face-down in the sand. 'I'm a podcaster, I did go to university in Cardiff to study media, and I'm interested in strange events. Hence, the subject of my podcast.'

'You know, I could take all that. After your childhood experiences, I could believe that you'd have an interest in odd happenings and wanted to investigate them. Expose the real facts, even. That's an honourable thing to do. But you've duped your listeners by presenting them with the facts of what happened at Pant Meinog as a neutral observer when, in fact, you were there. You were already in the story.'

Luke made a face. 'I wasn't happy about doing it. You're right, it's unethical and the only good thing is that none of my regulars made the connection. I mean, why should they?'

'But why? There are millions of strange incidents out there. You could have just focused on those. Why use Pant Meinog?'

Luke picked up a handful of sand and let it trickle through his fingers. 'Because Bev asked me to.'

'Bev?'

'As I told you before, I contacted her about another case and she directed me towards this one. She loves the publicity around her deliverance work. Thinks she provides a real service to the community but she's usually called in by fantasists and the mentally ill. She wants more genuine cases.'

'So she asked you to highlight Pant Meinog and her role in helping to get rid of the spirit.'

'Exactly.'

'That's not what she told me. She said you asked her for recommendations for local hauntings and she directed you towards Pant Meinog.'

'That's what I just said, wasn't it?'

Well, not exactly, thought Mallory. In Dylan's account the agency was with Bev, not himself. 'But the Pant Meinog haunting wasn't genuine, was it? It's an odd case for Bev to focus on to promote her work in cases of supernatural activity.'

Luke exhaled. 'Bev is positive that there was a genuine case of haunting and nothing I say can get her to change that belief.'

'And she didn't realise who you are?' asked Mallory.

Luke shook his head. 'Of course not – all our contact was over the phone. I haven't seen the woman since I was a child.'

'What about Gwenllian and Carys? Have they stayed in touch with Bev?'

'I doubt it. Gwenllian moved away and has a family of her own, so I can't imagine why she'd want to stay in touch with Bev. As far as I can tell, she doesn't want to rake up the past and Carys also hates talking about what happened in 2003.'

'Are you in touch with them? Carys said she doesn't know where you live.'

'That's technically true, as I move around a lot. We're in touch occasionally, though, so I'm surprised she put it like that. Gwenllian, I've not seen in years.'

'Then there's something I need to tell you. I'm afraid we found Gwenllian's body this afternoon.'

Luke froze, his sunglasses hiding his reaction to the news.

'Where did you find the body?'

'In the woods near Pant Meinog. Gwenllian, you see, went back to stay at the house where you grew up.'

Luke stood, brushing the sand from his legs. 'So that's why you came to see me on Saturday. It's not only me who's been hiding the truth, then, is it?'

Mallory reached out an arm and grabbed his wrist. 'Luke, listen, I'm sorry but when we met, I didn't realise both David and your sister were dead. Didn't you see the appeal for information?'

Luke shook his head. 'I live a little off-grid. I'm not interested in the news.'

'I need you to go back to your time in the forest so I can understand what went on. The impression I've been

160

given is that you weren't involved in the pretence there was a poltergeist. Is that true?'

Luke shook her off but sat back down, gazing at the water's edge. 'I hated it all, right from the beginning.'

23

Dylan heard his sisters giggling behind Carys's bedroom door. He was excluded, as usual, a fact that Gwenllian in particular enjoyed. He guessed they were practising their tricks. There had been jokes with string and wire, splashes of water where there shouldn't be any, and things, including his toys, going missing. This was the most upsetting. His bedroom was private – he'd even put up a 'no entry' sign on the door that he made with his crayons – but he was sure his sisters went in there anyway. He'd lost his favourite Action Man, the one dressed not in combat gear but as an adventurer, with a thick jumper and jeans, like the loggers who came to harvest the forest trees.

He didn't like being excluded from his sisters' tricks but when they were found out, there would be big trouble – and not just from their parents either. There were others who didn't like Carys and Gwenllian messing around. He turned the handle of the door and pushed it open. There were no locks in the house; no one had any privacy. He caught Gwenllian with her arm in the air, a vase he hadn't seen before in her hand. She paused for a moment as he stood staring at her, his eyes wide with shock. Carys, who viewed him as little more than an irritant, snatched the vase from her hand.

'Look, a robin in the tree outside,' she said.

Despite himself, his eyes slid to the window and, next, he winced at the crash the china made as it hit the wall, smashing into three solid chunks.

'See, you never saw anything, did you?' said Carys.

'Please, don't keep doing this.'

Carys turned a pair of mocking eyes on him. 'Carys! Carys! Let me have my fun.'

She ran to pick up the remains of the vase and studied the breaks. 'It would be more fun if it smashed into lots of small pieces. Perhaps we should try a glass.'

Gwenllian's eyes lit up. 'Get a wine glass. It'll be easier to break.' She refused to look at him, in case she saw the expression in his eyes. He ran out of the room, away from his sisters' merciless glee.

It had been fun at first, watching them throw things across a room when their parents' back was turned. They'd seen the trick on the TV. You held something by your side and acted like you were reading or eating your dinner. Then, when the adults were distracted, you threw the object in your hand across the room, all while you carried on with your task. It worked every time, although Mum and Dad proved difficult to scare, only moaning that they'd have to buy more crockery.

So, they'd come up with new ways of causing havoc, but Dylan felt left out of the deceit. It was Gwenllian and Carys having all the fun, and now the police were involved. They'd been visited by police officers who'd acted concerned but hadn't believed them; they'd questioned all three children about 'telling lies', although he, Dylan, had nothing to do with it.

Dylan lay awake night after night, worrying about his things. His father didn't like buying him his action figures but, when pressed about what he wanted for Christmas or his birthday, he insisted that he wanted nothing but the latest Spider-Man model – and he usually got his way. They were his precious toys and if it was his Action Man figure today, what would be gone tomorrow? His sisters were unconcerned about the police visits. Excited even, and now wanted more attention.

Dylan slipped out of bed and pulled from underneath it his latest present, bought for him by Gethin and Cathy after a day trip to Cardiff. He thought he was their favourite, as they'd bought his sisters a book each which, in Dylan's eyes, was nothing much. For him, they'd been into a toy shop and bought him something he could wear. This was unheard of – he even had to wear second-hand clothes from the local charity shop. He slipped on his present and admired himself in the mirror across from his bed. Now, this really was something.

24

Mallory stared at the sea, Luke's words churning over in her mind. He was portraying himself as an unwilling participant in the deception, which was a possibility. A boy at the mercy of the antics of his two teenage sisters and unable to confess the truth. That would leave its mark. In Mallory's experience, children of around ten were still at the stage where rules were meant to be obeyed. Perhaps it was drilled into them at school. Cross the road at the lights, don't go down the private road, stand to the left on the escalator. Mallory could remember Toby tugging at her sleeve, telling her she wasn't allowed to take photographs at a pantomime they'd gone to. He'd been mortified when she'd done so anyway. There was definitely a scenario where Luke's story held true.

On the other hand, he'd shown himself as an adept liar when he'd first spoken to her, concealing his true identity, and she wasn't sure how much she could now trust him.

'Give me your impressions of Pant Meinog,' she asked him. 'You mentioned in your podcast that it had a strange atmosphere, which I can relate to. Was that bit true?'

Luke shrugged. 'I liked the setting and loved playing amongst the trees.'

Mallory started, wishing he'd take his sunglasses off. 'You actually played in the forest? Didn't you find it a bit creepy?'

'Not really.' Luke lay on his back, staring at the sky. 'I found it inspiring and it meant I was out of the house a lot, especially when the haunting started. Then I heard that there was a woman who was coming to try and exorcise the poltergeist, which was a bit embarrassing, considering it didn't exist, so I'd get the hell out of there.'

Mallory considered. 'So you didn't meet Bev when you contacted her about the podcast and you didn't see her in 2003.'

Luke shrugged. 'I actually *did* meet her once, when she came to Pant Meinog. It was when the press was hovering around the house, so it was difficult for me to get out to play. She came to my bedroom, which I thought was a bit of a bloody cheek, and just stood there in the doorway, looking at me.'

Mallory frowned. 'Didn't she say anything?'

Luke shook his head. 'Nothing at all. After that, I made myself scarce whenever she was around.'

'Luke, what happened that final day when Gwenllian was attacked?'

'I swear I don't know. It was a strange day, anyway, hot like today but muggier. We were all trying to keep cool, except for Carys, who was sunbathing in the garden, as she liked a tan. Gwenllian was in her room and I watched Carys come in with a glass in her hand. I assumed she was getting a drink but I thought I heard her talking to someone.'

'Who? Who would she be talking to?'

'I don't know and now I'm wondering if she was just muttering to herself or something.'

'OK, so there's the three of you in the house, plus possibly someone else?'

'Exactly. Then everything went quiet, so I stayed in my bedroom, playing with my action figures and then I heard this blood–curdling scream. At first, I thought Gwenllian was playing tricks, so I stayed where I was but then she screamed again and ran out into the landing, shouting that she needed help. I opened the door and I swear I nearly vomited when I saw the state of her. She said she was attacked and to call the police, and I did.'

'Did you see the person who might have been talking to Carys?'

'No – Carys came out by herself, so I must have been mistaken. If anyone attacked Gwenllian it would have been herself. It's the sort of thing she'd do. She always wanted the attention on her.'

Mallory thought this a little harsh, but then Luke was regressing to the little boy he had been. 'More so than Carys?'

'Definitely.' Luke finally took off his sunglasses, folding them neatly and placing them in the pocket of his jeans. 'Do you want to go for a swim?'

Mallory shook her head. 'I haven't brought my costume. Look, I need to ask you about your parents' death. Can you just go over what happened?'

'If we must. I was at university when their car came off a road in Brecon. The tyres were bald, according to the inquest, which isn't surprising. They were never fussed about the upkeep of the vehicle, too busy doing their own thing. I'm amazed nothing happened before.'

Mallory wasn't fooled by his nonchalant tone. The loss of a parent is upsetting, two in an accident was a tragedy that he would have felt keenly at that age. Her heart went out to a little boy playing with his action figures while his teenage sisters wove a web of deceit, in the same way as she had been moved by Pippa's row of Lego figures lined up in the room that had probably belonged to Luke. Uncle and niece had more in common than they realised. She hoped, whatever happened, that Luke would get to know the brave Pippa.

As if guessing her thoughts, Luke said, 'Where do you think the children are?'

Mallory was distracted from replying by a familiar figure walking across the beach in front of the shoreline. She stood and called across to a group of teenagers.

'Toby!'

Her son turned and she expected him to look embarrassed, which was his default expression when dealing with her when he was with his friends. To her surprise, he came over.

'Mum? What are you doing here?'

'Chatting to a friend. Luke, this is my son Toby.'

'Hi. We met in July.' Luke waved an arm and smiled at her son. Toby was wearing a pair of knee-length trunks and a vest which hung off his frame but suited him more than his everyday clothes.

'Hi Luke.' Toby looked back to his friends. 'Are you out this evening? I thought I'd take my friends back to the caravan.'

That was a hint and gave Mallory a good excuse to get back to the station to see how the interview was progressing and share the news that she'd found Dylan Prytherch. 'I've left food in the fridge. Give your friends something to eat. I'll be back later.'

'Sure. Bye!'

'See you around, Toby,' shouted Luke.

Mallory realised that Toby was holding hands with Megan. This was progress, as far as she was concerned, and she would tell Joe once he was back from holiday with his new girlfriend. She watched as Toby and his gaggle of friends continued along the beach.

'You don't look old enough to have a son that age,' said Luke. 'He'd told me his mother lived nearby in a caravan. You're not what I had in mind, to be honest.'

Mallory snorted, suddenly irritated by his flattery. 'I've got to go. Look, can I have your address? We're going to need you to make a statement about your whereabouts last Friday.'

'I told you, I largely live off-grid. I have a shed that I use as my recording studio and I sleep over there sometimes. If you want me, you'll find me here on the beach most afternoons. I'm a night owl – the real work starts when the sun goes down.'

'You sure the children aren't with you?'

'Of course not. I hardly know them and they wouldn't come to me if they were in trouble.'

His face had a set look and Mallory tried to relax, keen to keep him on side. 'That's fine. Maybe it'll be me who comes back tomorrow to take a statement. What's your next podcast on?'

Luke smiled. 'A UFO sighting over Anglesey.'

25

Mallory arrived at the station as they were preparing to interview Pippa after a break. As she turned the corner towards the interview room, she spotted Steph stalking down the corridor, the set of her back suggesting Pippa's appearance hadn't delivered any significant answers to the Pant Meinog mystery yet. Harri was alone in the observation room, which was fortunately air-conditioned, although set a little low for Mallory's taste. He was looking dishevelled, his tie loosened and his curly hair in need of a brush. He moved along to give her a view through the observation window but didn't speak to her. She could smell the soap, or maybe shampoo, he used, its scent overpowered by the aroma of endless cups of coffee.

'We're not getting as much out of her as we'd like, so Siân suggested a break. The impression I'm getting is of a little girl who liked to listen at doors, eavesdrop on arguments, and so on. I used to do it as a boy myself.'

'Me too,' said Mallory, 'but the problem is that you sometimes get the wrong end of the stick. I remember hearing what I thought was my parents agreeing to separate, when in fact they were talking about temporarily sleeping in separate beds after my mother's hysterectomy.'

Harri nodded. 'Exactly, but given how little we do have, we're going to have to see where Pippa's admittedly fractured story gets us. She told us there was a visitor to the house and that's where we're going to pick it up.'

'Sure.' Mallory folded her arms.

Pippa was sitting in a chair, looking more composed than when Mallory had found her. She'd been given a can of regular Coke and a cereal bar but they sat untouched on the table, although her eyes kept straying to the snacks. Mallory could well understand her inability to eat while an interview was taking place and, hopefully, she'd be given a proper meal once the session was over. A door opened, and Siân and Freddy walked in, and Mallory's estimation of them increased when she saw they were carrying a plate of sandwiches, which they put in the middle of the table.

'About teatime,' said Siân brightly, picking up a sandwich and pushing the plate towards the social worker. 'Fancy one? There's cheese if you're vegetarian.'

The social worker picked one up and offered the plate to Pippa, who hesitated for a moment. Freddie was writing on a notepad and Siân made a fuss of getting something out of her bag. Mallory watched as Pippa snatched a sandwich without looking at the filling and wolfed it down.

Siân looked up. 'We'll start in a minute. Let's have another, shall we, and then we'll get going.'

Pippa was clearly starving, given she ate the second sandwich with equal speed. It gave her the courage to open the can of Coke, from which she drank deeply.

'OK,' said Siân, 'I want to talk to you about the visitor who, you said, came to the house. Can you tell us a little more about them? Whether it was a man or woman, for example.'

Pippa shook her head. 'They came late at night, long after I'd gone to bed. It was dark and the sun doesn't set until after ten p.m. in August, does it?'

Mallory smiled at the girl's pride at her knowledge of this fact. She was a clever girl whose intelligence shone despite her obvious trauma.

'Why were you awake?' asked Freddie. 'It's late for you to be up.'

'I was bored. We never went anywhere and I thought Dad might end up recording me with all his equipment so I kept as quiet as I could.'

'Did you hear either your mum or dad talking to this visitor?'

'Not Dad, just Mum.'

Mallory looked at Harri, who leant in towards the screen, concentrating on Pippa's words.

'Where was your dad when your mum spoke to this visitor?' asked Siân.

'In the bedroom. They'd had a row.'

'Who had been rowing? Your mum and dad or your dad and the visitor?'

'Mum and Dad. I heard Dad go upstairs and bang the door, and then the visitor came.'

'Did you see when the visitor left?'

'After an hour, I think. I heard the front door close.'

'Did you look out of the window then?' asked Siân.

Of course she did, thought Mallory. Pippa nodded.

'But I couldn't see anything.'

'Do you think they came on foot?' asked Freddie.

'I don't know.'

'There's the track at the back,' murmured Harri next to Mallory. 'Anyone with knowledge of Pant Meinog would be aware of it.'

'Who do you think it might have been?' asked Mallory.

'Anyone on that list I gave you,' said Harri. 'Or someone we don't know about yet.'

'Interesting David and Gwenllian were arguing before the visitor, though. I wonder what that was about?' Mallory turned her attention back to the screen, worried she was missing Pippa's words.

'What I want to go through with you now,' said Siân, 'is what happened last Friday. If anything upsets you, we'll stop for a little break, OK?'

'The day Dad died,' said Pippa in a small voice. Mallory glanced at Harri. No mention of her mother.

'That's right,' agreed Siân. 'The day your dad died. Let's go back to the morning, shall we? Can you remember what time you woke up?'

Pippa shrugged. 'I'm not sure. Maybe eight o'clock. My bedroom faces east so the sun came onto my bed. The curtains were really thin.'

Freddie smiled at her. 'How do you know about the direction of the room?'

'You can tell by where the sun rises.'

'OK,' said Siân, 'so you woke up with the sun in your room. Were the rest of the family up?'

'Mum and Dad were in the kitchen, but Matty and Ava were still in their rooms. I don't know if they were awake.' She sounded apologetic and Mallory felt her eyes fill up. Nothing to apologise for, she silently told the girl.

'You got up and then what happened?' asked Siân.

'I had a shower and put on my clothes. I went downstairs into the kitchen and Mum had started making some sandwiches, but she wasn't yet dressed. She was wearing her new nightie, the one she bought for the trip.'

The nightshirt she had been found in. Again, Elsa's description of a woman running in the woods came to mind. Mallory shook away the thought and concentrated on Pippa, who was continuing to describe her morning.

'We were finally going to go to the beach. I poured some cereal into a bowl and started eating it.'

'That's great,' said Siân. 'Can you remember which chair you were in?'

'Of course. The one facing the door to upstairs.'

'That's well remembered,' said Siân. 'So, you had your back to the window, that's right, isn't it?'

'Yes.'

'Was anyone sitting opposite you?'

'Dad. Dad was sitting opposite me, and Mum was making the sandwiches.'

'What happened then?'

Pippa looked confused. 'What do you mean what happened? Nothing happened. I went upstairs and started drawing.'

'OK. And Matty and Ava were still in their room?'

'Yes, but I heard a door open, so maybe Ava went down.'

'OK, so you were doing some drawing. Then what happened?'

'I heard shouting, but I didn't think anything of it.' She looked across at Siân. 'I thought Mum and Dad were arguing again.'

'Could you hear what they were shouting about?' asked Siân.

'I couldn't hear so I went to the door. I heard these heavy footsteps on the stairs, and Dad grabbed me and pulled me out of the room. He also pushed open Matty's door and told him to get in the car.'

'OK, so that means Ava and your mum were down-stairs, weren't they?'

'I… I think so. I don't know for sure because when I got to the car, Ava was sitting in it.'

'Where was your mum?'

'I… I don't know. Dad made me get in the car next to him, and Matty and Ava were in the back.'

'OK, I understand that. Did your dad drive off?'

'Yes, but not down the usual driveway – he took us through a track at the back.'

Freddie asked, 'Did your dad say anything about your mum not being with you all? You must have wondered why she wasn't there.'

'I was… I was scared to ask.'

Mallory noticed that Pippa's speech had become more hesitant as she relived the trauma of that morning.

'That's OK, Pippa, don't worry. What do you remember next?'

'Dad drove for a bit. Ava was crying because she'd left her mobile phone in her room, but Matty said he had his. We were going very fast, not like Dad usually drove, and I was scared.'

'Do you think your dad was scared too?' asked Siân.

'I… I don't know. The thing was, after a while, he started slowing down and the driving was really weird. He said that he had to stop the car. I was feeling sick too which was weird.'

'And where did he stop?'

'In the lay-by where he died.' Tears had begun to flow down Pippa's cheeks.

'Do you want to stop for a moment?' asked Siân. Pippa shook her head. 'OK. So, your dad stopped the car. Then what happened?'

'He said, "I don't feel well. You have to hide. Don't go back to your mother."'

Mallory looked at Harri, aware this was pushing the case in a new direction.

'Why do you think he said that? Why shouldn't you have gone back to your mother?'

'I don't know.'

'Are you sure you don't know, Pippa?'

'Maybe because she gets angry sometimes. That might have been it.'

'You think he was worried she would be angry. Why might she be angry?'

'Because we all ran away in the car.'

Siân took a pause. 'When you were told to run away for the second time, from the car not the house, what happened?'

'Ava and Matty ran.' Tears coursed down Pippa's face.

'They just left you?' asked Siân, her voice calm.

Pippa hesitated. 'I wouldn't leave Dad. He was sick. Matty tried to pull me away – he's big but not very strong. I pushed him away, and Dad was shouting to run and hide.'

'Run and hide?' asked Freddie. 'Were those his exact words? Not "run and get help", for example?'

Pippa shook her head. 'He told us to run and hide. Then we heard a scream, and Matty and Ava gave up trying to persuade me to come with them, and they ran off. I climbed in next to Dad, who was breathing funny, but he pushed me back out through the door. He told me to stay away and run, and I did. I ran and ran in the woods.'

Pippa was shouting and the social worker spoke for the first time. 'I think we need a break.'

'I've just a few more questions this evening for Pippa and then I suggest we call it a day,' said Siân. 'Pippa, I know this is hard, but do you know where your mother is?'

Pippa accepted a wodge of tissues from a box. 'I thought she'd still be at the house, which is why I went there. I went into the village first, because I thought I might be able to get something to eat, but I realised I had no money.'

'It doesn't matter about the food,' said Siân. 'You went back to Pant Meinog after you'd had something to eat, is that right?'

Pippa nodded. 'It was her home. Did you know that?'

'We know she used to live there. Did she tell you that?'

Pippa froze. 'Only after I found out last year. I found out about Mum and Auntie Carys, and the things they did.'

'How did you find out?'

'I googled it all.'

Of course she did, thought Mallory. The internet was a boon to an inquisitive child such as Pippa.

'Did Matty and Ava know about your mum?'

'I... I'm not sure.'

'Do you know where they might be? Somewhere they might be hiding?'

'I don't know.'

'But you think Matty has his phone on him?'

'That's what he said.'

'That's fine. Now, Pippa, I want you to think very hard. When your dad grabbed you and you all went into the car, did you see anyone else other than your mother?'

Pippa for the first time looked not distraught, but frightened. 'I never saw anyone. I looked and looked but there was no one there. So why was everyone so frightened?'

26

Tuesday

Mallory had expected to get no sleep, as she had been buzzing when she returned to the caravan. Toby, however, exhausted by his train journey and afternoon on the beach, was already tucked up on the pull-out bed when she crept through the door. Mallory, too tired even to check the food situation, had fallen asleep as soon as her head hit the pillow and she'd woken with a clear head, raring to go. Toby too had been anxious to get out and had accepted a lift from her to New Quay to start his day's work. In Carmarthen HQ, Siân and Freddie crammed into Harri's office alongside Mallory to mull over Pippa's account.

'Let's start with the most urgent,' said Harri, who also looked refreshed in the cooler morning. 'The whereabouts of Matty and Ava. Pippa, as far as I could tell, was unable to give any indication of their location. Agreed?'

Siân nodded, pursing her lips in disappointment. 'No, but the fact they ran off suggests they too sensed danger. Pippa, for all her intelligence, is still a child. What is most shocking for her is that they went without her, even after attempts to get her to go with them. That suggests that the sense of danger overrode their desire to bring their sister along.'

'Given they're the children of David's first marriage,' said Freddie, 'they're probably closer, especially given the fact that they're twins. They were determined to stick together at all costs, even if that cost was Pippa.'

'You know...' Mallory took a sip of her instant coffee and made a face. 'I'd be happier with that explanation if it had been Gwenllian in the car, but it was their own father. It's surely easier to leave your dying stepmother behind than your own flesh and blood. Their actions aren't making much sense to me, unless we assume that there was an acute sense of danger. The type that makes individuals leave loved ones behind in their panic.'

'I'd be inclined to go along with that,' said Harri, 'but my guess is also that they had somewhere to go in an emergency. Someone they wouldn't need to ring. We know from phone records that Matty didn't make a call to anyone except Ava's phone. He was probably just checking its whereabouts for his sister. That shows that, despite patchy coverage in the forest, he could have called someone but decided against it. Either they knew where they were going or they didn't want anyone to discover their location, possibly both.'

'But where?' asked Siân.

Mallory thought of the list of names Harri had given her. 'I think we need to reinterview witnesses in the old case connected to the family and undertake searches of their properties. Can we get warrants for those?'

Harri nodded. 'I'll get that in hand. What do you think the likelihood is that it was Gwenllian who was the danger to the children? David may have been running away with the children from her.'

'But they'd been there a week,' said Siân. 'Why rush out of the house at that moment in time? It suggests the presence of an external agent.'

'And who killed Gwenllian?' Mallory turned to Siân. 'When did you decide not to inform Pippa about her mother's death?'

'At the interview strategy meeting, which sounds more formal than it was, given it lasted ten minutes in a side office, the social worker suggested telling her this morning, when Pippa's eaten properly and has had a night's sleep. She's in emergency accommodation at the moment. I know the foster family, who are great.'

'One thing I've been able to clear up,' said Harri, 'is where David went on the Thursday. Despite his suspension, he still had swipe access to his department. There's no CCTV, alas, but a colleague saw him coming out of one of the IT rooms on Thursday. He thought nothing of it, as he knew David only briefly, but it seems he was making use of the university's recording equipment for his visit to Pant Meinog.'

'Can they check the swipe records for the previous week to show when he picked it up?' asked Siân.

'They're doing so now. What I don't understand is why he interrupted his holiday to take the equipment back. The person I spoke to thought it unlikely anyone would have noticed it gone, given it's the summer holidays. David had gone to the house to try to prove that the Brechfa poltergeist existed but by Thursday of the following week, it was all over. What happened in between?'

'I wonder if it was to do with Gwenllian's comment about a cuckoo in the nest. Did you manage to get any more information on this?' asked Mallory.

'Unfortunately, not,' said Siân. 'It could have referred to her children or, of course, the siblings from 2003, Carys and Dylan. Or even Gwenllian herself, who might have felt apart from her family after her disfigurement.'

'It was an interesting exchange with Luke Parry, formerly Dylan Prytherch, but I doubt he's the cuckoo. If anything, he appeared a little cross by his sisters' activities. However, he's proved himself a liar and says he lives off-grid. I'd be inclined to send Freddie down to interview him, as I got the impression he wasn't taking my questions seriously.'

'Good idea,' said Harri. 'I don't like the sound of some-where off-grid, as there'll be no near neighbours or ways for the twins to contact us if they're being held against their will. I'll send Freddie this morning. What about you, Mallory? Any suggestions in relation to discovering who our cuckoo is?'

'I could try Bev Christie,' said Mallory. 'She was pretty accommodating when I met her, but I'll be giving her some unpleasant news when I tell her how she's been duped by Luke. She should be a relatively neutral witness, and I doubt Gwenllian would have been talking about cuckoos in relation to her. She may have inveigled herself into the family but she's not, as far we're aware, actually related to them.'

'You go there now, Mallory,' said Harri. 'This is a two-hander – we're questioning them about the contents of Pippa's statement but I also want to ensure that Matty and Ava aren't hiding out with them. Will your lad be all right without you?'

'He's at work and will be fine.'

'Good. When you've finished with Bev, go back to Carys and do the same. With both of them, I'd be inclined to wait outside their homes for half an hour first. See if it looks like there's more than one person in the place.'

'What about the others on my list?' asked Mallory. 'The Thomas family, for example.'

'I'm going to pay a visit to Gethin and Cathy, as I'm curious what they've been up to in the intervening years. Tom can wait, as I'm pretty sure the twins aren't with him. What is it, Mallory?'

Mallory had been paying little attention to his reply, as her mind had begun turning over the discussion from a few minutes earlier. The reference to recording equipment designed to pick up sounds of the supernatural that David had been determined to return, despite its lack of urgency.

'Can we put in a request,' she asked, 'to see if anything's been recorded on the equipment returned to the university?'

Siân looked at Harri. 'It'll be in a computer file, surely.'

'Did we find a laptop at the house?' asked Mallory. 'I never saw anything.'

Siân shook her head. 'Nothing.'

'You think the equipment might have picked up sounds of a more human nature?' asked Harri.

'It's got to be a possibility,' said Mallory. 'I'd really like to get to the bottom of why David was so keen to give up his original intention for visiting the house.'

'Siân, get onto it.' Harri took a swig of water. 'It would be brilliant if it gave us an insight into why Gwenllian wanted David to steal someone else's ID. Maybe all roads lead from Cardiff to Pant Meinog.'

27

When Harri had met Gethin and Cathy Thomas back in 2003, they'd struck him as a young, lively couple happily settled in Tom Thomas's house. It wasn't that unusual for multiple generations of families to live together in rural Wales, and it always struck him as funny when he read about 'boomerang kids' in newspaper articles that articulated parents' despair at their offspring returning to the family home. Ben was at the local college, studying graphic design, and wanted to go to university once he'd got his T Level. Ellie, bright and motivated, was already talking about a career in law, probably inspired by his sister Fran's work. But if they decided to come home after studying, Harri would have no problem with it – in fact, it would make holding on to his roomy semi-detached house easier to justify.

Interestingly, according to Land Registry records, Gethin and Cathy Thomas had bought their terraced house in Brechfa in the spring of 2004, a mere eight months after the alleged hauntings at Pant Meinog. Given it could take on average four to six months to buy a property, it appeared that Gethin and Cathy had looked to move not long after the Prytherchs had left the house next door.

As Harri approached the property, he noticed all the front windows had been left open, with the music of

Radio 2 escaping through the front room. He rapped hard on the door and waited as the shadow behind the glass came closer. Gethin Thomas looked largely unchanged from the man he'd met twenty years earlier – he'd aged better than most and, by that, Harri meant he'd kept his hair. Aware of his own ageing body, Harri was nevertheless proud of his head of curly hair. Gethin's was clipped short at the sides but longer on top, swept back in a style that reminded Harri of Tom Thomas.

'Can I come in?' Harri showed him his warrant card.

Gethin's eyes widened in alarm. 'It's not Cathy, is it?'

'No, not Cathy. I've come in relation to a body found today in the forest.'

Gethin stepped back. 'Oh God, that's fine. I mean, it's not fine, but I worry about Cathy on those roads. People are always overtaking without looking properly. I thought something had happened.'

Gethin took him into the living room and switched off the radio. He'd made a living driving farm machinery back in the day and the muscles on his arms suggested he was still employed doing manual labour, possibly in the forest.

'We've met before, haven't we?' he asked. 'You look familiar.'

Harri nodded. 'A long time ago. I was one of the officers who came out when the girls claimed they were being haunted.'

'This is about her, isn't it? Gwenllian. She's the body you found in the woods – I saw on the news you were looking for her.'

'We think so, although identification is going to take time, due to the state of the body. We're pretty sure it's not one of the children.'

'That's something, anyway.'

Gethin slumped on the sofa and Harri took the chair opposite him. He listened for sounds upstairs but if Gethin were hiding the teenagers, he'd surely have left the radio on to mask any noise.

'You sure the children aren't here with you? You are related, aren't you?'

Gethin's hard currant-brown eyes stared at him. 'Distantly, but we never had much to do with that side of the family, so why would they come here? Anyway, I thought you'd found the little girl. I heard something on the radio.'

'We have, but not her siblings.'

'Are they Gwenllian's too? She'll have had them young.'

Harri shook his head. 'Her husband's.'

'Then I'm not related to them at all and, as I said, I'm not in touch with the family. How are the others – Carys and Dylan – doing?'

'All right,' said Harri, not wanting to give much away. 'Can I ask when you last saw Gwenllian, or any of the siblings for that matter?'

Gethin fiddled with the sleeve of his shirt. 'I haven't seen any of them for years. We were never that pally, so I'm not sure what you're doing here.'

Gethin's tone was wrong, his manner altered from a relaxed casualness to a watchful demeanour.

'Are you sure about that?'

Gethin, Harri decided, was someone who'd make an awful liar. A beetroot flush crept up his cheeks as he shrugged.

'I promise you, I've not had contact with them since they left all those years ago.'

'I think you're holding something back, Gethin, and I'd like to know what it is.'

'I'm not grassing up anyone, but you need to speak to Dad.'

'Tom? Do you think he's sheltering the children?'

'Of course not.' Gethin rolled his eyes. 'But he recognised Pippa – she looks the spit of her mum at that age and he came to me, worried about what trouble was going to be thrown up.'

'He thought the hauntings might start over again?'

Gethin snorted. 'Something like that. Trouble comes in all guises.'

Harri heard a thud coming from above. 'What was that?'

'The cat jumping down from the bed, probably.'

'Mind if I take a look? It's nothing personal but there are children missing.'

'If you like. As I said, they wouldn't come here.'

Gethin didn't follow him but stayed picking at the armrest as Harri went upstairs. There were two bedrooms, both with double beds, and a bathroom, its glass shelves stuffed with shampoo bottles, face creams and shower gel. A ginger cat lay on the floor of one of the bedrooms, its tail thumping on the carpet. Feeling a fool, Harri flung open the wardrobes of the main bedroom, but no one was there. He went back downstairs.

'Where's Cathy?'

'Visiting her mum in a nursing home in Carmarthen. She won't be back for another hour or so.'

'Do you think the children might have contacted her without you knowing?'

'No way.' Gethin folded his arms. 'And she'd ring you lot if they did. That family have brought enough trouble as it stands. Carys, Gwenllian, Dylan. Even their parents were a nightmare for us.'

Harri, who had been about to leave, sat back down. 'Gethin. Go through with me one more time what happened in 2003.'

28

Carys lay on the sunlounger, wearing jeans and her bra. She was already nut-brown from a summer of unusually hot weather and seemed determined to take advantage of any rays permeating the dense forest. Gethin had told her before that she shouldn't lie out in the garden like that. It was all right around family, but tourists would sometimes take the shortcut through the woods, following the path of an ancient track which passed by their house. These people had become more inquisitive when the story of the haunting had made it into the newspapers. All nonsense, of course – the Prytherchs were known for their strange ways – but you never knew who might come up the track to take a gander at the infamous house. Carys didn't care, though, giving him a wave as he passed by on his way to take a shower, the sweat of the day slapping his shirt to his chest.

He motioned towards the house with his thumb. 'You need to put some clothes on.'

With a sigh, she threw her magazine on the floor and flounced towards the front door. In the house, Gethin shed his own clothes next to the washing machine in the utility room, and switched it on, jumping into the adjacent shower. As he let the water cascade over him, he heard the bathroom open and Cathy come in.

'How was your day?' She sat on the toilet, her dark hair pulled back and held by a plastic clip. Her job in the hotel kitchen in Carmarthen was a nightmare in this heat and she liked to keep the hair away from her face.

Gethin closed his eyes. 'Same as usual. Yours?'

'Same. I…' She stopped after hearing a noise outside, inclining her head as she listened. 'What's that? It sounds like screaming. Oh God, I hope those girls aren't pissing around again.'

'Carys has only just gone into the house. Surely, there hasn't been enough time for them to start throwing stuff around.'

'I wouldn't put anything past those two.' Cathy turned to open the window, leaning out to see what the commotion was. She pulled her head back, her face white. 'Gethin, quick, it sounds as if there's something seriously wrong with Gwenllian.'

Gethin scrabbled round for a clean shirt and fresh jeans and dressed hurriedly, the clothes difficult to put on while he was still damp from the shower. He pulled on a pair of trainers and ran out of the house, noticing that his dad was coming out of the front door of Pant Meinog. Kneeling on the ground was Gwenllian, her face in her hands like the statues he saw in the parish churchyards of the villages he passed through. Except, carmine-coloured blood seeped through Gwenllian's fingertips like in a scene from the late-night horror movies he liked to watch.

He rushed over to her, as Dylan came hurtling out of the door. 'I've dialled 999 like I've seen in the films. The police are coming.'

'The lass needs an ambulance,' said Tom. 'I'll call from the house.'

Gethin watched his father walk back to the cottage, his shoulders hunched.

'What happened, Da?' he shouted after his retreating back. 'What did you see?'

Cathy was looking at Carys's head burrowed into Gethin's shoulder, her expression fixed. 'What's the matter?' he asked her. 'The lass is injured.'

'You never usually turn on the washing machine,' Cathy told him. 'Why today?'

29

As Harri had instructed, Mallory sat in her car outside Bev Christie's house, watching for any movement in the tall building. The teenagers would have been told to stay away from the windows but Mallory was convinced they weren't there. There's an odd emptiness to an unoccupied house, and this one looked as if it were waiting for its owner to return. After thirty minutes, Mallory swung open the gate and rapped on the door. She was surprised to see a movement – perhaps she had called it wrong – but Bev's ancient dog stuck its head behind the net curtains and gave a half-hearted woof. Mallory wondered if Luke had been in touch with Bev since yesterday and tried to imagine how she'd taken the news of his real identity. She wouldn't find out today, that much was clear. Bev, she thought, was a bit part in this tragedy, a supporting actor, and she would leave the interview for another time.

Mallory started her car and drove across town to Carys's flat. An interview with Gwenllian's sister was likely to be more productive but, despite noticing a light shining in the first-storey window, Mallory waited again in the car, keeping an eye on the apartment. She decided there was nothing so dull as watching a property – she clearly had no future in stake-outs. She'd been trained in them, once upon a time, but now she'd heard there were dedicated teams specialising in watching people come and go. With one eye still on the window, she sent a message to Toby, checking he was OK. She got a terse *Fine* in return and decided to leave it at that. In the end, after a passing couple gave her an odd look, Mallory got out of the car, desperate to stretch her legs.

Carys buzzed her into the building and stood on the landing as Mallory climbed the steps.

'I saw on the news that you've found Pippa. Is she all right?'

'As far as I can tell, she seems to be doing OK. She spent the night with a local foster family, in case you were wondering where she's staying.'

'And after that?'

'I don't know, I'm sorry,' said Mallory, slipping through the front door. Carys was cooking a stew and the smell of braising beef infused the small flat.

'There's no room for her here.'

If Mallory thought the statement a little bold, she refrained from being too judgemental. Carys had lost her sister and brother-in-law, and grief rarely brought the best out in people. In any case, Mallory thought there was little chance of Pippa spending time with her aunt. Carys was a possible suspect, and more importantly, Pippa hadn't asked for her. It seemed that Carys's account was truthful in that respect: she wasn't close to her sister's family.

They settled in the sitting room but, unlike the previous visit, no offer of tea was forthcoming. Carys had been crying, her eyes rimmed red as she chewed her lip.

'I assume you were informed about the discovery of Gwenllian's body yesterday?'

'Two officers knocked on the door. They were very nice but didn't tell me much. Are you sure it's Gwenllian?'

'Pretty much, but we need to wait for forensics to complete their work.'

'The officer took a swab from me.'

'That's standard practice for DNA analysis, but we'll know for definite in a day or so, once we've matched the dental profile with Gwenllian's records. These results usually come through more quickly. Pippa gave us a good description of what her mother was wearing, which matches the victim's clothes.'

Carys reached for a box of tissues and blew her nose. 'Did you want something else from me?'

'I need to ask you again whether Gwenllian or David made contact with you. I know what you told me yesterday but now Gwenllian is dead and I want you to tell me anything you omitted from your previous account.'

Carys turned her head away. 'I promise you no one got in touch.'

'Are you sure about that?'

'I was on holiday in Italy, remember? I only came back yesterday. Even if Gwenllian had called me, I wouldn't have been able to meet her. You can check my flight details. Whatever happened to my sister, it wasn't anything to do with me.'

'You know...' Mallory watched Carys's face carefully. 'I've found Dylan. He's living in New Quay.'

'Is he? Well, he always liked beach life, so that's not surprising. It was a disappointment to him that we moved further inland after Pant Meinog.'

'I don't have an address for him, but I can tell you where to find him? He chooses the same spot on the beach each day.'

Carys, for the first time, met Mallory's eyes. 'I don't think I want to meet him. We're not close and I can't see that changing any time soon. He knows where I am, if he wants to speak to me.'

'He says Gwenllian didn't contact him either.'

'Well, there we are. Whatever these deaths are about, it's nothing to do with either of us.'

'Why weren't you close as adults? You must have been as children, living in that place.'

'Thrown together, more like,' said Carys. 'Look, there's something I want to tell you. There was all sorts of stuff going on in that house and it all focused around Gwenllian. When her face was attacked, it wasn't the first time she'd done something on her own.'

'What do you mean?' asked Mallory.

'I had this camera that we'd been playing around with. Gwenllian wanted me to photograph her levitating from the bed, which I thought would be fun, but afterwards she locked herself in the bedroom and claimed a spirit had attacked her. She showed me the bruises.'

'How long before the scratches on her face did this happen?'

'I'm pretty sure it was days. Dylan was with me in the house, and he was pretty shaken up by it too, but what I'm trying to tell you is that I wasn't in on that, just like I wasn't involved in making the scratches on Gwenllian's face.'

'You're positive she did it herself?'

'Of course.' Carys sighed. 'Of course, I am.'

'So basically, an attack had already happened on Gwenllian. I think we've all been assuming that it was a joke between the pair of you before the final day, when something went too far. But you're saying she had already been the subject of a supposedly violent assault.'

'Exactly. Gwenllian was taking all of us for a ride, me included. You've repeatedly asked me why Gwenllian and I weren't close, and I'm telling you why. It was embarrassing enough that we pretended we were being haunted at Pant Meinog. Even worse is that Gwenllian believed our own story.'

'Do you have the photos from the day of the first attack on Gwenllian?'

'I have not. I deleted them straight away. I was already sick of the whole caper by then.'

'You know, when I spoke to Dylan about the attack on Gwenllian, the final time, he said he thought he heard you talking to someone in the house. Who was that?'

'Me?' Carys's face clouded. 'I don't remember.'

'He's adamant that someone else was in the house.'

'It could have been Gethin,' said Carys, refusing to meet Mallory's gaze. 'He used to pop by a lot – Cathy and Uncle Tom, too.'

'Gethin more than Cathy and Tom?'

Carys shrugged. 'Maybe.'

'Nothing weird, though?' asked Mallory.

Carys met her gaze. 'Nothing weird.'

–

Toby was on his own by the time Mallory got back to the caravan, and he had done a decent job of clearing up. He was hunched over his mobile, the hood of his sweatshirt pulled up as he took swigs from a brightly coloured bottle.

'Have a good day?' asked Mallory cheerfully, resisting the urge to go to the fridge to check if the food had gone.

'It was all right.'

Mallory took this as approval and dumped her bag on the table. 'I'm going to take a shower. Do you want something to eat?'

Toby pointed to the recycling dumped by the door. 'We shared a pizza.'

Mallory grunted. Sharing made it more difficult to monitor Toby's food intake but there wasn't much she could do without making a fuss. He saw her expression.

'I had a slice, all right?'

'Fine. You need to go easy on that energy drink at this time of night, though. The caffeine will stop you sleeping.'

'I'm going for a run first, before bed.'

'Christ. You've got work tomorrow. Can't you just relax for a bit?'

'Running relaxes me.' To her surprise, he followed her into the bedroom, clutching his energy drink. 'I saw Luke on the beach again today. He never moves from that spot.'

'That's not exactly true, given he has his own podcast that he records. Did he say anything to you?'

'I was just leaving work and waiting for a friend. We had a quick chat about things, and he was telling me about all the other decent beaches around here which I should visit. He was also asking a lot about you.'

'*Was he?*' Mallory flipped open a can and took a long swig. 'What was he asking?'

'Nothing to do with your work. Just, I dunno, how long you'd been living around here. I just wanted to tell you. My friends came along and I moved on.'

Mallory picked up on his mood. 'Why are you telling me this? Did one of your friends say something?'

Toby shrugged. 'Only that he was a bit strange, which I kind of knew from when I met him before. He just sort of sits there every day in the same spot, reading the same book.'

'That must be a bit of an exaggeration – I don't think for a moment it's the same book. And anyway, I can understand why someone would choose the same spot on a beach. You get kind of attached to a place.'

Toby pulled a face. 'They say he likes older women too.'

So that's what it was all about. Mallory kept her expression neutral but was secretly amused. 'I wasn't passing the time of day with him, Toby. I was interviewing him as part of the investigation into those missing children.'

'I thought they'd found them?'

'They've found the youngest, Pippa, which is a massive relief to everyone. The two teenagers are still missing, though.' Mallory looked at Toby and wondered how she'd feel if he'd been missing that length of time. It seemed inconceivable that their biological mother wasn't a tiny bit worried about their fate, but there had been no communication from her at all.

'Right.' Toby took a final swig from his bottle and threw it into the wastepaper bin in her bedroom. 'I'm off for a run.'

'Hold on.' Mallory's shower would have to wait. 'Did your friends say anything about Luke, apart from the fact that he likes older women?'

Toby paused. 'Not much, but he has a wife and kid, so why spend so much time on the beach?'

'He's married?' Luke had never mentioned a family, who must be living off-grid with him too.

'Yeah, sorry, Mum. Plenty more fish in the sea.'

Mallory threw a pillow at his departing back and stripped off for her shower. Afterwards, she lay on the

bed in her dressing gown, enjoying the quiet before Toby
returned, wondering why she was so certain, despite the
confessional nature of her account, that Carys had been
lying to her.

30

Wednesday

Harri was in the office early the following morning, waiting on the results of Gwenllian's post-mortem. He'd given the task of observing the autopsy to Freddie, as he wanted Siân on standby in case Pippa needed reinterviewing. He, personally, wanted to give the little girl a break; the events of the last few days were a lot to take in and she must be desperately worried about her future. The good news was that her father, David, had a brother, who was travelling up that morning with a view to taking her back to his family once social workers were happy with the arrangements. He claimed to have been in regular contact with the Andersons and had recently lent David some money, following his dip in fortunes. If it all checked out, then Harri would have no problem with Pippa returning to Cardiff with her uncle, although it wasn't really his call to make. What was in his remit was whether Pippa would need to be reinterviewed, and that was difficult to judge because he still thought all the answers lay in the past. The late-night visitor to the house, he thought, was almost certainly the killer but none of the suspects, in his mind at least, induced the kind of terror that Pippa had described on that Friday morning.

Harri put his head in his hands, trying to decide if his queasiness and aching head were due to his diabetes or the fact he wasn't eating properly. Possibly both. Not for the first time, he wondered if he was the best person to lead this investigation. If he'd had no history with Pant Meinog, perhaps he'd have approached things differently. He couldn't decide if his knowledge of the house's dark past was hindering the investigation. If he'd had another boss, someone less inclined to look after her own back, he might have confided some of these doubts to Steph. As it was, he was without a confidante. He'd have loved to confide in Mallory, who was full of common sense and knew the stresses of the job. Something, however, was holding him back. Confidences were a form of closeness and Harri sometimes felt the veil between them was gossamer-thin. They were both lonely, damaged by the past and unsure what the future looked like. Harri would have loved to know what Mallory thought of him, but she was difficult to read.

Harri sighed and focused on the timeline constructed by the team for the week leading up to the killings. The family had arrived on Friday and the car had not been seen until the following Tuesday, when all of them had gone shopping in Carmarthen. Pippa had confirmed the trip in her interview and Harri suspected the family had gone en masse to ensure the place was empty while David's recording equipment monitored any activity. Harri picked up the phone and called DC Sioned Cross, who had gone to Cardiff to look at the recording equipment returned by David. She'd promised to ring him if she found anything, and her silence suggested the trip had been useless.

'Sorry, boss,' said Sioned when she answered his call. 'I'm on the way back. There's this big storage room in the psychology department and it's impossible to tell what was taken and returned. I managed to collar a technician, who pointed out what the things were, but it's all digital. Any images, sound recordings or text will have been uploaded onto David's cloud and they absolutely don't have access to that, although the IT department will.'

'If we got a warrant asking for it, you think it possible we could take a look?'

'Definitely, boss. Shall I put in a request?'

'As a priority. Try and do it today, would you?'

After cutting the call, he picked up Mallory's update from the previous day and read through Carys's account. Mallory's note that Carys was almost certainly with-holding information rang true and he turned to look at the clock above his desk, wondering if he could slip away for an hour. His seniority in the CID meant it was perfectly appropriate for him to leave the interviewing to his team – both full-time personnel and civilian investigators like Mallory. However, he detected in himself a deep-seated reluctance to see Carys again, even though she had been the one to admit to the deception. Mallory had said she showed little grief over the death of her sister and Harri, the product of a close-knit family, was inclined to find this odd. The fact Mallory had not been able to detect any traces of the twins in Carys's flat didn't necessarily mean that they hadn't been there, although the potential dynamics between Matty and Ava and their step-aunt were difficult to fathom. When questioned, Pippa had not been forthcoming with the name of anyone she should contact if there was trouble, and yet Harri was convinced the twins had known where to go. He picked up his jacket and slipped out of his office.

Carys's voice held a note of surprise when he announced his presence through the intercom at her apartment building. She recognised his name, he was sure.

Either Mallory had mentioned his role in the investigation or she remembered him from the past, and he was about to find out which. It was a new apartment block with a utilitarian feel to it, although the stair carpet was thick and well maintained. Carys opened the door and gave him a searching look. She hadn't changed much in the intervening years. With her sandy, curly hair, she would likely look the same when she was fifty, seventy even. She'd been the shorter of the two girls and the more pragmatic. Her confession to creating the poltergeist activity had been willingly made when she realised things had gone too far.

'I remember you from the house,' she told him.

'I *do* need to talk to you. I'm sorry, as I know this is a difficult time,' said Harri.

Carys nodded. 'It's OK. Come inside.'

Mallory had been right when she'd said that the flat was devoid of much personality for someone employed in the creative industries. In fact, Harri was sure his house had more artistic flair, although that was largely down to his sister, Fran. Carys took him to the living room but remained standing.

'They're not here. The twins, I mean. If they'd called me, I'd have gone to help them, but I'd have let you know they were safe. What little I knew of them I liked and, in any case, they're family, aren't they?'

'They never even tried to contact you?'

'I swear I've heard nothing from them.'

She sounded disappointed but unsurprised. Harri nodded, satisfied that in this respect she was telling the truth. He was sure, however, there was still something to be extracted from the interview, and it started in the past.

'I'm very sorry about what happened to Gwenllian,' he said. 'It really wasn't the outcome we were hoping for.'

'Outcome?' queried Carys.

Harri lifted his hands. 'Police speak, you're right to call me out on it. I just wanted to say I'm sorry she died.'

Carys nodded. 'I appreciate that. We weren't particularly close anymore, not in the way we had been as children, but it's still a blow. You kind of expect, as the eldest, to be the first one to go and it's a shock when your younger sibling goes first.'

'Was it the attack on Gwenllian that split you apart?'

Carys frowned. 'I suppose so, but things had been getting more and more weird with Gwenllian. I began to fear for her mental health and that's quite a responsibility when you're only fifteen. My parents, as you've probably heard, weren't around much.'

'From Mallory's report, I understand that you think Gwenllian herself was responsible for the attack on her face.'

'I do, however hard that is to believe.'

'The thing is, Carys, in the constabulary, we have access to a wide range of support services. Social services, psychiatrists, and so on. At every stage, I've asked my team to make sure they're being consulted and there's a consensus that people who self-harm rarely attack their faces. Wounds are usually found on limbs or their torso.'

Carys shrugged. 'Gwenllian was always an outlier in these things.'

Harri masked his shock and he hoped to God his own kids never spoke about each other in this cold-hearted way.

'I want you, for the moment, to run with the scenario that Gwenllian was actually attacked by a human being. Who might that be?'

Carys blanched. 'I have no idea. The thought is ridiculous.'

'Was it you?' asked Harri.

'I promise you it wasn't.'

'What about Dylan?'

Carys shook her heard. 'Dylan? You saw the scratches on her face. They weren't made by a child.'

'What about one of the Thomases? Gethin, for example, might have been in the house.'

'Definitely not Gethin.' Carys's voice was firm.

'You seem pretty sure about that.'

'The thing is, Gethin was there to see me.' The words came out in a rush, a confession years in the making. 'I thought you guessed at the time.'

Harri sat back in his chair. 'You and Gethin were an item? No, I never picked it up. How close a relation are you?' Harri frowned, trying to remember the dynamics of that hot August day. He was sure nothing had suggested an affair between the two family members.

'Third cousins, I think. Not close family, certainly, although we are related on my mother's side.'

'Had it been going on for long?'

'Not long and, before you make any snap judgements, the fling was consensual.'

'You were fifteen, Carys. Consent isn't a term I like to use for a relationship between an adult and a child.'

She brushed away his words. 'Nevertheless, it was consensual. Anyway, it all stopped after that afternoon. It had all got too much, and we subsequently moved away, and I never heard from the Thomas family again.'

'Do you think Gethin might have been interested in Gwenllian too?'

'No!' shouted Carys. 'I told you it wasn't like that. Gwenllian was still a child.'

'And did either Cathy or Tom know about the affair?'

'I don't think so.'

I do think so, thought Harri. It'd be hard to keep something like that secret for long. 'And how was your own family afterwards? When you moved to Brecon, did you become close again?'

'No, because Gwenllian was sent away to school. She was traumatised by the attack and she initially went to two state schools, but both insisted she was too damaged for them to teach her. So, they found a small religious school near New Town and she boarded there.'

'Boarded?' asked Harri. 'That sounds expensive. I got the impression your parents didn't have a huge amount of money.'

'They didn't,' said Carys. 'The fees were paid for but don't ask me by whom, because I don't know.'

'Do you think Tom Thomas might have paid them?'

Carys snorted. 'Him? I very much doubt it. He couldn't wait to get us out of the house. The day of the attack, he was in the kitchen, moaning at me to keep the noise of my radio down. No, some other benefactor helped Gwenllian out for the three years it took her to finish school. It did her good: she went to university in Cardiff, met David and the rest is history.'

Harri thought meeting David did Gwenllian no good whatsoever.

'Religious school, did you say?' asked Harri, an idea forming in his mind.

'That's right. Not nuns or anything, a sort of Presbyterian place.'

'Not Baptist?'

Carys frowned. 'You know, it might have been a Baptist school.'

Harri felt his pulse quicken. 'Do you remember deliverance minister Bev Christie?'

'Of course. You don't think *she* paid for Gwenllian's schooling. She gave the impression of not having any money either.'

'No, but these schools have places paid for by assistance or subscription. Do you know if she kept in touch with Gwenllian?'

Harri watched as Carys massaged her temples. 'Do you know, I don't think she kept in touch with her, but Bev definitely knew David.'

'How? How did she know David?'

Carys stared at him. 'Through his work, of course.'

Harri sat back. Bev knew David through his academic work and Gwenllian through the 2003 haunting. It was entirely possible that she had met David's children. Bev, after all, was essentially a trustworthy person, so why hadn't she told any of this to Mallory?

–

Back in his office, Harri had barely sat down when there was a knock on the door and Freddie came in, looking a little green around the gills after the autopsy.

'Unpleasant?' asked Harri, having seen enough of Gwenllian's remains to be glad it wasn't him attending the post–mortem.

'Awful. I had a light breakfast, which is just as well, and I won't be eating for the rest of the day.'

'What have you got for me?'

'Evidence of a blow to the head with a sharp implement like a carving knife. There's a fracture about here…' Freddie pointed to a spot above his ear.

'There's been no discovery of the weapon. Can they give us any more info?' asked Harri.

'A long, smooth blade, according to Doctor Griffiths, at least nine centimetres in length.'

'Not much bloody use, is it?'

'There is something, though,' said Freddie, still looking queasy. 'The pathologist showed me the head wound and explained why she could tell me it had happened recently. There's no evidence of healing whatsoever and apparently the regenerative process starts almost immediately after an injury.'

'Right, so how does that help us?'

'Because Gwenllian's skeleton shows evidence of much older injuries. There are signs of broken fingers, on both of her hands, a fractured elbow and two of her ribs had clearly been broken at some point.'

'How long ago?' Harri thought about the dynamics of the Andersons' marriage, a family who kept themselves to themselves.

'This is the thing. It's hard to tell how old an injury is – just that it's not happened recently. Most of the injuries show signs of complete healing, so we're not talking very recent. She thinks we're talking about decades.'

'Decades?' Harri sat up. 'That means we're unlikely to be looking at domestic abuse in a marital setting.'

Freddie shook his head. 'We need to go back further into Gwenllian's past than that.'

'Shit. Maybe Lewis and Sally Prytherch abused their kids, although neither Carys nor Dylan have mentioned it.' Harri picked up a can of full-sugar Coke that he shouldn't really be drinking. 'I've been sitting here, trying to convince myself I'm on the wrong track looking at the past.' He took a deep swig of the fizzy drink. 'Right, we call in Carys and Dylan, or whatever name he's going by now, for questioning. You do it, Freddie, and take Sioned or another duty DC in with you. I want Siân to be here for Pippa. I'd like her to dig a little deeper into the Andersons' marriage with their daughter, just so we can rule out recent domestic abuse. I want you to push hard with Carys and Dylan, who are running rings around Mallory and me. I'm getting very tired of people lying to us about the dynamics of 2003.'

31

2003 – Gwenllian's story

Once it started, it wouldn't stop. Gwenllian could never work out what she'd done wrong. It had begun a few years earlier, coinciding with a new school and more logging work taking place in the hateful forest. It had upset the order of things around the Pant Meinog clearing. Lewis and Sally had complained the money coming from the local farmers' markets had shrunk; Carys's periods had started giving her wracking, shooting pains every month; and Dylan had retreated to his room, modifying and adorning his model toys to reflect the images in his enormous imagination. When the loggers had left, nothing was the same. The forest had taken on a new, monstrous enormity and Gwenllian had shrunk from its presence. Carys had new secrets and Dylan, although drawn back to the now-silent woodland, kept himself more to himself.

Then the attacks started on her. At first, pinches and scratches. Then she would be on the ground, a heel in her ribs or her fingers bent backwards until she heard a bone snap. She could tell no one, as everyone was pretending not to notice as the assaults on her grew. Across the way, Tom, Gethin and Cathy were regular visitors to the house and still no one looked, actually looked, at her and saw her trauma.

The poltergeist story had been her idea, not Carys's, although her sister liked to claim credit for it. For her birthday in April, she'd received a novel from her parents about a girl in America whose farmhouse was haunted by a poltergeist. The book wasn't new – nothing in their house was – but it had set Gwenllian's imagination alight, and she had crept into Carys's room and suggested creating their own story. It had been a futile attempt to get closer to her older sister, to regain some of the connection they'd once had. At first it had been fun. Carys had a brilliant imagination and had gone to the library in Carmarthen to look at a book on tricks. How to throw a cup, for example, without anyone knowing it had come from your direction.

The problem was that Gwenllian's bruises were being put down to the poltergeist by Carys. There was one police officer, a short man with a head of thick brown curls, she desperately wanted to show them to – he'd arrived at the beginning, and his gaze into her eyes had been straight and honest. How she wished he'd come out again and maybe, just maybe, she'd have told him how she was terrorised – not every day, but most. There was no one else she could tell – everyone had their own obsessions – but surely it was time to call an end to it all. Tom next door had once told her that this place was bad land and now she agreed with him. But the ground on which they stood wasn't the only problem. The badness came from within and there was nothing, absolutely nothing, she could do because she was sure her assailant would never leave her in peace. Sometimes spirits could be a source of comfort, not fear. Far better to hold on to them.

32

Toby had already left for work by the time Mallory woke. Although she had driven him to New Quay for his first morning at the office, Toby was at the age where he craved independence and had informed her that he wanted to walk to work in future. To get to the ticket office on foot, he needed to take the coastal path dotted in parts with sheer rocky drops to the sea. Safe enough, Mallory supposed, but still she fretted over him. If he wasn't eating properly, he could pass out and it'd be an age until he was found. Bad weather was also a worry. She opened an app on her phone and saw the heatwave was due to break the following day. More to worry about.

Mallory pulled on her walking sandals, the ones that Toby hated on her, and flexed her feet. Like her son, she used to enjoy running but her leg, injured in a stabbing in her former police role, was temperamental and a brisk walk was as much as she could usually manage. She'd get the exercise in before her working day started and perhaps this would ease her worry over her son.

Mallory opened the door and stepped out into the sunshine. At eight o'clock, the campsite was already humming with activity. The aroma of bacon and eggs wafted in the air and, in the distance, came the sound of excited cries as the outdoor pool opened. Mallory locked the caravan and headed inland, hoping as the distance between herself and the sea widened, she'd find some much-needed peace. After half an hour of brisk walking, she found herself in the hamlet of Llanina, a place that consisted of a huddle of houses and a striking church with a turreted bell tower. The door was locked and Mallory sat down on the stone steps, enjoying the sensation of the sun beating down on her face, until she was interrupted by the shrill of her ringing phone.

Mallory listened to Harri's update, her mood darkening. She doubted Freddie would have better luck with either Carys or Dylan in finding out who might be responsible for Gwenllian's injuries. The siblings might not be in touch, but they were united by a common talent for keeping their emotions tightly sealed. The other possibility was that one of the parents had been assaulting Gwenllian. Lewis and Sally were an unknown in the investigation and despite their repeated absences, they must surely have noticed Gwenllian's broken fingers. It might be possible to unpick the dynamics within that family, even after all this time. Tom Thomas might be able to give some insight and, after speaking to Bev Christie, she would track him down. Harri was happy for her to follow this trail and, after cutting the call, she girded herself for the long walk back to her caravan. Mallory's reverie was broken by the sound of keys jangling. She looked up to see a young woman with a small child in a pushchair.

'Sorry, am I in your way?'

'You are a bit,' said the woman, pushing the hair out of her eyes. 'I just need to open up.'

Mallory stood, brushing down her trousers. 'Are you the vicar?'

The woman's laugh was closely followed by her little boy's, whose chuckles rang across the graveyard. 'I just open up the church, as I live nearby, and shut it in the evening. Would you like a look inside?'

Mallory wasn't particularly interested in churches but, aware she might come across as rude, nodded. The air was cold inside the building; there were fresh flowers on the altar and a visitors' book had a comment left in it the previous day. The woman pushed the stroller back towards the door and dipped her fingers in a nook in the wall, before lightly touching her son's face. She caught Mallory's gaze on her and flushed.

'Sorry, old habits die hard. My mam used to do the same to me.'

'What is it? Some kind of anointing?'

The mother looked like she wanted to laugh again. 'It's holy water, blessed. It keeps us from harm.'

'From evil spirits, you mean?' asked Mallory.

The woman, who had been about to leave, stopped, a frown on her face. 'I suppose so, but I've never really looked at it like that. More sort of a general protection. From bad things out there.'

'Even bad people?'

The woman shrugged. 'Of course. It might be just superstition but even if it does no good, it doesn't actually do any harm, does it?'

Mallory personally thought religion, whether official or not, could do a lot of harm but now wasn't the time to express her opinions.

'Wanna play outside.' The little boy's shout echoed around the church.

'Sorry, I'm keeping you,' said Mallory. 'By the way, given your interest in protection from spirits, you don't actually know someone called Bev Christie, do you?'

'Her?' The woman's tone was dismissive. 'She's famous round here. Infamous. You a friend of hers?'

'Not at all. I met her the other day, that's all.'

'I'd steer clear if I were you. I've heard that she likes to make things up. A drama queen.'

'You mean in relation to the hauntings she investigates?'

'Hauntings,' the woman scoffed. 'It's always the worst with her – poltergeists, evil spirits. The dead don't want to harm us.'

'So, hold on.' Mallory frowned. 'You believe in ghosts but not that they're out to harm us.'

'That's for the horror films and Bev Christie. Don't listen to her stories, that's all. Take the Beast of Brechfa. It's been the talk of that village for decades and we have one nearby too called the Beast of Bont. But even if the animals exist, and I think they do, they're not out to harm us. Humans are a threat to them.'

'And how does Bev Christie come into this?'

'She's trying to impose her beliefs on something much older, and no good will come of it.'

–

Bev didn't sound thrilled to hear from Mallory but she agreed to a meeting at her house. Harri had updated Mallory on news of Gwenllian's private schooling and she would push this line of inquiry but all it suggested to Mallory was Bev's pastoral care of a girl suffering.

Bev's face was high in colour when she answered the door and she was breathing with a heavy wheeze.

'Is everything all right?' asked Mallory, following her into the living room where the dog snoozed on a rug.

'This weather is playing havoc with my chest. I'll be glad when summer is over.'

'Rain is due tomorrow.' Mallory too was finding the heat oppressive, but autumn would bring its own problems and decisions to be made. She wasn't going to be wishing the summer away. The room was a little messier than on Mallory's previous visit but that was due to the reams of paper scattered around. Church notices, flyers for events and magazines were piled onto side tables and across the sofa. None of the publications looked the type to appeal to a teenager, although Mallory still kept an ear on any sounds coming from upstairs.

'You're aware,' said Mallory, 'that we haven't yet found the missing Anderson twins.'

'Of course, and I'm very sorry to hear that. I've been keeping them in my prayers.'

'Did you know them?' asked Mallory sharply.

'Not at all. I only knew Gwenllian as a child, and I knew of David through his work. I've told you all this.'

'Well, this is the thing. You didn't mention you knew David. It's come as a surprise.'

Bev was dismissive about the revelation. 'Take it from me, I know everyone in these parts who has an interest in paranormal investigation. We weren't close at all.'

'It's just that we believe someone is sheltering Matty and Ava, who might hold important information in respect of the killing of David and Gwenllian.'

Bev winced and pulled a blue inhaler out of her pocket, drawing deeply on the device. 'I can't help you. I'm sorry.'

'I also need,' said Mallory slowly, 'to pick your brains about the dynamics of the Prytherch household in 2003.'

Bev frowned. 'I thought we'd gone through that.'

'We now believe that Gwenllian may have been subject to abuse from within the household. Obviously, you knew the dynamics between the children. How were they together?'

'Abuse? Who from?'

'That's what we're trying to find out.'

'Well, I only met the parents twice so I can't really give you any insight into how they treated their children in private. All I'll say is that they were two of the most selfish people I've ever met and that's something, given my role.'

'Selfish in what way?'

'They were a couple who put their own pursuits above anything else. Although Lewis was a teacher, I don't think his heart was in it, but someone needed to support the family. He was always in the garden, tilling the ground, growing his plants, which was ridiculous as the soil there is nutrient poor. It's why the farmland was used for trees even before the new forest was planted.'

'He did grow stuff to sell at the market, though, didn't he, along with Sally's crafts?'

'They did. Sally would do the round of markets during the week and Lewis would join her at weekends. The kids were basically left to fend for themselves and that's when the trouble started.'

'You mean the fabrication of a poltergeist.'

'I mean exactly that, although as I said to you last time, there was plenty that was left unexplained by the incidents.'

Mallory was uninterested in this. 'What about the dynamics between the children? You spent more time with them.'

Bev took a moment to reflect, her eyes on Mallory. 'Gwenllian and Carys had the competitiveness I'd expect between sisters close in age. Carys was the obviously more mature of the two girls, both physically and in her manner, but the two seemed fond of each other. Dylan, I think, felt a little left out of things and I actually only met him the once. He wasn't really involved in the haunting deception and, if anything, was a bit frightened by what the girls were saying happened.'

'Do you think he was shocked when he realised that Carys and Gwenllian had made everything up?'

Bev shrugged. 'I think it would have been harder to pull the wool over Dylan's eyes. He was there in the house with the girls and must have seen what was going on. As I said, he appeared frightened, though.'

'Did you know he is Luke Parry, the person you suggested look up the Brechfa haunting?'

Bev sighed. 'I do know now. He called me after speaking to you to confess.'

'Don't you feel betrayed? He's rather good at deception, I'd say.'

'We all are, in our own way. I wouldn't read too much into him adopting a new identity – lots of people change their names.'

'The thing is, Pippa overheard her parents refer to someone who was a "cuckoo in the nest". As much as I agree with you about the culpability of the Prytherch parents in terms of how they looked after the children, I'm wondering if the phrase doesn't refer to one of Gwenllian's siblings.'

Bev frowned. 'Cuckoo in the nest? I don't know what you mean. I wouldn't have applied that term to any of the Prytherch children.'

Mallory leant forward. 'Was it you who arranged for Gwenllian to attend boarding school when she left Brechfa?'

Bev took a deep breath. 'OK, yes, but don't read much into that. It only involved me pointing Lewis Prytherch to the subsidies on offer when I heard Gwenllian was struggling. We'd taught together, don't forget, and despite his failings, he knew how to work the education system.'

'We've also recently discovered there may have been a relationship between Carys and Gethin. Did you know about that?'

Bev frowned. 'No, I didn't, but all the Thomas family seemed to be unusually interested in what was going on in the other house, so I'm not that surprised. Carys was a very attractive girl. Have you spoken to her about it?'

'I can't answer that, I'm sorry. Is there anything you can add to the information we already have?'

Bev shrugged. 'You might want to speak to Cathy, Gethin's wife. I got the impression that she wasn't very happy about what was going on at Pant Meinog, and it might not have been to do with the haunting.'

33

Mallory left Bev, who began busying herself in preparation for a funeral at her chapel. At least she was certain as she could be that the twins weren't in the house. Bev hadn't seemed that shocked when Mallory had mentioned a cuckoo in the nest, and she wondered if pointing her towards Cathy Thomas was nothing more than a diversionary tactic, but she couldn't see what Bev had to gain from lying about the dynamics in the house. Mallory swung by the station to speak to Harri, since she couldn't reach him on the phone. He was emerging from a press conference, dark smudges underneath his eyes and a patch of stubble on his cheek that his shaver had missed that morning. He tried to shrug her off, keen to return to his office for an update with his team but she stayed by his side, repeating Bev's words.

Harri stopped. 'Cathy? Go and interview her, and ask her in particular about the injuries found on Gwenllian.'

'Can I reinterview Gethin about the allegation? If he was regularly in the house with Carys, he's got to be a potential suspect for any injuries to Gwenllian.'

'He'll deny it, though, won't he? I would, in his position. He could be facing prosecution if he admits to a sexual relationship with a minor. Carys has admitted to a relationship, though... Look, begin with Cathy and let me know what she says, and then speak to Tom. When we have their statements, we'll compare them with what Gethin has to say.'

'Is Carys at the station yet?'

'Freddie is interviewing her now. We've also brought in Luke Parry. He was, as you said, at the beach but I want his official address as a matter of urgency. Now, I have to get on.'

Mallory watched him go with a sinking feeling. She preferred it when she had his entire attention, as it wasn't creepy or disconcerting as with some men. She enjoyed his intelligence as much as the intensity of his gaze. His distraction was harder to take and she wondered if her status as civilian investigator was keeping her out of the inner circle. She pushed open the door of the detective room and sat down at her desk. A colleague she didn't recognise was studying something intently on the computer.

'Do you think you could look up something for me? I want the contact details for Gethin Thomas's wife, Cathy. Could you get me their address?'

–

'Of course, I knew about Gethin and Carys. I'm not blind and I'm certainly not stupid.'

Harri had been right that Gethin would be likely to deny any relationship with Carys – but wives, in Mallory's experience, usually knew if their husbands were up to no good. Gethin had been shitting on his own doorstep, playing around with a teenage girl who lived next door in an isolated area. Carys was family, too, however distantly they were related. It was a powder-keg situation and might account for the violence pulsating in the background of the 2003 events.

'How did you find out about the relationship?' asked Mallory. Cathy had given her lemonade in a long glass and the cool liquid trickled down her throat, relieving her parched mouth. Cathy herself was restless, refusing to sit down and roaming the room, picking up ornaments and setting them down in a slightly different spot. She was in her mid-forties, with dyed blonde hair and a full face of make-up that suited her. Women like her always made Mallory wish she made more of an effort herself.

'I never exactly found out. I just noticed Gethin had been acting a little strange and I kept my eyes open. He works with other blokes on farms around the area and I didn't think he was involved with someone through his job, so I looked a little closer to home.'

'You thought it was Carys straight away, not Gwenllian?'

'Gwenllian?' Cathy started to laugh. 'She was a child. Gethin might like to think of himself as a stallion but he's no paedophile.'

'If the relationship with Carys was sexual in any way, then that's exactly what he is.'

Cathy looked unconvinced. 'She was nearly sixteen and full of it, like you are at that age. She'd parade around with next to nothing on and Gethin would make a big show of shouting for her to cover herself up in a brotherly kind of way. But then I noticed he'd disappear and I wouldn't be able to find him. You've been up to the valley. There's fuck-all place to go, so it got me thinking about this *brotherly* thing with Carys.'

'You didn't actually catch them out, though.'

'No, but once the suspicion was there, I kept my eyes open. There were enough signs to convince me I was on the right track.' Cathy paused. 'And what does Carys have to say about it?'

'That it was brief and ended the day Gwenllian was injured. You stayed together, then, after you found out about the affair.'

Cathy laughed, a bitter tinkle. 'Oh, we did it the Welsh way by not talking about it at all. Gethin never admitted the affair to me, and I never told him I'd pretty much guessed the truth.'

'Why do you think the attack on Gwenllian brought everything to an end?'

Cathy frowned. 'I'm not sure. I think we were all shocked by how many police cars turned up after what happened. It made us all think about what the bloody hell we were doing in that isolated clearing. Not long afterwards, the Prytherchs left. Lewis got a job in Brecon and they departed pretty much without saying goodbye. Gethin didn't seem heartbroken and I decided it was likely to be a blip in our otherwise happy marriage.'

'He hasn't had any affairs since then?'

'Oh yes,' said Cathy, flicking her hair. 'I was young and naive then. Blip my arse. As I said, he thinks he's a stallion.'

'You both left the valley shortly after too, didn't you?'

'That's right. We'd been saving up for a house and this one came up, so we decided to go for it. I thought it was a stepping stone to something bigger, maybe livelier, but no, this is it.'

Mallory looked around the homely room that probably hadn't been decorated since Gethin and Cathy had moved in twenty years earlier. She thought it better not to say she was currently living in a caravan. It was all about perspective, wasn't it? Mallory might not know what her future held, but she didn't actually feel trapped.

'Let me ask you about Gethin's moods: is he violent at all?'

'Now, hold on.' Cathy put her hands on her hips. 'Are you asking me if Gethin had anything to do with Gwenllian's death?'

'Well, did he?'

'Of course not, we had no idea Gwenllian was coming back to rent that house.'

'You're sure Gwenllian didn't try to get in touch with you?'

Cathy was silent, fiddling with the zip on her cardigan.

'Well?' asked Mallory.

'I occasionally look at Gethin's emails. Don't look at me like that. When you live with a serial philanderer, that's what you do. I'm not proud of it. There *was* an email from Gwenllian, asking if Tom was still living at Dan Y Derw.'

'Did Gethin mention the email to you?'

'No, he bloody well didn't. That's why I have to scour through his emails, just so I know what's going on.'

'Did you look to see if he'd replied?'

Cathy finally sat down, as if the memory had exhausted her. 'There was no reply when I first looked. When I logged in next, the email had gone and he'd deleted all his sent items.'

'Does he usually do that?' asked Mallory.

Cathy shook her head in misery.

'Why do you think Gwenllian wanted to know if Tom was there? Did she want to meet him?'

'I don't know. The thing is, the tone of the email implied she didn't want him to be still living there.'

'Do you know how she might have got Gethin's email?'

'That's easy: search Gethin Thomas and Brechfa, and he comes up as the local councillor. He's easy to find.'

'So, Gethin knew that Gwenllian was coming back. Do you think he told Tom?'

'I have no idea.' Cathy's voice rose. 'I think I'd like you to leave now.'

'I'll go in a second. Can I ask again what Gethin's temper is like? Has he ever assaulted you?'

'Assau—' Cathy stopped. 'What's this about? Of course, he's not assaulted me.'

But Mallory could see calculation in her eyes. However shocked she was at Mallory's question, it had triggered a memory that she was fighting to suppress.

'Where was Gethin last Friday, Cathy?'

'At work, they were planting trees. You do it as a team. We've already worked out Gethin wasn't on his own all day.'

It should have been a triumphant statement, but Cathy was thinking furiously. Mallory waited a moment, but the woman wasn't giving up her secrets.

–

Mallory drove away from Cathy's house, convinced that given the nature of the divide between the couple, Cathy was unlikely to mention to Gethin about her visit. So, next up was Tom Thomas, to see if she could extract any information from him. He hardly fitted the description of 'cuckoo in the nest' and surely the sight of him appearing at the kitchen window was unlikely to send David and Gwenllian into a panic, given he lived in the house next door to their holiday cottage. Short of him wielding an axe, which Mallory definitely couldn't see happening, Tom was an unlikely suspect but a potentially very good witness to what life had been like at Pant Meinog in 2003

– and, in particular, tensions within the family. He might have an idea why Gwenllian wouldn't want to see him.

There was smoke coming out the chimney of the house again, despite the heat of the day. Mallory parked in the courtyard and cast a glance at the holiday house, which lay silent. Given it was peak season, the owners must have been doing their nut about the prospect of revenue loss. Mallory regarded the house thoughtfully, wondering if she could live there. It was academic, as she was unlikely to be able to afford a week's rent but, in theory, she wasn't put off by its turbulent past. Nevertheless, there was a forlornness to the building that all the interior design couldn't hide, and she wouldn't much fancy spending a night under its roof.

The door to Tom's house was open, and she could hear the rustling of newspaper, as if the occupant was banking up the fire. She knocked on the door and stepped inside, startling Tom, who dropped the papers he had under his arm onto the floor. A sheaf wafted across to Mallory, who bent down to pick it up. It was a newspaper clipping, but not recent, the paper yellowed with age. An article cut out from a Welsh-language newspaper, the words impossible for Mallory to read but the accompanying photo was equivalent to a thousand words. It showed Carys, Gwenllian and Dylan standing next to each other, Carys's hand on her brother's shoulder. Mallory looked at the other clippings strewn on the floor. All articles had been cut out, some with the old-fashioned sewing shears with serrated edges. This was no professional archivist: the names of the newspapers and the dates had not been scrawled on the clippings. It was just someone documenting the downward spiral of a family in crisis.

'Did you collect these?' she asked Tom.

He straightened, the effort making him wince, and looked in dismay at the mess around him. 'It's twenty years' work. They don't tell you anything you don't already know. I just don't want them in my house any longer.'

'Why did you collect all this stuff?'

'I couldn't help myself. The first time they were in the newspaper, I drove down to Carmarthen and bought every copy I could find with the story in it. Then it became a habit.'

'And you've kept them all these years?'

'On top of a wardrobe. I'd even occasionally look at them. When they were renovating the house across the way, I got them down for a look and decided it was finally time to get rid of them, but I couldn't do it. Back up they went.'

'So why now?'

Tom looked older than his seventy years, his wrinkled face grey. 'Because it's happening all again, isn't it?'

'What, though? What's happening again?'

34

'Once upon a time, there were two brothers...' Tom's hand trembled as he brushed a lock of hair back from his face. They'd retreated away from the fire, at the other end of the room where an ancient Rayburn continued to pump out heat. No wonder Cathy had been desperate to get away to a modern house. Mallory accepted the offer of tea, anything to keep herself hydrated, and settled back to listen to Tom's story.

'Once upon a time there were two brothers, Islwyn and Dafydd. Together, they bought a plot of land in the ancient Glyn Cothi Forest so their families could be brought up side by side. The older brother built the house across the way and called it Pant Meinog, while Dafydd, my grandfather, built this smaller cottage you're sitting in now and called it Dan Y Derw. Know what the names mean?'

Mallory smiled, feeling sleepy in the heat. His soft Welsh voice was perfect for storytelling and she was his captive audience. 'I know Pant Meinog means stony valley. I'm afraid Dan Y Derw is beyond my meagre Welsh.' In fact, Mallory had not had time to learn any Welsh, but she hoped Tom might be a little impressed she knew the meaning of Pant Meinog.

He sniffed. 'It means under the oaks. Glyn Cothi was a mixture of different trees, and the tenant farmers made a living from them – oak, ash, alder. It was only in the last century that they started planting those bloody pines.'

'You don't like them?'

'They're not native to here, are they? Imported.'

Like me, thought Mallory. 'I think it happened else-where in the UK.'

Tom wasn't interested in anywhere else, but what had happened on the land around him.

'Go on,' said Mallory.

'The two men married and had a daughter each. One child only, but for different reasons. Islwyn's wife wanted a brood but could only manage one, and was told another would kill her. My grandmother, however, had my mother and said that's it, no more.'

'Right, and the two cousins were brought up next to each other?'

'They were, and they inherited the houses in turn – only, my mam married and had me and my brother, but Anita, my aunt, remained unmarried. My brother died of cancer when he was twenty-one, so I not only inherited Dan Y Derw from my mother, but also Pant Meinog from Anita when she died.'

'That must have felt strange – I mean, all that history and it ends with you.'

'It didn't end with me, as I have Gethin, but he and Cathy never had kids, so it ends with him.'

'So, he'll inherit this house when you die.'

Tom shook his head. 'He doesn't want to live here. He'll sell it, which is fine by me, because I believe this land is cursed.'

'Because of what happened to Gwenllian?'

'To Gwenllian, yes, and to her husband.'

'The Prytherchs are relations of yours, though, aren't they? Where do they fit into the story you just told me?'

Tom smiled, happy to continue the tale. 'Islwyn and Dafydd had another brother, Henry. He was much younger and a bit of a mammy's boy, by all accounts. He stayed at home until his parents died but, you see, they didn't own the house or land. Once they were gone, he took on the rent, but the place had no heating or a bathroom. Most of the old families had migrated to Swansea and Cardiff, but Henry stayed behind, working as a labourer. Sally was his granddaughter and when she married Lewis, they asked if they could rent Pant Meinog. Gethin was only a teenager and I didn't need it for my family, so I agreed.'

'So, as Carys was almost sixteen in 2003, had the family been there at least that length of time?'

'Just a little longer. Carys came along seven months after the wedding.' Tom winked. 'The Welsh way.'

'And until 2003, did anything strange happen in the house?'

'They weren't a happy family, I know that. I'd hear shouting and crying, more than the usual married stuff, but I had my own problems, as my wife was sick. I just ignored them.'

'They sound like a volatile family. Do you know who in particular was argumentative? Lewis or Sally?'

Tom folded his arms. 'Both.'

'OK. And how did you feel when the girls started complaining about supernatural activity in the house?'

Tom puffed out his cheeks. 'They were messing about, weren't they?'

'From the witness accounts, I get the impression that your family and the Prytherch's were in and out of each other's houses. Do you think that's a fair comment?'

'They didn't come here much,' said Tom, folding his arms. 'Nothing for them here.'

'But Gethin went over there, didn't he? I know all about his fling with Carys, so if that's what you're hiding, there's no need.'

'Have you spoken to Geth?' asked Tom.

'Not yet. Did he tell you that Gwenllian had emailed him, asking if you still lived here?'

Tom nodded. 'Must have been when she decided to come here on holiday.'

'But she came and never got in contact with you, did she? It's almost as if she was hoping you *wouldn't* be here. Do you know why that might have been the case?'

'Maybe she didn't want me recognising her.'

'That would be the natural conclusion, but who did she think you were going to tell? Gethin? It can't be him, as she'd emailed him herself. So, who?'

Tom didn't answer her but got up and poked the fire ineffectually with a stick. Masses of paper make ultimately poor fuel and the air in the cottage was thick with smoke.

'Tom.' Mallory leant forward. 'Do you know what happened in 2003?'

Tom turned his face away towards the spitting fire. 'I think all the bad blood spilled out that afternoon.'

35

2003 – Tom's story

Tom was glad when Gethin told him he wanted to leave the valley. Families were busy letting go of houses that had been in their possession for generations and most did it without a backwards glance. Pant Meinog was better serviced than some of the farmhouses. It had a decent-enough working bathroom and kitchen, but he knew that wasn't enough to entice Gethin and Cathy to live there. They wanted somewhere modern on the mains gas network, with double glazing and a shower that pumped out hot water. They were staying with him while they saved up for one of the houses on the new estate in Brechfa, and he couldn't blame them. He'd told his son that once the Prytherchs had left Pant Meinog, he'd sell up and the money was Gethin's to pay off his mortgage. He only wished the family would move sooner. Lewis and Sally paid their rent on time, but Tom detected an undercurrent of annoyance that, as family, they were paying any rent at all. Except, they weren't really family. Second or third cousins, and he'd only agreed to let the house to them when he'd heard how hard-up they were.

Since the press had arrived, the shrieks and groans from the house had intensified but what they didn't know, and he couldn't tell them, was that the terror had always been there. Bad blood will out. It had been the same with Henry, although no one talked about it much, and the strain had clearly passed down through the generations. Tom didn't much like having people hanging around the valley, but there wasn't much he could do other than watching and waiting.

When that final agonising scream came, it was the sound he'd been waiting for. He was already in the kitchen, leaving a note for Lewis, who was late in paying his rent that month. He pulled the screaming Gwenllian out from the house, hardly noticing the blood as he deposited the girl on the grass and rushed back in. Carys and Dylan were white-faced, the little boy pointing upwards, his eyes full of tears. Tom rushed up the stairs and flung open the bedroom door. He knew which room it would be, didn't need to ask.

It was a teenager's bedroom, posters of a band on the wall he didn't recognise. It had been Nirvana when Gethin was young; this lot looked cleaner-cut but the essence of the room was the same. A messy space belonging to a fourteen-year-old.

Tom crossed to the window and flung it open, letting in the warm sticky air. Across the meadow, he could see Lewis and Sally at the vegetable garden, arguing, their own raised voices drowning out the screams of their daughter. Either that or they were making a good job of ignoring her. He started at a sound behind him and whirled round to see that the children had followed him up the stairs, their gazes fixed on the cupboard in the corner.

'You think someone's in there?' His voice sounded harsh to his ears as he pulled open the door. The cupboard was stuffed full of clothes, most of them thrown in. He knew Sally was a slut with the housekeeping and this was the proof.

There was no sign of relief on the children's faces as he'd opened up the cupboard, only a resignation that their deepest fears had not yet found their origin.

'Listen.' Tom put his arms around the pair, noticing neither of them flinched. 'You need to get your mam and da to leave here. I'm going to give notice and you need to go.'

36

Mallory frowned, confused.

'You actually think it's the house. You believe in malignant spirits?' She was disappointed, as she'd taken to Tom and didn't want him spouting the same nonsense as Bev.

'It's not the house. It's a combination of the house and the family. It amplifies everything. The house on its own is fine. The family, away from the house, are also OK. It's when the two meet that things get deadly.'

Mallory shook her head in disbelief. 'The autopsy on Gwenllian's body was completed this morning. It shows signs of old fractures. Gwenllian was regularly being abused by someone and I don't think a house can do that.'

Tom stared at her, his expression hard to read. 'Abused?'

'She had broken bones, fingers and ribs mainly. Any idea who might have carried out these attacks?'

'Her husband?'

'Tom, they're older than that.'

Tom stood, his chair scraping across the tiled floor. 'I need you to leave. I know nothing about broken bones.'

Mallory got up. She would get nothing useful out of Tom if, in his heart, he believed there were malign spirits at work. She was certain, would stake her life on it in fact, that there was a more prosaic explanation for what had happened to Gwenllian. However, Tom had made one interesting statement. Lewis and Sally were in the garden when Gwenllian was attacked, not at the market, as Harri had told her. Either his recollection was flawed – which was unlikely, as he'd recently looked at the files again on the police computer – or the children had lied when they'd claimed to have been alone in the house.

So, the question was, where were Lewis and Sally when the police arrived? Harri would surely have noticed a car in the driveway, unless the family had more than one. It suggested that while their daughter was lying injured in front of their house, Lewis and Sally had either driven off or made themselves scarce. As far as Mallory was concerned, it put the pair of them in the frame for the attack in 2003. She would go back to the file detailing their accident and see what she could find.

–

Harri was nowhere to be seen when Mallory entered the detective room. His office blinds were closed and, unless he was sitting in a darkened office, he was clearly away. Mallory managed to get the info from a duty officer that both Carys and Luke were still being spoken to separately about the old injuries to Gwenllian. Mallory didn't envy the interviewing officers, as the siblings could also be victims of that same abuse. Or perpetrators. Or both. The line between abuser and victim was often paper-thin. Mallory, feeling restless, wasn't inclined to observe the interviews.

Siân came into the detective room, stuffing a bacon sandwich into her mouth.

'You'll give yourself indigestion,' Mallory shouted over to her.

Siân nodded in agreement while sitting down at her desk. 'I need to get something inside me, as I missed breakfast. I want to have a full stomach before speaking to Pippa again.'

'How is she?' asked Mallory, wondering whether to nip out and get herself something for lunch. There was something about the smell of bacon that was irresistible.

Siân shrugged. 'She's worried about her future now that her immediate needs have been met. She's been fed and had a good night's sleep, but she's a bright child and wants to know what happens next.'

'Do we know that?'

'David's brother has arrived and is waiting at a nearby Costa. I suppose Carys and Luke might express an interest in the girl but given they're both potential suspects, they're not a viable option for taking in Pippa. David's brother is the best bet.'

'Perhaps he'll also be able to give an insight into David,' said Mallory, checking her purse for change. She'd definitely be buying herself a bacon sandwich.

'Maybe. We're waiting on Cardiff University's IT department getting back to us, as we want to see what turned up on the recording. Remember, David was under suspension for lack of academic rigour. He had begun to believe in the existence of the supernatural, so we assume he had finally persuaded Gwenllian to return to her home, and yet, by Thursday it was all over. What happened?'

'The late-night visitor?' asked Mallory.

'Who we think David didn't see but might have heard.'

'Shit, I hadn't thought of that. Surely, Gwenllian knew the house was under surveillance?'

'Sure, but David was an experienced psychologist. He might have told her he'd switched off any cameras or digital recorders but kept one running.'

'Will we get access to David's cloud today?' asked Mallory.

'Bloody hope so.'

—

At her desk, stuffing the sandwich into her mouth with the same finesse Siân had employed, Mallory called up the file on the deaths of Lewis and Sally Prytherch. The facts were pretty much as Harri had summarised. After leaving Pant Meinog, Lewis had got a job in a school in Brecon and the family had rented a property in the town, clearly wanting a change from the isolation of their former home. Gwenllian had failed to settle and had attended a boarding school, where she'd attained good grades; she'd attended Cardiff University and then secured a job in the central library before being made redundant and working in retail. Her two siblings, meanwhile, had drifted back to West Wales, and Dylan morphed into Luke Parry.

In Brecon, Lewis and Sally had lived a similar life to that in the forest: Lewis teaching and Sally selling her home-made crafts at the market. There was nothing to suggest any ongoing issues, but an official report was unlikely to have gained any insight into the undercurrents of that family. It would be pointless, thought Mallory, for her to chase down former colleagues and neighbours. Any abuse that had taken place in the home had gone undetected at Pant Meinog, and that pattern had likely been repeated in Brecon.

Out of the corner of her eye, she saw Freddie flop down in his chair. 'How's it going?' she called over to him.

'We're having a break. Carys swears she knows nothing of the injuries Gwenllian sustained, and we're now going to take her through everyone who might have had access to her sister to cause the broken bones.'

'You don't think she was responsible?'

'I'm not sure. I can't crack her cool exterior. She doesn't give much away, does she?'

'She doesn't. And Luke?'

'We've finished with him. Again, he says he knows nothing about Gwenllian's injuries and suggests they might have occurred within her marriage.'

'If he hasn't kept in touch with his sister, how the hell would he know that?'

Mallory turned back to the screen and read the report of the car accident that took the lives of Lewis and Sally. The car had been poorly maintained. Its MOT was due the following month and investigators could find no evidence of it having been recently serviced. The front offside tyre was nearly down to its thread and the three other tyres were worn beyond their legal limit. Although it was only lightly raining, the road was wet; Lewis took a bend too fast, skidded off the tarmac, through a barrier, and plunged down the mountain. Sally had been thrown from the car and investigators had concluded that the seatbelt was defective. This made Mallory pause. Defective? It had admittedly been almost a year since the previous MOT but could a seatbelt really become dangerously damaged within eleven months of a manual check? Mallory read on and saw that the anchorage of the belt had been deemed faulty. The place where the belt buckle was slotted into its cradle had become loose and the belt had not held. When the car rolled off the road, Sally had been catapulted out of the vehicle. Lewis, it appeared, had not even been wearing his, and discussions with the Prytherch children had revealed this was not an uncommon occurrence.

Mallory picked up the phone and rang the garage where she'd had her car serviced in April. The mechanic, Alfie, remembered her and listened to her query, answering to the best of his ability. Mallory put the phone down, convinced that Sally's seatbelt malfunction was not the result of poor maintenance but deliberate sabotage. The question was, by whom?

'Can you do me a favour?' she shouted over to Freddy. 'Ask Carys how recently she'd seen her parents before their fatal car crash. Try not to make too much of it, I just want a time frame. Days, weeks. Then call Luke and ask him the same question.'

–

When she got back to the caravan that evening, Toby had come home from work and was in unnaturally high spirits. It took a minute or two of disjointed and rambling conversation, a marked contrast to his usual mumblings, to realise that he was tipsy.

'Have you been drinking?' she asked.

'Just the one,' he said, 'to celebrate the end of my second day.'

'Right.'

Toby was turning sixteen that autumn and, like much of his generation, had shown little interest in alcohol. Was him having a beer a good thing? Mallory liked the idea of him socialising with friends and he had said he'd only had one. Given the little he ate, she was unsurprised the drink had gone straight to his head. She opened the fridge and scanned its contents. 'I can make cheese on toast. Does that appeal?'

Toby scrunched up his face. 'Do you have any salad?'

Mallory extracted tomatoes and a cucumber that was just about OK, chopped them up and added some olives from a jar. 'Seriously, Tobe, you need carbs too.'

'Stop going on.' She watched him wolf down the salad and had to turn away, as the sight of his thin body induced a dart of pain. When his bulimia had first been diagnosed, she was certain that together – Toby, his dad Joe and herself – they could conquer Toby's demons. Now, however, she was unsure this was achievable. Toby had not opened up to them and his counselling sessions had been intermittent. Not his fault, but there was a shortage of staff in NHS paediatrics. She'd been warned that it would be worse once he reached eighteen. She'd half-heartedly suggested medication, such as antidepress-ants, but this again had been turned down. Toby's body and brain were still developing, and they had no wish to interfere with this. Of course, if there was a crisis…

What a strange situation to be in, thought Mallory. To be hoping for a crisis so Toby could get the intervention he needed. As she lay on her bed, to give Toby some privacy while he was eating, she wondered what had persuaded him to have a drink.

37

Thursday

Mallory woke to the shrill of her phone and she stumbled around until she located it in the back pocket of her trousers. She could hear an unfamiliar sound on the roof of her caravan and realised with a jolt that it was rain. Harri began talking to her before she'd even put the phone to her ear.

'You need to get down to Tom's house. We've found him dead – it looks like he had a visitor last night. What time did you leave him?'

Shocked, Mallory sat down on the bed. 'Around lunchtime, after which I came into the station. He gave no indication he was expecting anyone, only—'

'Only what?'

'When I told him about Gwenllian's injuries, he was determined to get rid of me. I'd clearly touched a nerve with my questions.'

Mallory was pulling off her pyjamas so she could get in the shower immediately. 'It's possible he contacted someone after I left, and my guess is that it's the same person Gwenllian was worried he was in touch with. At least we can strike Gethin from this.'

'Gethin has an alibi for most of the evening, anyway. Get down here, Mallory, and see if anything's different to when you left.'

Tom Thomas, the keeper of secrets, lay sprawled on the floor. Unlike the cunning murder of David Anderson, no such ingenuity had been needed for this crime. Tom had been beaten around the head with a rock, probably picked up from the path outside. Pant Meinog, thought Mallory – stony valley, and she wondered if the neatness had gone unnoticed by the killer. She thought not. The scent of the forest was of a cloying dampness but inside the house the smell was much worse. She'd forgotten the stench of fresh blood, and it made her want to retch.

She glanced across at Harri, who looked furious. 'I blame myself. It was always going to be Tom who knew what really went on. He missed nothing. I remember that clearly from 2003 and he hadn't changed when we saw him recently.'

Mallory moved closer, as if to comfort him. 'You can't get people to talk when they don't want to. I tried yesterday. Remember the days of interviewing witnesses and suspects, day in, day out. Some talked, some refused. I was never much good at getting people to respond when they were dead set against it. Tom was one of those people.'

Harri inclined his head and Mallory followed him outside, where they stood in the softly falling rain.

'Do you think it could be one of the teenagers?' he asked her, his face pale. 'We've interviewed all the actors from 2003: Bev, Gethin and Cathy, Carys, Dylan. We can't unpick their statements. Maybe it's one of those kids.'

Mallory ran her hand across her face. 'I can't see it. Killing their parents, possibly, but why Tom? We will find those two, eventually, and then their stories will come out. They simply don't have the resources to disappear permanently. Murdering Tom doesn't help them at all.'

'Then who?' Mallory jumped at Harri's raised tone. 'Are we missing a key figure from the past? I went through the file thoroughly. The Prytherch parents are dead – they might have been able to shed light on what happened – but we've interviewed everyone else.'

'Not everyone,' said Mallory. 'We haven't talked to any of the police officers who attended the scenes. Some of them must be still serving.'

Harry folded his arms. 'I told you I went through the statements again the other day to refresh my memory of the case.'

'But we need more than that – we need their recollections too. Take the officer that accompanied you to the house. What was her name?'

'Delyth Jones?' Harri made a face. 'She's still in the force but she went in a different direction to me and took a job in computer forensics. She was always a bit of a geek and I think frontline policing, especially with cases like Gwenllian's, wasn't for her. You want to speak to her? I can assure you that everything Delyth saw, I did too.'

She'd dented his pride, Mallory noticed. 'I need to speak to her – and after that, any other officers we can track down. They'll have a different view to you as to what happened. Is Delyth still at Carmarthen?'

'I've seen her around in the last year, although she was heavily pregnant so she might be on maternity leave. Maybe I should go to visit her.'

'I think it would be better if it was me. You were there and you were her colleague – both factors will colour recollections.' Mallory was firm. 'I'll go.'

A quick call confirmed that Delyth was still on maternity leave, but her address was obtained easily. Mallory tapped it into her satnav, noticing it was only a couple of miles from the caravan park where she lived. Was this significant? She picked up her phone before setting off and typed in a message to Toby, asking him to call her when he was free. They'd left the caravan park together but he'd refused her offer of a lift, keen to make his own way to the ticket office despite the rain. She wanted to check that he was OK after his tipsy evening and also let him know she was likely to be late that evening. Three murders, and things were coming to a head finally. David and Gwenllian's deaths had been planned, she was sure. Tom, however, had known the identity of the killer and had refused to reveal it to her. Perhaps, after all, blood was thicker than water.

Delyth lived on a small cul-de-sac housing development that was likely built before cul-de-sacs became unfashionable and it was all about organically flowing routes. The house was the third to the left, made from a pinkish brick that would never have been seen in the natural environment, so maybe housebuilding had made some progress since the Eighties. There was a small car in the driveway, old but well looked-after, with none of the dust that was scattered across Mallory's vehicle. Mallory rang the doorbell, noticing it was a new type with a camera. Nothing unusual in that, she supposed. Delyth, as a serving officer, could well be security conscious.

The woman who answered the door was tall and reed-thin, her long legs encased in a pair of skintight jeans. Given she'd recently given birth, she must have got back into shape quickly. Mallory showed her ID but Delyth,

naturally, wasn't going to be cowed by a civilian investigator pass.

'Unless you've got a warrant, you're not coming in.'

'A warrant?' Mallory frowned. 'Why would I need a
warrant? Can't I even tell you why I'm here? I thought I
could have a chat with you over a cuppa. Harri, DI Evans,
and I thought you might be able to help us.'

Delyth folded her arms. 'I know why you're here. That
family has brought us nothing but trouble and you're not
coming in.'

So Delyth had been following the case even while on
maternity leave, which was interesting. 'I just wanted to
ask you about what went on in 2003. It's very important,
as there's been another murder, and I want to get your
recollections of the house and its occupants. It's a significant line of inquiry in our investigation.'

From inside the house, a baby began to wail. Delyth
made to shut the door. 'I'll ring through for a warrant
now,' called Mallory. 'They've sped up procedures since
you were in active policing. Do you have someone you
can leave your baby with while you accompany me to the
station?'

Mallory felt a wave of shame wash over her as she
watched Delyth's face. Twenty years is a long time to be
away from knocking on doors and although she would
have known the tricks police used to get inside a property,
she couldn't be sure Mallory wouldn't hold true to her
word. Delyth opened the door.

'You'd better come in.'

She took Mallory into a living room, its bamboo blinds
and fake-fur throws as dull as the exterior, although the
room had the reassuring smell of baby – Johnson's powder

and whiffy nappies. She left Mallory there and returned holding a baby, hushing it as it whimpered.

'How old are they?' asked Mallory, keeping her pronouns gender neutral, aware that a blue romper signified nothing in these enlightened times.

'Norah's five months on Saturday.'

At the sound of her name, Norah turned towards her mother and gave her a gummy smile. Mallory guessed Delyth was around Harri's age, so she must have had her baby late in life. The thought of doing motherhood all over again made Mallory's stomach lurch, but she guessed there must be some advantages to having a baby over the age of forty. She just couldn't think of one at that moment.

Delyth sat on the sofa and started nursing the child – a defence mechanism that Mallory forced herself to push beyond.

'It sounds like you've been following the case of the killing of David and Gwenllian Anderson.'

Delyth rolled her eyes. 'I could hardly ignore it when it comes to my own doorstep.'

Mallory, who had been mentally forming the next question, frowned. 'Has someone visited you already?'

'Of course they have. Yesterday afternoon.'

'Yesterday afternoon?' Mallory wondered if Siân had come to see Delyth on her own initiative.

'Of course. When they brought Luke home. He'd told them he'd get the bus to Aberaeron, and I could pick him up from there, but they insisted on coming here to check his address was genuine.'

Mallory's heart missed a beat. 'Luke lives here? Luke Parry, formally Dylan Prytherch.'

It was Delyth's turn to freeze. 'Isn't that why you're here?'

'I had no idea that Luke was married to you. I came here because I wanted to talk to you about the events of 2003.' So much for Luke telling her he lived off-grid. This house was hardly Mallory's definition of carefree living.

'You mean the hauntings. Why don't you ask Harri Evans? He was there too.'

'Harri's given up all he knows. I wanted to speak to you about that time. When did they bring Luke home yesterday?'

'Around three, I think. Maybe a little earlier. He was in a foul mood when he got here, I can tell you.'

'Did he say anything about the interview?'

'I tried to ask but then he went out to his shack to record another podcast.'

Delyth spoke easily, which suggested she didn't know Tom Thomas was dead, as she was failing to provide her partner with an alibi.

'What time did he get back?' asked Mallory, trying to match Delyth's casual tone. 'He's not here, is he?'

'He came back well after midnight but I was up with the baby. He told me the recording hadn't gone well and he needed to go back to the shack early to finish it off.'

'The shack... Is it nearby?'

Delyth shook her head. 'It's up near the forest in Carmarthenshire – not far, now I think of it, from the house he grew up in. What's this all about?'

'I just need to make a quick call. I'll go to the other room.' Mallory went through to the kitchen and called Harri, who wasn't answering his mobile. She managed to get hold of Siân, who swore under her breath.

'We need to get hold of Luke urgently, as it's not looking good for him. Look, there's something else. We've finally got hold of David Anderson's sound and audio files from his university cloud. There's an awful lot to go through – days of the family going about their daily lives – but we've concentrated on the Tuesday evening, when Gwenllian received her visitor. It's definitely Luke who arrives at Tall Pines, but they spoke outside. That's all we've got: him arriving at the house. We were coming down to reinterview him this morning.'

'Delyth can take me to his recording studio.'

'Wait for backup – I'll send a car to Delyth's, and she can direct us to Dylan's shed.'

'I'm going there right away.'

'Wait for backup!' shouted Siân, as Mallory cut the call.

Mallory looked at Delyth. 'You need to give me directions to the shack.'

The woman shook her head. 'You'll never find it. It doesn't have a postcode or anything. I'll have to come with you if I can put Norah's seat in the back. Luke's in trouble, isn't he?'

'I think so. You can tell me what you remember in the car.'

38

2003 – Delyth's story

When the message came in that there had been yet another incident at Pant Meinog, Delyth was surprised that Harri responded immediately to say they would attend the scene. They'd just left a burglary in Llandovery and would be passing Brechfa Forest on their way back to Carmarthen, so really there was nothing unremarkable about them taking the job. But the speed with which Harri had spoken into his radio left her in no doubt he wanted to be there, despite the proximity of other patrol vehicles to that weird forest clearing. Harri put his foot down on the drive up the mountain, clearly anxious to get to the stricken girl. Delyth wondered what new trick Gwenllian had come up with this time. The thinking was that it was an elaborate fraud, which should surely have downgraded the call, except that it was an ambulance crew who had asked for their assistance. Paramedics, in Delyth's opinion, were not easily spooked, which meant something significant had happened.

As they drew into the clearing, a huddle of people was standing around a figure lying on the ground. Delyth recognised Carys and Dylan from her previous visit – both were standing apart from the group, although they seemed to draw no comfort from each other. Carys was chewing her bottom lip, her eyes on the adults standing over Gwenllian, while Dylan, his face chalk-white, pushed his hands deeper into his pockets, his little shoulders hunched up.

It took a few moments to see the extent of Gwenllian's injuries and she noticed Harri was deeply affected by it.

'Who was in the house with you?' he asked the hysterical girl.

'What does it matter?' she screamed back. 'It was the spirit.'

Harri looked up then, his expression difficult to read.

'You don't actually believe that stuff?' Delyth asked him. Her uniform felt itchy in the heat and she longed to take off her jacket. 'It's all a big sham.'

'You think she did that to herself?'

'If she didn't, someone else did. We'll have to interview the children again. Shall I take Carys and you Dylan?' She suggested this pairing, as Carys might open up to another woman but Harri, she saw, viewed the teenager as the greater prize. Carys would probably know more than her younger brother about what had been happening in the house. Delyth approached Dylan and led him into the house, turning him away from the trail of blood.

'Where do you feel safest here, Dylan?' she asked him.

'My room,' he whispered, taking her up the stairs to the room at the front of the house, overlooking the forest. It was full of action models, she saw, some of which were hard to identify. He was obviously creative, as bits of cardboard, plastic and stone had been attached to some of the models, making what might have been a bland toy far more evil-looking. Dylan sat on the bed, passive and incurious about what was happening outside.

'Can you tell me what happened, Dylan? I need to know how Gwenllian got injured.'

'I was reading my comic,' he pointed to a Spider-Man magazine on the bed, 'and I heard screaming. At first, I stayed here.'

'Why was that?' asked Delyth.

He didn't reply, his eyes on his action figures.

'Was it because you thought Carys and Gwenllian were playing the joke again?'

Dylan nodded. 'When did you leave this room, Dylan?'

'When I heard Carys asking what she had done. Then I came out and saw Gwenllian standing there. Her face was... was...'

'That's OK,' said Delyth. 'Do you know who did that to Gwenllian?'

'She said that it was the spirit but I think she was lying.'

'What makes you think that?' Delyth had her eyes on what looked like a suit of armour Dylan was constructing. He'd got as far as the chest plate and arms, a hard plastic casing leading to some kind of modified glove.

'Because she was laughing too. Like she'd won something.'

'She was laughing?'

'Yes. She kept saying, "This is the end, this is the end."'

'Do you know what she meant by that?'

Dylan slowly shook his head.

–

And that was the end of that sad story – or it would have been if Delyth hadn't gone to that nightclub in Carmarthen three years ago. Stinking of alcopops and cheap perfume, she'd been persuaded to go by members of her spin class. She'd felt like a fish out of water, ten years older than the next oldest member of the group, but considerably fitter. She might be stuck behind a desk in the IT fraud department but she kept herself trim and passed her annual fitness checks with impressive ease.

Luke had made a beeline for her, and she'd spotted that he was younger than her – much younger – straight away. It hadn't bothered him, though. Generation Z, according to an article in a newspaper, didn't care about age gaps in the way that her age group did. Well, that was easy to say, unless you were the older woman. Then you had to put up with speculation and bemusement in the eyes of your contemporaries, with their balding husbands and teenage tearaways. But, despite her reservations, things had got serious with Luke and she'd soon found herself pregnant with Norah. Was he a good father? It was difficult to judge. Neither good nor bad, she'd say. A little indifferent and cool but maybe the baby had taken him by surprise too.

Funny that he'd turned out to be little Dylan from all those years ago. He'd been open about it when he realised who she was. He hadn't recognised her but when watching a TV programme about the case, he'd confessed he had once been Dylan Prytherch and she'd almost had the breath pushed out of her body. She'd known her young lover as a little boy, frightened at the deception drummed up by his sisters. The knowledge had given her a jolt, but this was West Wales. Connections were common and unremarked upon. He'd laughed when she told him she was the police officer who'd spoken to him in his room after that final attack on Gwenllian, but he'd been silent for a while afterwards, digesting the information. The next morning, he was back to his usual self.

After news came out that David and Gwenllian had died, she had been surprised he was so unaffected. She knew he had little time for his family, but she'd expected more grief from him. She'd decided then and there that if she had more children, she would encourage sibling closeness, which had been so lacking in the Prytherch family. Because, after all, these things often were down to the parents, weren't they?

39

Mallory kept her eyes on the road as she sped through the countryside towards the forest. She supposed it was inevitable that Dylan would be attracted back to the place where he'd explored his darkest fears. Would she find the twins in his shack? She hoped not, as those who crossed Dylan usually met a very grisly end. Delyth's story matched Harri's almost word for word, but their responses had been very different: Harri had reacted with shock, Delyth with practicality. And at the heart of this maelstrom was one person: Luke.

'You know, I'm finding it hard to believe that you didn't recognise Luke. I identified him straight away from the photos Carys gave me. You can detect the child in the man.'

Delyth, to her surprise, didn't bristle at Mallory's words. 'The thing is, I agree with you. When Luke told me who he was, I looked him up online and he is like the child I interviewed. But I'm a serving police officer, specialising in online security and, believe me, I interview a lot of teenagers. I hardly remembered the Pant Meinog hauntings, let alone the physical appearance of one of the witnesses.'

Mallory was silent, mulling over Delyth's words. The woman had a lot to lose, given the nature of her job, but it was entirely possible she hadn't realised who Luke was. Luke not recognising Delyth was another matter.

Delyth turned to her. 'I know what you're thinking but I'm not attracted to children. Luke was a grown man by the time I met him.'

'When he revealed his identity to you, did you decide between you to keep your past history quiet?'

'Of course. I technically was part of the investigating team for the attacks on Gwenllian and these things sometimes have repercussions, even if it was twenty years ago.'

How Luke must have loved romancing one of the police officers he'd had a hand in duping. She didn't think for a minute that Luke hadn't recognised Delyth. Christ. The thought turned her stomach. As if reading her thoughts, Delyth grasped her arm.

'He's not responsible for those deaths.'

'I'm afraid I think he is. He paid a visit to Gwenllian at Pant Meinog on the first week of her holiday and, whatever was discussed, changed the course of everything. We need to get to him quickly. How far away is this place?'

'Another five minutes, I'll tell you when to turn.'

Delyth directed her off the main road, up a thin track barely tarmacked, with high hedgerows on either side. The car got hotter despite the rain and Mallory fiddled with the air conditioning, which was clearly playing up.

'You need to park up here,' said Delyth, pointing at a small lay-by. 'It's a short walk to the shack but he's not there.'

'How do you know?'

'His bike's not here. He parks it in the lay-by and walks up. The track's not great, even for a bike.'

'Fine.' As the wipers squealed against her windscreen, Mallory looked at the baby asleep in her seat. 'I want you to wait here with your daughter while I take a look. It's up the path, you say?'

'It won't take you longer than a couple of minutes.'

'Give me fifteen. If I'm not back then, call for help.'

'Jesus. This is Luke we're talking about. Look, maybe I should come with you and bring Norah. He loves her.'

'I'd rather you stayed.'

Mallory left as Delyth climbed into the back seat to join her daughter. She was on the mountain and Pant Meinog was about a fifteen-minute walk to the other side of the hill. Luke, despite his protestations, had been drawn back to his childhood home. She entered the woodland and saw, set against an old oak, a small shack. It was probably a loggers' rest, equipped with the bare essentials for a day in the woods but, most importantly, connected to the electricity network, which Luke needed for his recordings. It was unclear whether Luke actually had permission to use the place. She very much doubted it, given its location on public land. It had the air of being deserted and, when she went up to the door, she noticed it was fastened by a padlock.

Mallory rattled the lock, but Luke was adept at shielding his secrets, and the door failed to budge. The window was clean but obscured by a curtain or blind. To be sure no one was locked inside, Mallory banged on the door.

'Is anyone in there? It's Mallory Dawson.'

There was only silence, although a starling was watching her from a nearby tree, its gaze inquisitive. The only course of action was to take Delyth back to her home and call for backup. Luke needed to be hunted down as a matter of urgency.

Mallory decided to make a circuit of the building as a final check, feeling she needed to cross this location off her list. The wet, stony ground was slippery underfoot and yielded nothing, until she came back to the front door. On the ground, she saw a bracelet made of a deep coral, like the one Toby had been wearing. She bent down and picked it up. Coral. Her heart gave a lurch and she fumbled for her phone, praying that she'd get a signal. She tried Toby's number, but his phone was switched off. It took an age to open up the internet but she finally found the number for New Quay boat cruises and asked to speak to a manager, explaining she was Toby's mum. After she'd been kept on hold for five interminable minutes, a female voice came on the phone, introducing herself as Andrea.

'Is everything all right with Toby?' asked Andrea.

Mallory's heart lurched in her chest. 'Why do you ask?'

'It's just he hasn't returned from lunch yet. We wondered if he'd got lost. He said he was meeting a friend.'

'I can't get hold of him by phone. Did he say who this friend was?'

'He didn't but last night he was out drinking with Luke Parry, the guy who sunbathes by the lifeboat station. You might want to try him.'

Mallory felt her world spin. 'Thanks.'

She could barely remember the walk back to the car. Her sore leg and aching head were forgotten as she stumbled back down the path in the intensifying rain, praying that Toby would come to no harm. It was her fault he was with Luke. How that man would enjoy playing God with someone else's life now Gwenllian was dead. Anyone would do – and why not start with her?

Mallory yanked open the rear door and stared down at Delyth. 'He has my son.'

'What do you mean?'

'I have a teenage son and I think he's with Luke.'

Delyth began chewing her lip – unbelievably, little Norah had fallen asleep and was gently snoring in her car seat.

'Where might he go, Delyth?' asked Mallory. 'Where's his safe place?'

'Here. It's the place he loves. I can't think where else he might go.'

'Might he go back to Pant Meinog? The forensic team will be there, but he might be in the woods nearby. Should we try there?'

'He says he hates the place.'

'I don't think that's true but…' The sound of a shotgun sliced through the forest. 'What was that?'

'It sounded like a gun.' Delyth swallowed. 'It could be a hunter.'

Mallory experienced a stab of visceral fear. 'I've not heard shooting before in this forest. It sounded like it came from Pant Meinog. How long do you think it'll take me to walk down the hill?'

'I'm not sure. Ten minutes if you run.' Both eyes turned to Norah, sleeping in the car. Each woman worrying about their child. Mallory made a quick calculation.

'You need to drive away and find help. Your child needs to be safe.' Mallory handed over her car keys. 'I'll follow the sound. Is there a path?'

'An ancient one, I think. It's not easy to find but there is one. You need to walk towards the clearing and find a gap in the trees. Then just go downhill.'

'Right. Dial 999 and say it's an emergency. You know the drill. You've heard a shot in a tourist area, and they should send help quickly. Stress it's urgent and to do with the current murder investigation.'

'You think Luke…?' Delyth's eyes were wide with desperation, torn between her child and lover.

'You need to get Norah to safety. That's your priority. Does Luke have a gun?'

'No, of course not.'

'Would he know how to use one?'

'I… I don't think so.'

'What colour is his motorbike?'

'A dark blue.'

'Call that in, too, just in case, but I think I know where I'll find it.'

Mallory sped away to the sound of her car engine starting. She halted for a second. Luke had tampered with David's car and possibly that of his parents. Was her car safe? They had driven here without harm but there was always a risk. Delyth, however, had already sped off, leaving Mallory to rush to the clearing and look for the opening in the trees.

As someone who had grown up in the city, nature held no attractions for Mallory, and it threw up no landmarks. The rain was beginning to fall more intensely, obscuring her view of the undergrowth. Finally, she found what *might* be an opening and pushed through it, running as fast as she could on the path clogged with thicket and knee-high nettles. As she ran over a ridge, the old wound in her thigh groaning in protest, she saw the valley stretch out in front of her, and the houses of Pant Meinog and Dan Y Derw nestled within it. She could see no one, and no further shots came from that direction.

Shit. Mallory hoped she wasn't lost, but it was too late to turn back now. She pushed onwards, gravity and fear propelling her down the hill until she heard the sound of a siren in the distance. As she reached the bottom of the hill, she saw a motorbike had been parked under a tree, near to a pick-up truck. There was no sign of the forensic team, who must have finished their work. Mallory plunged forward, desperate to call for Toby but fearful it might make things worse. She entered the courtyard and saw a huddle of figures near Tom's cottage. As she came closer, the scene coalesced in front of her eyes and she stopped.

40

Harri crossed the courtyard in front of Bev Christie's house and went past the front door, slipping down the side passage that smelt of weed, probably wafting out of the open window of the house that backed onto the garden. The side gate was shut but unlocked and he made his way noiselessly into the yard, being careful not to kick the bike that had been left propped up against the wall. He'd spent the morning in a meeting to update Steph, and her words were still ringing in his ears. Three killings and three different causes of death – and yet he was sure it was the same person. He understood Steph's scepticism. A rag in the exhaust is different to a knife in the head. The latter suggested revenge and anger, which were also mirrored in the killing of Tom. Siân's revelation that Luke had visited the house on the Tuesday evening had finally suggested a sequence of events that might just be possible.

David, a once respected parapsychologist, had become increasingly convinced in the presence of the paranormal and had married, by accident or design, someone who might help him to prove his theory. Harri, ever the romantic, was inclined to believe it was a love match, given the length of time it had taken for Gwenllian to be persuaded to return to Pant Meinog. Except 'persuaded' was the wrong word because, if Pippa was to be believed, it had been Gwenllian who had decided it was time to return to her old family home. What Harri didn't know yet was the reason for this – perhaps another conversation with Luke, this time under arrest, would reveal why Gwenllian was so desperate to return to see her childhood tormentor. He did, however, think he knew who might be able to shed some insight into this and, if his hunch was right, she was on the side of angels.

Harri crossed the yard, keeping his back to the wall, and headed towards the French doors, rotting around the frame but adorned with fairy lights possibly left over from Christmas. One door was open and he could hear low voices and muted laughter, the occupants at ease with each other. When he reached the doors, he stood to one side, out of view, listening until he was satisfied he knew who'd be inside: an older woman, her voice bold and confident, a young man, laughing, and a girl. Harri swung round and stepped into the room, enjoying the startled expressions on the faces that turned to greet him. They were eating buttered bara brith on a wooden table, its stripped pine top worn with the scores of endless knives.

'Hello Matty, hello Ava.'

He kept his eyes on Bev. They'd wasted a lot of police time and energy looking for these two when they'd been safe all along. Steph would be furious when she discovered they'd been sequestered a mere two miles from the station, in the home of one of the people they'd interviewed. Mallory had visited twice but they'd been hidden some-where, probably upstairs or in the cellar. He would have to get to the root of Bev's involvement, but Steph would ensure the minister was prosecuted for hiding the children. Harri would bet his police pension on it, because his boss liked to settle scores.

Matty stood, as if to run, but Bev stopped him by placing a hand on his shoulder. 'Harri's one of the good guys from what I've heard.'

'I think you are too?' said Harri, pulling up a chair. 'Although you did a pretty good job of convincing my colleague Mallory that you weren't in touch with the family.'

Bev smiled. 'I wasn't at all until Gwenllian met David, who I knew slightly. Before that I'd lost touch with all the Prytherchs and I just couldn't believe it when David turned up with Gwenllian at an academic conference. She was instantly recognisable and not because of the scars. She still looked like a teenager when she married David.'

Harri's eyes drifted to Matty and Ava. 'How long have they been with you?'

'Since Friday. They called from a phone box on the outskirts of Brechfa – clever, I thought – and I went to pick them up.'

'How did they have your number?'

Bev sighed. 'Gwenllian gave it to them. David thought it was all nonsense, but Gwenllian was agitated before returning to Pant Meinog. She'd been terrorised by an online stalker for years, although she claimed to David that she had no idea of the person's identity. Despite her having no online presence, she implied it was starting all over again. I was the person to call if there was ever any trouble. It was news to me, of course, but when the twins called, I went to Brechfa to pick them up.'

'I can understand that in the first instance,' said Harri. 'But once we were involved, why not let us know. We've wasted a lot of time looking for Matty and Ava.'

Bev shook her head. 'With David and Gwenllian gone, they would have been the responsibility of their next of kin, and there was no way I was going to hand them to either Carys or Dylan. I had no proof, but something was going on back in 2003.'

'You could have told us this.'

Bev's gaze hardened. 'I'm a minister first and upright citizen second. I have no proof about the danger one of those siblings poses.'

Ava turned to him, her pale blue eyes on his face. 'They're not really our family, are they? We won't be going to stay with them.'

'You most definitely will not. I've requested a warrant for the arrest of Luke Parry, who Gwenllian knew as her brother Dylan, for the murder of David and Gwenllian.' Harri heard Bev sigh. 'We think we can build a good case on how he terrorised Gwenllian for years. It'll take time but there are officers experienced in forensically charting how domestic abuse ends in murder.'

There was no reaction from either of them, but Harri noticed how Ava leant towards Matty, gaining comfort from his presence.

'I think,' said Harri, 'that we'll also be able to build a case against Luke for the murder of your father, but I need your help. Can you tell me what happened?'

To his surprise, it was Ava who spoke, and he realised that perhaps he'd got the dynamic wrong between them. Ava had leant forward not to receive reassurance, but to give it.

'How long have you got?' she asked.

Harri reached over to pick up a piece of bara brith liberally spread with butter. He'd be in trouble with his diabetic nurse, but so what?

'Take your time. Start at the beginning, or wherever you think the beginning is. There's no right or wrong way to do this.'

Ava took a deep breath, shooting a look at Matty. 'We can start when he met Gwenllian. That's as good a place as any. Everything was fine until Dad and Gwenllian married. It was just us and Dad for a long time.'

'But Gwenllian married your father in 2012. You must have been young when they met.'

Ava shrugged. 'We were used to it being the three of us.'

'Did you miss your mother?'

'Mum left us when we were babies and is living in Italy. We went out twice when we were younger, but she leads a different life out there. An apartment in a city. We could tell she didn't want us there, so we stopped going.'

Harri bit his lip, aware that Ava had touched a nerve. Missing mothers was something that kept him awake at night and he didn't doubt for a moment that Ava had been affected by an absent parent.

'So, your dad met Gwenllian and they married quite quickly, did they?'

'She was pregnant with Pippa, so they made it legal.'

Her harsh words shocked Harri. Perhaps when she was older, she'd appreciate the complexities of relationships and bringing up children alone. There was no recognition in her words about how David, her father, might have felt. The mention of Pippa had also given him a jolt, but he'd have to wait a little before he was able to quiz her about why they'd left their younger sister in the forest.

'Carry on with your story, Ava. David married Gwenllian. How was it afterwards?'

'Dad changed. He worked at the university and really enjoyed his job, but he became obsessed with Gwenllian's story. I mean, we knew about it, it's all over the internet, but we thought it was all a hoax. But according to Dad, the case contained the X factor.'

'The X factor?' Harri thought she was referring to the TV show that his daughter had been obsessed with when she was younger.

'He thought,' Matty looked at Harri as if to back up Ava's story, 'that Gwenllian was the case that would prove the existence of the supernatural. The scratches on her face were the X factor.'

'Even though she'd admitted to making some of the story up?'

'Some of it. That was the point. It was the bits that she hadn't made up that David was fascinated by.'

'You call your dad by his first name?' asked Harri, unable to stop himself interrupting.

'I do,' said Matty.

Harri kept his expression neutral, wondering once more about the dynamics within the family.

'David was hoping to use Gwenllian as proof of the supernatural. How did he do that?'

'Everything.' Ava's voice rose. 'Seances, visits from spiritualists, diviners. And all the while, he wanted to go back to Pant Meinog, but she wouldn't let him.'

'Gwenllian didn't want to go back to her old home?'

'She would get hysterical when he suggested it, which meant Dad was even more keen. He thought the place held the key to an explanation of what happened to her.'

'So how come Gwenllian changed her mind?'

'We're not sure. Carys, her sister, rang her up and they spent ages on the phone. That was strange, because I thought they didn't get on. After that phone call, there was a lot of chat between Dad and Gwenllian, and the next thing we knew, we were here on holiday.'

'Did you know that, according to Pippa, Gwenllian persuaded your dad to use a false identity to hire both the car and the cottage?'

Ava looked to Matty. 'No, but something was up because he asked us not to tell our friends where we were going.'

'So, in essence, your father had been fascinated by your mother's case for a number of years but the decision to visit Pant Meinog happened recently, possibly following a conversation with Carys.'

'Yes,' said Matty. Ava nodded, her lip trembling a little, and Bev held out an arm to comfort her.

Ava said, 'We usually went on holiday to Cornwall and that's where we thought we were going, until we saw we were heading west, not east. Matty was gutted because he likes to surf but Dad said there would be beaches where we were going, although we'd have to wait. It was why he'd booked the cottage for three weeks. A week to do some stuff and then two weeks' holiday.'

He'd booked the cottage for three weeks, thought Harri, because that was the length of time of the original booking. 'Did you know you were going to Gwenllian's childhood home?'

'No,' said Matty, 'but as soon as we got there, we realised where we were. It's all over the internet. The house looks more or less the same, except maybe a bit nicer.'

'And how were David and Gwenllian?'

Ava said, 'David was really excited, and Gwenllian... She looked determined, which was unusual for her.'

'How was that unusual?' asked Harri.

'She was so remote. She didn't pay us much attention, which didn't bother us but I'm sure Pippa would have been upset.'

'She didn't bother much with Pippa, then?'

For the first time, Harri saw shame in Ava's eyes. 'None of us did.'

He had to ask the question. He should have let Ava carry on with the story, but the father in him was desperate to know.

'We found Pippa on Monday,' he cut in. 'She says you ran off.'

Matty interrupted Ava, who was about to speak. 'We were obeying what Dad said to us when we drove away. He said that, if anything happened to him, we were to run. It had been agreed with Gwenllian too. If we were afraid, we were to run.'

'I tried to make her come with us, but she didn't understand. She said she was going to stay with David. I honestly did try. She doesn't hate me, does she?' There were tears in Ava's eyes.

'I'm sure she doesn't hate you, but you'll have to explain your actions to her. She stayed with her father, even though it could have come at a terrible cost to her.'

'How did David die?' asked Bev.

'From carbon monoxide poisoning – it nearly took Pippa too. She got out of the car in time.'

'I don't understand,' said Bev. 'If she got out of the car, why didn't David?'

'I think David's spirit had been broken – and I need to hear the rest of Matty and Ava's story to find out why.'

There was a brief silence, as if the twins were digesting his words. Ava picked up her mug, a signal to her brother that he could take the lead.

'Things were weird the first week,' said Matty. 'Dad put all his electronic stuff out, which we were kind of used to. His work was also a hobby, he liked to stay in old houses and see if his monitoring equipment picked up anything.'

'How did your father seem?' asked Harri.

'Focused,' interrupted Ava.

'This went on for a few days,' said Matty. 'We were desperate to go to the beach and then, on Wednesday, there was a huge row and I heard first Mum crying and then Dad. Don't ask me what it was about because I don't know. Pippa might, because she was always listening at doors.'

'She doesn't know, but there was, according to her, a visitor late on Tuesday night, which we now know was Gwenllian's brother, Dylan.'

'We didn't know that,' said Matty. 'After the row was over, Gwenllian came to see us. She said if anything bad happened, anything at all, we were to run and ring Bev. She explained that David didn't think there was anything to worry about, but she did. She gave us the number to call.'

'How did Gwenllian look when she told you this?'

'Scared,' said Ava. 'I thought maybe her old stalker had found her, but she wouldn't answer me when I asked. David left the next day and was out all day. He told us he was returning the equipment and that our holiday would start soon.'

'Do you think it is fair to say...' Harri began slowly, 'that Gwenllian knew that David was underestimating how dangerous someone could be?'

Matty and Ava shrugged.

'Was Pippa in the room when Gwenllian told you to run if anything happened?'

'No,' said Matty. 'We asked about her and Gwenllian said not to worry, David would look after her. In the car, though, when he was ill and we were feeling sick too, he shouted at us all to run. And we did. We ran and ran.'

41

Present day – David's story

His colleagues called it his midlife crisis, but he was indifferent to their scorn. People didn't realise what a career in academia could do to you. Those endless meetings and a cabal each year of indifferent students whose only reason for taking his classes was to add a bit of spice to their psychology degree. Very, very few cared about paranormal psychology and wanted to pursue a career in the field. His most able students, he'd soon discovered, were the sceptics who looked for the trickery and cold readings to unmask the fraudulent. Twenty years ago, David would have been amongst the best of them, but the intervening years had brought the realisation that there were some things that just couldn't be explained. At first, he'd mentally filed away these anomalies, categorising them as baffling but not without a rational cause. They just hadn't been able to prove anything. Gradually, however, two cases had kept him awake at night.

The first was the appearance of a blue figure in the bedroom of a small boy, which had continued through adolescence and into the man's twenties. The man had been referred to David by a colleague who'd readily admitted to being stumped by the case. David had been impressed by the man's apparent honesty and the photographs he'd taken of the phenomena. He might have used this as a test case to prove that sometimes the veil between this world and the next could be as thin as gossamer, but the man had moved to America and had not responded to David's emails. So he had reluctantly shelved his study into the individual and had cast around for other subjects.

He had heard of the Pant Meinog hauntings, of course, had even taught a module earlier in his career. The case had echoes of the Enfield poltergeist but, while those children had remained tight-lipped into adulthood, Carys and Gwenllian had willingly admitted to making it all up. Except, of course, for that final time. David hadn't at first understood the significance of Gwenllian insisting that she had not been responsible for the scratches on her face. He'd lumped her account into the wider deception and had not paid the case much interest as his career progressed.

What changed everything was meeting Gwenllian. She had come along to one of his public lectures, which the university insisted he give once a year, and he'd recognised her straight away. There was only one person she could be, with those deep, angry grooves scored into her face, and he'd been unable to keep his eyes off her. He'd felt he was delivering his lecture to her only and afterwards she'd sought him out, desperate to talk about the link between the teenage years and apparent hauntings, even when they weren't true.

What David hadn't realised was that Gwenllian would be the catalyst for a revival in his passion for parapsychology. Finally, he had a case where a subject had willingly admitted to making things up, but events had happened despite the deception. However, there was a stumbling block and that was Gwenllian, who didn't want to return to the house of her past. He'd pleaded and threatened to rent the house anyway, but he knew he needed her to be there, that nothing would happen without her presence. Finally, by what he thought was some miracle, Gwenllian had agreed to come. It had been her who'd suggested it and, in his elation, he hadn't thought to question her change of heart – he had even gone along with her plan to make sure no one knew their identity.

On the website, Tall Pines looked a perfect place to revisit the past. Down a solitary track, with just one other house nearby – he'd checked the approach on Google Earth – and with enough space in the house to keep out of each other's way. But they'd arrived too early. Unwilling to stop at services, with their prominent CCTV cameras, they'd pressed on until they'd reached a lay-by where they'd eaten the sandwiches prepared by Gwenllian that morning as dawn was breaking. At the bottom of the drive was an old man, leaning heavily on his stick. David thought he must be the occupant of the other house, Tom Thomas. He waved his walking stick in greeting as they passed but didn't turn his head. Gwenllian had been furious with him and had refused to lift her head from her magazine.

There was another car in the drive, a battered Fiesta. They'd been asked not to arrive before four p.m. but David had taken a chance that the holiday let would be ready anyway. It was a mistake as, winding down the car window, he could hear the sounds of a hoover being swept around one of the upstairs rooms.

'Wait in the car.'

'I can't,' moaned Pippa. 'My legs have gone to sleep.'

Matty leant forward. 'I need to stretch my legs too.'

'OK, you can get out but don't wander far. You know how important it is.' David turned to Gwenllian. 'How are you feeling?'

'Tired.' She turned towards him, her huge sunglasses covering her face. She picked up her magazine, signalling the conversation was over. 'I'll be happier when we're inside the house.'

'Well, that's a good thing at least.'

In response, Gwenllian lifted her magazine a little higher. David opened the car door and heard the children clamber out behind him. Matty and Ava would be fine, but he wasn't sure about Pippa, who still liked to wander off.

When he'd finally got into the house, he'd been in his element, setting up the cameras and recording devices in each room. He was more interested in upstairs, as this was where the attack on Gwenllian had taken place, but all he'd picked up in the first few days were the muted sounds of his kids messing around, despite the fact he'd told them to keep quiet. Then had come the late-night visitor that Gwenllian had refused to discuss, sending him upstairs like a naughty schoolboy. He wasn't even allowed to meet his own brother-in-law and, despite keeping the digital recorder on downstairs, nothing had been picked up.

Afterwards, she'd trembled with terror and revealed the story of his assaults on her and her belief that, with a new daughter, Norah, it would all start again. For it was Luke, with the mechanical glove modelled on the hand of one of his favourite action figures, who had scored those marks into his sister's face. At first, David couldn't make sense of what Gwenllian was telling him, until she'd screamed at him and mimicked the putting on of a gauntlet like armour and scratching down her face. He'd shrunk from the action but a glance at her expression had convinced him she was telling the truth.

David couldn't believe that by chasing what he thought would be his greatest triumph he had put himself and his family in danger, and his first reaction was fury. Gwenllian had deceived him. There was no supernatural entity here, but a human being with a black heart. Her fear had propelled her away from the family, but had brought her back too. While he'd thought it was him who was shaping the plans for that hot August, it was Gwenllian who had intended to confront her past.

'What are we going to do?' he asked her.

Gwenllian's face was chalk-white, the grooves a pale pink, as if painted on with nail varnish.

'We can go back to Cardiff if you think we're in danger.'

'I don't think you are in peril, only me.'

'I'm not leaving you behind.' David's voice was firm.

Gwenllian crossed to him. 'If he comes here, you have to go. Leave me behind, it's me he wants. Just go. I've already told Matty and Ava that they need to run, even if it means leaving you and me behind.'

But David would never have left Matty, Ava and Pippa to fend for themselves. Whatever his weaknesses, he loved his children and when Dylan appeared that afternoon with a knife in his hand, David's first thought was to protect his children. He'd bundled them into the car, but Gwenllian had refused to accompany him. She had waited for this moment, dreamt of it, she told him. And he had gone.

As he was driving along the forest road, though, elation and fear had turned to something more sickening. He couldn't understand what was wrong. Had he been poisoned? They had never thought of that and had taken no precautions. He pulled over and turned to the children.

'You have to run.' He was aware of Matty and Ava unclipping their belts and pushing open the door, their movements strangely slow. He turned and released Pippa from the front seat. 'Go with them. Run.'

Pippa opened the door but didn't move from the car. Ava was pulling at her and had managed to drag her through the door but Pippa fought her. 'I'm staying here.'

She made to climb back in, but David held out his hand. 'Go. Run… and… hide…'

Then he was gone.

42

Mallory saw through the rain that there were three of them. Toby, Luke and a much younger version of Tom Thomas. This must be Gethin, Tom's son. He looked devastated by the loss of his father, his back to the cottage where Tom had been found earlier that morning. Her eyes met Toby's and she saw he was injured, his left hand holding his temple as blood and rainwater seeped through his fingers. Mallory, her legs paralysed with fear, knew it was of the utmost importance not to show alarm. Luke had killed Tom and now had her son in his sight.

'Are you OK, Toby?' she called to him.

Toby turned to her, relief and shock in his expression. She wanted to go to him, and it took all her willpower to stand firm.

'Go away, Mum.'

Gethin swung round and it took her a moment to understand the dynamics between the three. It was he who was holding the gun — a hunting rifle perhaps, its barrel worn from frequent use. Luke, who had assumed giant malevolent proportions in Mallory's brain, stared in fury at the weapon, shocked at his predicament. He was at the mercy of Gethin and without a means of defending himself.

'I'd like you to release my son, please, Gethin.'

Gethin kept his gun trained on Luke. 'Who are you?'

'I'm Mallory Dawson, a civilian investigator at Dyfed-Powys police. I spoke to your wife, Cathy.'

'She never mentioned anything.' Gethin curled his lip. 'How do I know you're who you say you are? You know Harri Evans?'

'I do and I'm a member of the team investigating your father's death. I've called for help and they know that someone is armed. We can work this out but I'm asking that you release my son first. Please, he's only fifteen and has nothing to do with this.'

'I'm not going without you, Mum.' Toby looked terrified, a catch in his throat as he spoke.

Gethin kept his eyes on Luke but nodded. 'The lad can go. He needs to see a doctor and it wasn't my doing.'

'I'm not...'

But Mallory was interested only in his safety. 'You need to get away,' she shouted at him. The rain was beginning to pelt down and, in the distance, she could hear the rumble of thunder. A storm was coming in from the coast. 'Go across the fields and get help. It's urgent.'

'I'm not going.'

'Get lost lad, listen to your mother,' bellowed Gethin, shocking them all with his fury. It propelled Toby forward and he stumbled towards her.

'You're injured,' she said to him. 'Get help and call Harri if you can. He'll know what to do.'

He nodded briefly, a hurt expression as she sent him away. Luke stood watching the exchange, his expression neutral as Toby ran off.

Mallory saw Gethin pull back the catch on the shotgun. 'Put the gun down, please.'

'I've nothing against you, copper, so stay out of my way. It's him I want. He killed my father. I knew he'd come back here – can't stay away from the place, according to Da.'

Luke was standing still, his hands by his side. At that moment, he reminded Mallory of Toby, an angst-ridden teenager, and she had to tell herself that this was a man of thirty-one, and a killer of at least three people. She'd been duped by him, with his casual manner and promises that he was completely out of the poltergeist deception. But Luke had been the cuckoo in the nest, allowed to terrorise his sister by parents who had spent too much time away from the family home, their self-absorption preventing them from seeing the psychosis in their son. He had relished the chaos created by Carys and Gwenllian, and fed on it.

'Why kill Tom?' she asked. 'I can understand Gwen-llian – David, even – but why Tom?'

'Because he knew it was me who had killed Gwenllian and David. He never liked me, even as a child, and said I reminded him of Henry, my ancestor, like I give a fuck about that loser.'

'But why kill him?' In the distance, Mallory could hear the siren getting louder. The response car knew a shot had been fired and would keep its distance. It was a good hour from Bridgend, where the armed response team for three Welsh police forces was housed. It would be too late by then.

'Because he told me to leave this place and never come back. That was never going to happen.'

'Bad blood,' said Gethin, raising his rifle. 'It always comes out.'

43

Harri was back in his car before he discovered there was a hostage situation taking place in the grounds of Pant Meinog and, according to the patrol car who had radioed for the armed response unit, it appeared Luke Parry – Harri's suspect for the murder of David and Gwenllian Anderson – was the hostage rather than the kidnapper. Harri's head hurt as he sped towards the scene, partly due to his poor eating habits over the last couple of days, which meant that his blood sugars were all over the place. That morning's finger-prick test had recorded a high reading but he had been unable to stop himself ordering a chocolate croissant with his coffee. The other reason his head hurt, though, was because of the twins' story, which for him had been as heartbreaking as Pippa's.

He believed their account of David's descent into depression and academic mockery, and his fixation on Gwenllian – or rather Gwenllian's story – as the route to redemption. He'd seen these types of obsessives throughout his career – they usually ended up in a file involving harassment, assault or worse. David was an outlier in the fact he was the victim. Harri also worried about what would become of the three children – Ava, Matty and Pippa – knowing how difficult it was to deal with the loss of one parent, let alone two. And, finally, what was making his head thump in pain was the worry about what he would find when he got to the small valley. Mallory was already at the scene, but he wasn't sure if that was a good thing. She had the unnerving ability to find herself at the centre of any crisis, and it rarely ended well. As Harri sped down the country lanes, he finally managed to get through to Siân.

'What's the latest?' he asked without preamble.

Siân, unusually for her, sounded flustered. 'A negotiator has just arrived at the scene and armed response are on their way from Bridgend. The Super has also just got there. Do you want me to come down? They've cordoned off the valley and I doubt they'll let either of us through in a hostage situation.'

Harri was approaching Brechfa and, despite the rain, he could see, just beyond the church near to the village shop, that the road had been closed.

'I'm just arriving now and there's a cordon, as you say. I can't see Steph yet. Let me check what I can find out and I'll call you in a bit.'

Harri drove to the tape and showed his warrant card to the officer; the PC's youthful face flushed with the excitement of the drama unfolding across the valley. 'I can't let you through, sir. Only the negotiator, who will join the armed response team. You can speak to the Super over there, if you like.'

Steph was in her own car, a dark blue Jaguar, speaking on her mobile while her eyes were fixed on the forest.

'Fine. I'll just park up.' Harri reversed his car into a parking spot, a plan hatching in his mind. He'd visited the village many times over the years, as his great-grandparents were buried in the churchyard. He retrieved his waterproof coat from the back of the car and pulled up the hood, hoping the ground wasn't too boggy. Checking that no one was following his progress, he opened the gate into the field behind the church hall. If he spoke to Steph, he'd be forced to wait with her, far from the action, and there was too much at risk for him to stand still.

It was rough going through scrub and undulating grass mounds. He came to a small well, probably once used to water cattle and now just a sludge of brown. He stopped for a second, listening for any activity, but all he could hear was the steady fall of rain. If the negotiator was there, the discussion was taking place without a megaphone. Harri ploughed on, frowning as a movement caught his eye. He saw a figure in front of him, slender as a reed, and at first thought it was a young girl. As the person approached, he saw it was Toby, clutching his head, his face haggard.

'Christ, Toby. What are you doing here?'

Toby staggered and Harri reached out an arm to steady the boy.

'Luke brought me here on his motorbike. He suggested taking me for a spin during my lunch hour. By the time I realised he was taking me away from New Quay, there was nothing I could do. He took me to this hut, but he realised he'd forgotten the keys and wanted to lock me in that house in the forest. What have I done?'

The boy was near tears and Harri put his arm around Toby's shoulders. 'He's a devious bastard, that Luke Parry. He's had people fooled for years. Where's your mum?'

'There. She asked the man with the gun to let me go and he agreed.'

'So, what happened to your head?'

'I tried to get away when we arrived at Luke's den. He hit me over the head with something. I think it was a cricket bat.'

Harri very much doubted that. Cricket bats could kill, and Toby looked concussed but coherent. You never really knew with head injuries, though.

'What does the man with the gun look like? Tall, full head of sandy hair, muscular?'

'Yeah, that's a good description. He's silently angry, if you see what I mean. He looks like he hates Luke.'

'I'm sure he does, as Luke killed his father. Only, I don't understand why Luke isn't dead yet. Do you have any ideas why that might be?'

'I... I'm not sure. I don't think he wants to shoot him in front of Mum. She's stayed there, even though the man said she could go too.'

Harri felt his heart swell at Mallory's courage. She'd sent her son away but stayed to see the crisis through to its conclusion, wherever that led her. Luke needed bringing to justice, and not the rough kind Gethin was intending to mete out.

'Toby, I need you to follow the field. In ten minutes, you'll come to the village. Go to the pub and call an ambulance for yourself. You can wait there for them to arrive. If not, knock on the door of any house and ask to use the phone.'

Toby mumbled, 'Can't I come with you?'

Harri turned the boy by his shoulders and faced him away from Pant Meinog. 'I know you've helped your mum before, but this time the danger's too great. Gethin has a gun and he could kill everyone. Mallory and I are professionals. You need to leave us to get on with things.'

Toby was nobody's fool. 'Why are you creeping about in these fields, then? It doesn't look much like an operation to me.'

'I want to make sure Mallory comes out of this alive.'

Toby stared at him for a moment, before finally nodding. He headed towards the village, still clutching his head, his back and legs painfully thin. Harri crept on through the fields, his feet occasionally slipping on the grass, feeling his resolve harden as he reached the woodland. The forest smelt fresh and offered shelter from the rain, but Harri's spirits revolted. All his ancestral fears over this forest came to the fore. This was the place of legends and drama, and a twentieth-first-century one was about to play out. After a quarter of a mile, he saw the edge of the trees and could hear someone speaking loudly. Perhaps megaphones were out these days. They'd always seemed a blunt instrument in a precariously balanced situation. Harri approached, wishing to God he hadn't picked out his burgundy pinstriped shirt to wear. He might as well have worn a T-shirt with a target on it. There was nothing else to do but keep behind the trees and hope Gethin's gaze was focused away from the forest.

As he edged nearer, a thought came to him. Perhaps the cuckoo in the nest was Gethin too — perhaps looking for a single cuckoo in the nest had blinded them to the fact that Gethin also wasn't a patch on his father. Two lines of the same family and two lethal strains. Harri didn't usually hold much truck with the idea that evil passed down the generations. His own father had liked a drop of alcohol a little too much for Harri's liking, but a propensity to drink to excess hadn't been passed down to Harri or to his own son.

As he reached the edge of the wood, he stopped and watched the three figures from a distance. Mallory was easy to identify: slim, with her dark hair pulled back into a ponytail. The fair-haired child Dylan was just about distinguishable in the form of Luke Parry, with his loose curls. Gethin was holding a gun at the pair of them, probably a hunting rifle similar to the one Harri's grandfather had used on the farm. No one would survive a shot to the chest or stomach, and Harri felt helpless in the face of the standoff.

Luke, to his surprise, appeared by his gestures to be pleading with Gethin, although his words were indistinct. Perhaps he was appealing to Gethin's memories of the little boy he'd been, but his entreaties were falling on deaf ears. Harri looked beyond the three figures, to the two patrol cars barely visible at the top of the drive. They were right not to come any closer. The wide clearing made hiding impossible, and any negotiations would have to be conducted across the vast space. Harri watched as another car approached in the distance and parked away from the other vehicles. A woman in a high-vis jacket emerged, followed by two officers with rifles. They couldn't have made it from Bridgend so quickly and must have been deployed in the region. He assumed the woman was the negotiator, who would have been briefed about the three people standing there, and the dynamics between them. Sure enough, he heard her call across the courtyard on her megaphone, introducing herself.

The abrupt sound caught Gethin by surprise and, as a defence, he lifted his gun, aiming it towards the noise. It was a fatal move. Luke took the opportunity, charging towards Gethin, who was quick on his feet and used to handling the weapon. He swung round and blasted Luke, hitting him not in the torso, but in the legs. It was enough for the armed response to take action, and Harri watched Gethin fall to the floor.

It took all of Harri's willpower not to plunge down the hill. The armed officers were running towards the figures, and the danger was not over. Mallory, it appeared, knew this too and stayed stock-still, her hands in the air. Only when he saw the officers tending to the two wounded men did Harri cautiously advance down the hill, his gaze focused on his colleague.

'Mallory! Over here!'

Mallory turned and ran towards him, her face pale.

'Are you OK?'

'I… I think so. God, that was awful when the shots rang out. I thought I was going to go down too.'

'You did everything right. Did Gethin or Luke say anything to you?'

'Luke very little, and only in relation to Tom Thomas. He clearly didn't think he had to explain himself to me about Gwenllian or David.' Mallory looked heartsick. 'I need to find Toby – I hope to God he's made it to safety. Luke must have punched him in the face, as he was holding his head like he was in agony.'

Mallory had begun to hyperventilate; the thought of her son, rather than her own safety, had finally allowed the fear to overflow. 'I saw him when I crossed the fields. I told him to call for help from Brechfa, so he'll hopefully be on his way to hospital by now. He'll be easy to track down.'

'Then I need to go to him.'

Harri watched as Mallory ran towards a patrol car and had a discussion with a uniformed officer. The officer nodded, conferring with one of the negotiators, and Mallory slid into the front seat of the car and the vehicle sped off. It left Harri feeling curiously abandoned. Finishing a case, especially one as dramatic as this one had been, usually brought with it a sense of exhilaration. But his team was not close to hand and, worse, he was aware that, if things had turned out differently, he might have put his whole career on the line rather than leave the hostage situation to the professionals.

Harri turned and decided to return to his car by the way he'd come. The rest of the day would be spent debriefing and overseeing the interviews of both Luke and Gethin. The thought of it all left him exhausted. He entered the wood, remembering the drawings that Pippa had left behind on her bed. He wondered how she was doing and hoped that there would be some reconciliation between her and the twins. Given what he knew of families, however, he wouldn't bet on it.

He was glad to be back in the shelter of the forest despite its oppressive atmosphere. Above him, the trees were motionless in the breezeless air, and he experienced the pull of an old protection as he plunged on. His nerves, however, were shot and he jumped at the sound of something rustling through the thicket. A fox, possibly, and he turned to see what was creeping through the undergrowth. In front of him, he saw a large panther-like animal staring at him, its yellow eyes incurious. They locked gazes for a moment, before the large cat moved on, gracefully disappearing amongst the pine trees.

44

Six days earlier – Luke's story

Luke parked his motorbike at the bottom of the track and climbed up the path where he'd played as a child. This was sacred ground and the source of everything he loved about the forest. It was his home, his inspiration and his destiny. If it wasn't for his useless parents, he'd still be living here and not in some loser starter-house in a cul-de-sac – although, if truth be told, there was some nice symmetry in tracking down Delyth and starting a family with her. He'd do a better job with young Norah once he got Gwenllian and David out of the way. Lewis and Sally hadn't been able to hold anything together, least of all keep track of what their children were up to. It had also helped that Carys and Gethin had been too busy fucking to know what had been going on underneath their noses. It had left him and Gwenllian to amuse themselves, although only he had been amused, he suspected.

The problem was that nothing lasts. Their stay at Pant Meinog had come to an end after he had attacked Gwenllian with the glove he had painstakingly assembled. That outcome was something he hadn't accounted for, and it was a major slip-up on his part. Worse, Gwenllian had gone away to a new school once they'd moved to Brecon, and he'd been left alone and far away from where his heart lay. The long road home had been tortuous and uncertain, and only the continued taunting of Gwenllian had kept his spirits raised.

Had she known those online messages were from him? He suspected she'd guessed, given she'd refused to meet him and lately Carys had been giving him the cold shoulder too. It suggested that Gwenllian had finally told Carys of her past – and Carys, more worryingly, had told Gwenllian about his relationship with Delyth and the birth of their daughter. Clever Gwenllian had nearly returned to Pant Meinog without him knowing. He liked to keep an eye on who was coming and going in the place, driving by on his motorbike and occasionally prevailing on Delyth to run the occupant's number plates through the police system. He'd never have known that blue jeep was Gwenllian's if he hadn't seen the little girl running down the path he'd once used, the very image of her mother.

He'd gone to see Gwenllian that very night, appearing at the doorway of the home that was rightfully his. She'd pulled him outside and he'd been surprised at her strength. As a child, Gwenllian had been fragile, but she'd pulled him into the hot night air and told him she was going to confess all to her husband. She would then go to the police and make sure it never happened again – to her, to Norah, to anyone – and consequences be damned.

Damned. That's what they all were – they just didn't know it yet. In his hand, he held the knife he'd brought from his kitchen. Delyth hardly cooked these days so was unlikely to notice it was missing. In his other hand he had a piece of rag he'd picked up from near the shack. He wore plastic gloves so there would be nothing for the forensic team to pore over when they discovered its presence. If

Gwenllian and David escaped from the house, the car would see them off; it had worked, after all, rather well in relation to his parents.

As he neared the house, he looked at his watch. Just gone eleven on a Friday morning. Time for everything to begin.

45

Friday

The midday sun beat onto the roof of Mallory's caravan, heating the interior – according to the living-room thermometer – to nearly thirty degrees Celsius. Mallory was dressed in cut-off jeans and a shocking pink T-shirt, her feet shoved into a pair of flimsy flip-flops. After a long search for Toby, a debrief to the team, and an interminable wait for the results of the CT scan on Toby's head, she'd finally come home at six a.m. for a shower, knowing that there was no way she'd be able to sleep. The difficult phone call to Joe had been made and, to her surprise, he'd sounded more resigned than angry. She hadn't wanted to ask him if he was enjoying his holiday, but this mellowness was a new one on her. It must be his new girlfriend, and good luck to her. Toby would be coming home after eight hours of observation on the paediatric ward. He hadn't wanted to stay and if Mallory had been in possession of her car, then she doubted she'd have been able to stop him coming home with her. It was only when he learnt that Harri was picking her up to take her to the caravan that his protests subsided.

'Where *is* my car, come to think of it?' she asked Harri, as she uncorked a bottle of white wine.

They'd been for a swim, the sea chilly and refreshing even during such a warm day. She'd expected Harri to be ashamed of his body – he had none of Luke's tanned leanness – but she'd got him wrong, and not for the first time. He'd stripped off to his bathers and waded in, splashing water over his pale chest until he plucked up courage to submerge himself. It was Mallory who'd found herself shy in front of her colleague, getting under the water as soon as she could. Back in the caravan, she felt more at ease and flopped down beside Harri.

'I assume it's back at Delyth's house. You know, it's funny but we all made our way to Pant Meinog – Gethin, Luke, you, me, Toby, although that was unwillingly. However, Delyth couldn't wait to get away. Whatever bond there is between her and Luke isn't particularly strong.'

Mallory frowned, handing Harri a glass. 'She's a nursing mother and her priority is the baby. There's nothing strange about that.'

'True, but given Luke's hold over Gwenllian, I would have put money on him transferring that dynamic to the sexual relationships he had.'

Mallory pulled her T-shirt away from her skin, where it was sticking to her chest. 'I'm not so sure. Maybe he underestimated Delyth, or perhaps there is an element of control that's been loosened since her baby's birth.'

'Fair enough. Glad it's over, though. The kids are back to school in two weeks, and I fancy taking some time off. I might even book a trip to Spain.'

Mallory too was relieved it was over. It was seven days exactly since Elsa had called her – and what a week it had turned out to be.

'I must ring Elsa. She probably thinks we've forgotten her.' Mallory lifted her wine glass and took a sip of the cool Sauvignon. She'd only have half a glass – that would hopefully have left her bloodstream by the time she needed to pick up Toby. Really, she shouldn't be drinking at all, but there was something relaxing about sharing a bottle with Harri. She wondered what he'd say if she suggested they do it again, at a time when she wasn't wearing a T-shirt more suited to a teenager.

'Elsa will wait,' said Harri, unaware of Mallory's train of thought.

'Funny, though, that her vision turned out to be correct. We assume that Gwenllian did run out of the house the morning she died. Pippa said she was in her nightdress and she was most likely barefoot too. We're assuming Luke chased her through the woods before stabbing her. Strange that she didn't go with David when he fled.'

'She'd have likely ended up dead anyway. Please don't tell Elsa the details of Gwenllian's death when you see her. I don't want any defence lawyer starting to muddy the waters by suggesting we've been focused on anything but hard evidence. The main thing is that Luke has been charged with the murder of David and Gwenllian, but we'll still need you in Carmarthen until the case goes to trial.'

Helping the Crown Prosecution Service was an important role, but it wasn't the work Mallory liked. Harri was right: she preferred being in the thick of things, not stuck behind a desk. Not for the first time, she wondered what to do with the rest of her life. The first thing she needed to do was to get out of this bloody caravan. Come September, there would be more properties on the market, but she'd still be in the same position by the following summer. Perhaps she should look at finally buying a small terrace somewhere, maybe near a beach so Toby could visit more often.

Harri took a gulp of his wine and put his feet up on the table, his stocky frame filling the space.

'Gethin, I'm more sorry about. He's got some moral questions to answer. His affair with Carys, for example, was illegal – although, unless she herself makes a complaint, I can't see us making an issue of it.'

'You'll surely charge him under the Taking of Hostages Act. He'll be facing imprisonment for detaining both Luke and Toby.'

Harri grunted. 'Of course, although he did let Toby go. I have to say that boy of yours has the habit of being in the wrong place at the wrong time. As, in fact, do you.'

Mallory ran her hands through her hair, still damp from the sea. 'I got off lightly when I spoke to Toby's father, when I rang him to tell him what happened, but I'll never forgive myself.'

'You weren't to know Luke had befriended Toby. It's hardly an accident. Luke is a very devious character who liked to play God, when he wasn't torturing Gwenllian. He'll have deliberately targeted Toby once he discovered he was your son.'

'I just…' Mallory made a face. 'I just thought Toby was a bit more street-savvy, given he lives in central London. What the hell made him get on Luke's motorbike when he offered him a spin.'

'This place gets your defences down. Don't blame yourself or Toby. They'd already met over the summer and, as I said, Luke targeted Toby when he knew you were close on his heels.'

'Glad he spotted that I was onto him, because I certainly didn't.'

Harri pulled a face. 'Which brings us back to the fact that this has been an odd case where a decades-old tragedy has been revived. It's hard not to think of a sliding-doors scenario where David and Gwenllian failed to meet Luke, are having the second week of their holiday and the children are finally getting the surfing they were promised.'

'I wonder if Carys knew what she was doing when she told Gwenllian that Luke now had a child. Given the torture that Gwenllian had undergone, it's not surprising that she'd want to come back to Pant Meinog to see how things stood. She was probably planning to take things slowly in relation to contacting Luke, considering she emailed Gethin to see if Tom was still living there. She wanted to do things on her own terms. Do you think it was an act of altruism or was Gwenllian compelled by the past?'

'It doesn't have to be one or the other,' said Harri. 'Think of it from Gwenllian's point of view. David had been pushing her for years to return to the house. Here was a reason for Gwenllian to finally make the journey, but what did she really expect from her childhood tormentor? Can sociopaths turn over a new leaf? I doubt it – Gwenllian wanted a good look at Dylan but, to come here incognito, she had to persuade David to hide their identity.'

'You think she knew that Luke was with one of the police officers from the original case?'

'I think it's the only explanation for the fake ID for both the car and house rental, and again the information probably came from Carys. Luke has told us in his statement that he had kept a very close eye on Gwenllian but hadn't been compelled to visit her in Cardiff. Once he knew she'd returned to Pant Meinog, however, he couldn't keep away. Gwenllian was dead right to try and return incognito.'

Mallory took a gulp of her own wine. 'It's a lot to take in – I mean, stealing a wallet for all that. It doesn't sound like David Anderson at all.'

'The funny thing is that it appears that Robin Stevens, the owner of the wallet, and David were acquainted. They went to the same leisure centre. Mr Stevens was pretty sure he'd lost it on a night out in Cardiff, but it seems he went to the gym, showered and changed before going out. I think he lost it there and didn't realise until he went to pay for his first pint. It's a natural assumption.'

'Bloody hell, if we'd known it went missing at the gym, we might have found out David's identity sooner.'

'It wouldn't have stopped the deaths, Mallory. Gwenllian and David were already dead.'

'And Tom?'

'Tom should have told us what he suspected, rather than keeping it to himself. It was a decision that was to prove fatal.'

'Going on about the Beast of Brechfa… Too much mythology in this case.' Mallory stopped, noticing Harri flush slightly. 'What is it?'

Harri smiled slightly and shook his head. 'Nothing.'

'What were they doing, anyway, coming back here? If Gwenllian was worried about Luke's new relationship, there are ways to contact child protection services. Why put your family at risk?'

'Because only Gwenllian, and Gwenllian alone, knew the full extent of Luke's darkness and she couldn't tell anyone at the time. It was sealed inside her like the scars over her broken bones. However, when they finally met, she realised he hadn't changed at all. I also think that something he said convinced her that he'd had a hand in their parents' death too.'

Mallory shrugged. 'It's possible. I've looked at the file. That pair – Lewis and Sally Prytherch – played fast and loose with their safety. I know things are a bit laissez-faire around here but one of those tyres was so badly worn that I'm surprised the vehicle hadn't crashed before. The seatbelt is another thing, though.'

'It's going to be a bugger to prove but if Luke can interfere with an exhaust, I'm pretty sure he can mess with a seatbelt. Lewis and Sally would never have noticed. The pair went around in a world of their own. I suspect Steph will tell me to concentrate on David and Gwenllian but… you know… I'm sure he's killed before.'

'Do you think Carys had an inkling that Luke might be responsible for all this? Gwenllian, after all, kept quiet about the culprit responsible for the damage to her face.'

Harri made a face. 'Possibly. I think following the fake haunting, Carys's ability to play it straight with us is very much damaged.'

'Well.' Mallory threw the rest of the wine down the sink, suddenly restless. 'I think you'll be needing that holiday. Do you want me to make something to eat before you go? I don't think Toby has touched any of the food I left for him.'

'Actually, that's something I wanted to talk to you about. That lad of yours is really thin.'

Mallory, to her embarrassment, felt her eyes fill with tears. 'You think I haven't noticed?' she said, lifting the hem of her T-shirt to wipe her eyes. 'We're trying to sort it out, but you can't just click your fingers and get someone to start eating.'

To Harri's credit, he didn't reach out to her but let her reach across to a box of tissues she kept on the counter. She made a face. 'Maybe I shouldn't have chucked the rest of that wine away,' she said.

She felt Harri move a bit closer. 'It's not wine you need, but a break. You've been in Wales less than a year and you've been involved in three murder cases. It gets to you. You and Toby need a holiday.'

Mallory wafted her arm around the caravan. 'This is Toby's break.'

'Here? The pair of you on top of each other. You need to go further afield.'

'Like where?'

She felt Harri touch her arm, the warmth of his hand on her skin.

She looked up at him and he was smiling. 'How about Spain?'

Acknowledgements

Thank you to my agent, Kirsty McLachlan at Morgan Green Creatives, for her continued support. Siân Heap at Canelo has been an enthusiastic advocate of this series, along with Thanmai, Alicia, Hannah, Kate and Daniela Nava. Thanks, as ever, to Tony Butler for his forensic look at my writing and also to Judith Butler.

Thanks to continued supporters of my books Siân Hoyle and Gini Smith at Derby Book Festival, Niki and Karen at Gwisgo Bookworm in Aberaeron, Karen Meek, and Vicky Dawson at Buxton International Festival, to whom this book is dedicated. My fellow Canelo authors – Sheila Bugler, Julie-Ann Corrigan, Jeanette Hewitt, Rachel Lynch and Marion Todd – provide laughs and encouragement as do Crime Cymru pals including Bev Jones, Louise Mumford, Gail Williams, Phil Rowlands and Philip Gwynne Jones.

Thanks to all my family who read and recommend my books, especially Dad, and to my husband, Andy for his constant support and encouragement.

The Royal Literary Fund provided, through the Fellowship scheme, time for me to write, and heartfelt thanks to all my readers, especially those who chat on my Saturday morning Facebook posts. We have a lovely community talking about books, if you want to join in at: https://www.facebook.com/SarahWardCrime

CANELOCRIME

Do you love crime fiction and are always on the lookout for brilliant authors?

Canelo Crime is home to some of the most exciting novels around. Thousands of readers are already enjoying our compulsive stories. Are you ready to find your new favourite writer?

Find out more and sign up to our newsletter at canelocrime.com